THE SINGING SCHOOL TEACHER

Fighting Thieves and Kidnappers

Truett "T-Beau" West

THE SINGING SCHOOL TEACHER

Truett "T-Beau" West

© 2020 Truett "T-Beau" West.
ISBN: 9798647166609

Author: Truett "T-Beau" West

Edited by: Pam Eddings

Cover Design by: Harold Scherler

Prepared for Publication by:
Truett "T-Beau" West & Harold Scherler

TABLE OF CONTENTS

CHAPTER ONE
HARD TIMES

In the last village G. W. Broussard had noticed three shifty-eyed men sneaking long looks at his mule and the packs on his donkey. He always rode cautiously as a matter of long-practiced habit arising from his careful approach to life. Nothing could be taken for granted, and thinking ahead could avert unpleasant occurrences.

But now, with the country in the depths of economic depression in early June of 1934, desperate men could be expected to do desperate things. And of course, there were always those who needed no such excuse, if ever there was an excuse for doing wrong. His pistol, well-oiled with rounds in all six chambers, rode uncomfortably inside the deep left pocket of his overalls. Although the heat made the carrying of the firearm mildly irritating, when he gripped the butt of the pistol, he felt secure and at ease.

Although right-handed, at the urging of his father, he had practiced doing all kinds of things with his left hand throughout childhood. "Use the hand that you can use without having to change the position of your body," his father said. "Make the most of each hand."

His lever-action rifle rode in the saddle boot handy to his right hand, and he could use it effectively with that one hand. Flipping the barrel of the rifle upward with the natural recoil after a shot, he would lever another round into the barrel, and the weight of the rifle would bring it back into his hand ready to squeeze the trigger again.

Galen Wilson Broussard, known as "G.W.," had regularly used pistols, shotguns, and rifles from early boyhood on the river. Raised on a houseboat on the Mississippi River and its tributaries, guns had been an integral part of everyday life. The butt of his lever-action rifle protruded from the saddle boot, and he depended upon its obvious presence to deter casual would-be robbers. For those like the three would-be toughs he had seen in the last village, its presence would only prompt them to be careful and to perhaps recruit help.

He still had more than two hundred miles to travel to reach his destination in the rugged Ozarks of Northwest Arkansas. Although his purpose was to conduct singing schools at country churches, he had a secondary assignment. He was to keep his eyes and ears open for clues that might lead to the rescue of a kidnapped child. He wanted to put miles behind him while attracting as little attention as possible. Distance from the river reduced the possibility that someone would recognize him from his days of working the river as a federal agent.

Danger would continue after he reached the Ozarks, and he would ride carefully and thoughtfully, but it would sort of thin out because of the sparser population. From his previous experiences among the rocky ridges, he knew that strangers were regarded with curiosity, often mixed with suspicion. Among their foremost questions was, "What does this stranger do to feed and clothe himself?"

The large jack that followed his brown riding mule, Emma, had been dubbed the unimaginative name, "Jack," by his previous owner. He bore packs that contained, among other materials, recently received Rudiments of Music from Stamps-Baxter Music Company. After a couple weeks of instruction, his pupils would know their contents well, and they would be happily reading and singing the shaped notes.

He loved to see the delight and satisfaction written on the faces of young men and women when they realized they could make sense of the key signature, staff and notes, and could sound out songs they had never heard before. There was within him a strong desire to help others learn and understand.

The sound of hoof-beats made him aware of riders gaining on him from the rear. Their horses were moving at a needlessly rapid pace, especially for the hot day. He had glimpsed them twice several miles back as they carefully kept their distance, but now they drew steadily closer. He studied the road ahead, for they were probably working with one or more who had managed to get ahead of him.

The road had run mostly due west for miles across the flat delta country through a mix of fields of growing crops and dense wooded areas. Just over a mile ahead, he saw where the road changed direction abruptly, turning toward the north as it entered wetter ground marked by patches of switch cane. Locals familiar with other routes may have been able to get ahead of him, and his thoughts were not comforting as he considered who might await him when he made that abrupt right-angle turn ahead.

He decided to give his mule and jack a breather and gain a clearer idea of the intentions of the two riders gaining on him from behind. He would learn if they were two of the three who had shown interest in his outfit earlier.

There was a staging area on the right just ahead, alongside the cotton field that bordered the road on both sides. A cultivator, with shiny plow blades showing recent use, rested from its labors at the farther end of the area. At the nearer end, the shade of a big spreading white oak seemed to invite him to escape the rays of the sun for a few minutes. Its thick trunk would afford some protection in the event hot lead began to fly.

Upon reaching the shade of the tree, he dismounted and took an oily rag from a pocket sewn onto the saddle boot. Withdrawing the lever action rifle from the boot, he began to wipe the dust from it. He would have the rifle in hand when the riders approached him, saving perhaps critical time needed to make a move for it. One quick step, if necessary, would put him behind the tree.

Then he heard the sounds of rapidly moving horses north of the cotton field. Through the trees that grew on that side of the field, there must be a road or trail. His suspicions had been well founded. He dismounted and waited in the cool shade beside Emma.

The two following him stopped their horses, and beyond earshot, they began to talk with one another. Then they came on more slowly, a change that G.W. felt the horses must have appreciated. He was always thinking of the horses and mules.

"Hello, men. I know your horses appreciate that slower pace on this hot day." His voice was light and casual, but his words let them know that he was aware that they were stalking him. He continued to wipe the rifle with the oily rag as they reined to a stop.

The two would-be robbers had surely thought, since he had stopped, to take him without the help of their running mates he had heard in the wooded area. But they didn't like the way he held that rifle. Suddenly they felt very vulnerable, and they didn't like it.

"It's none of your business how we ride our horses," one of them declared resentfully. He was a tall slender young man with a neatly trimmed black beard, and not one of the three who had enviously eyed his outfit in town. A clean blue shirt and pressed khaki pants made him more presentable than those three. He held a new-looking pump-action shotgun across his saddle bow.

"Oh, don't take it personally," Galen answered. "I love horses, and I am always thinking of them. Those are good horses, and they look as if they are well cared for." His statement was honest, and he wondered if the horses belonged to them. The older partner, one of the three who had eyed his outfit, did not seem to be the kind of man who would take good care of his horse.

That older partner spoke. He appeared to be past fifty with tobacco juice stains below each corner of his mouth in a five-day growth of white whiskers. "Them packs on that donkey look like they got something heavy in them," he declared. The statement was actually a question, and he waited for a response.

Galen felt his patience wearing thin. He kept listening for the other riders. They had gone out of hearing, and he wanted to know where they were. "Speaking of none-of-your-business comments, that is one for sure. It's none of your business what is in those packs, but I am going to tell you anyway. I'm a singing-school teacher. Those packs are filled with instruction booklets and song-books for my students at the singing schools."

He stuck the wiping cloth back in its pouch and let the barrel of the rifle stray toward the slender one as he did so. "If you gentlemen—He put an ample supply of sarcasm into the word—plan to rob me for a pile of Rudiments of Music booklets, you had better get on with it. Otherwise, you can drop your guns on the ground where you can pick them up on your way back."

"On the way back?" the older one sputtered stupidly. "What you mean, on the way back?"

"The two of you are going to ride ahead of me to meet your friends around that bend in the road. And then we are all going to ride a few miles farther. All of you will walk back, and I will turn your horses loose about sundown."

"Don't try it, Biddy!" the younger one yelled desperately. "He's got that rifle pointed straight at my chest with the hammer cocked." He had seen his partner's right hand moving toward a pistol in his shirt front.

"You can go ahead and pull it out of your shirt," Galen said steadily. "Just do it slowly and drop it on the ground." Suddenly there was a pistol in Galen's left hand while his right hand still held the rifle steadily on the tall young man. Neither of the two culprits had seen how the pistol got into his hand, but Biddy found himself looking at the hole in the end of the barrel.

Galen patted them down for other firearms, and found a new, clean and well-oiled pistol on the younger one. He took a long thin knife from each of them. "I have an idea that both of you know how to throw these knives, so we will take temptation from you that would only get you killed."

"You shore don't talk nor act like no singing-school teacher," Biddy declared plaintively.

"Yes, I'm a singing-school teacher. And both of you would probably be different men if you spent some time listening to some good gospel music, whether you can sing or not. I was raised on the river, and I know a few things other than singing. I know, though, that singing gospel songs is good for a man."

"Slim, you used to go to them gospel singings," Biddy said. "Didn't seem to do you no good."

"I just went to see the girls," Slim answered. "But I did like to hear the people sing. Always wished I could sing like I heard them sing." Galen detected genuine wistfulness in his voice, and it touched a soft spot in his gospel-singing soul.

"You seem to have the voice for it," Galen opined. "It's not too late to learn. That is, if you don't get yourself killed before you mend your ways." He saw something flash across the young man's countenance that told him his remark had hit home. Robbers seldom considered the possibility that their wrongful actions might get them killed. He put their guns and knives behind a bush so that a passerby would not see them.

Before they reached the bend of the road, Galen heard low voices and a horse stomping its foot. The hoof seemed to land on a packed surface, and the sounds produced a mental picture of at least two men waiting in the road. They were only a short distance from where the road changed direction.

"I'm feeling pretty edgy right now," he told the two would-be robbers riding in front of him. He shortened the distance between him and them and made sure his pistol was ready to grasp as he held his rifle with his right hand. With his left hand he wound the reins around the saddle-horn, pulling the folded ends back through a loop and tightening.

He knew that Emma would respond to directions given with his knees, if she needed any directions at all. They had made many miles together, and she seemed to know where he wanted to go before he, himself, decided. She would not be spooked by gunshots or by the actions of the horses.

"I'm feeling edgy because anything can happen. I don't like it when things get out of control. One of us or all three of us could be killed. A good way that either of you could get yourself killed, would be to spur your horse or do anything at all but ride straight ahead. Any unusual move might activate my trigger finger."

Slim wailed, "If anything happens to these horses, I might as well be dead. Uncle Jim will kill me. He sets store by these horses."

As they rounded the curve he recognized two scruffy looking men on ill-kept horses, who stared at the three of them with puzzled faces. They were less than one hundred yards ahead. Then the one on the right, having sized up the situation, threw the butt of his shotgun to his right shoulder. As it made contact with his shoulder a rifle bullet struck that same shoulder. The shotgun fell to the road surface as he yelled in pain.

Biddy and Slim held a tight rein on their horses, remembering the warning Galen had given them. The bony horses ahead jumped at the sound of the shot, and the one ridden by the shotgunner reared up. The falling shotgun seemed to have bothered the horse more than the sound of the rifle. His rider slid off his back into the dirt while crying out from the pain in his shoulder.

The sudden action left the other rider wide-eyed and mouth hanging open. "Drop your gun! Now!" Galen yelled. Another old single-barreled shotgun hit the ground, and without waiting to be told, two hands were thrust into the air.

"Move forward slowly and carefully," Galen told Slim and Biddy. "This rifle has plenty of rounds left in the tube." They had heard him work the lever to put another round in the barrel in the next moment after he had fired the shot. When they reached the two with the skinny horses, the second one still held his hands high above his head. He quite obviously did not wish to give Galen any reason to fire another shot.

The familiar sound of a Model A Ford caught Galen's attention. It was approaching from the opposite direction Galen was traveling. About a mile ahead the road made a ninety-degree turn to the left to resume its generally westerly direction, and the vehicle was approaching that turn from the west. The thought ran through his mind. "Another complication. Another unknown. Could be good. Could be bad."

His shot had clipped the top of the bone on the culprit's shoulder, leaving him in much pain, but he would be okay. "Sorry about that old chap, but I didn't want any of that buckshot coming in our direction. You didn't care if you shot your friends. That buckshot would have scattered enough to hit all three of us." The only response from the culprit was to moan a little louder.

"We ain't got no buckshot," his scruffy partner volunteered. "We have short-brass squirrel shot. Ain't likely any of the shot would have made it that far. Jud was just stupid," he said in a voice filled with exasperation. "He's always been stupid. He's my brother, but he's stupid. Just plain stupid!"

"Your whole operation wasn't that bright," Galen responded. "Now I need to get free of you hoodlums, and I don't want to do anything stupid, myself. I don't want to have to deal with you farther down the road." A black Model A pickup negotiated the turn and headed in their direction. As it closed the distance they all moved to one side of the road to give it room to pass.

"Oh-my-gosh!" Slim moaned. "That's Uncle Jim. He's gonna have my hide."

True to his words, the pickup stopped and a stern-faced middle-aged man stepped out. "Slim, what are my horses doing here?" Without waiting for an answer, he turned to Galen.

"Are you that singing-school teacher I heard about? Are those packs filled with song books?"

"I am G. W. Broussard, Sir," he responded. "I'm on my way to secluded parts of the Ozarks where materials have to be packed in by mule or donkey. There are people there who love to sing good gospel harmony, and others who want to learn.”

“And these dimwits thought you were carrying something they could sell. They tried to waylay you and you got the upper hand. I have heard about you, Broussard. I know about your work on the river.” He turned to his nephew.

“Slim, get these horses home now. And don’t run them in this heat. I thought you had straightened up your act, and now I find you running with Biddy and these good-for-nothing Kreuger boys. You and I are going to have a talk. A short talk, straight to the point. Get moving.”

“Biddy!” Biddy flinched as if stung by a wasp. “You and these Kreuger boys walk home. These are the horses stolen from Mort Sensley back in February. If you Kreuger boys had them another two or three months, they would be dead. I’m going to find someone to pen them and feed them until Mort can come and get them.”

“Mr. Harding, I can’t walk. I’ve been shot. I need help.” Jud was in obvious pain and making the most of it in an effort to get sympathy. He was knocking on the wrong door. Jim Harding felt no sympathy for him.

“Yeah, I saw that right off the bat. You will live over it, but I doubt if you will learn anything from it. Just hold on a minute.” He stepped to his pickup and came back with a bottle of alcohol, gauze and tape.

He glanced at Galen. “When you have men working for you, Broussard, it’s a good idea to keep bandages and rubbing alcohol on hand.” He quickly washed and bandaged the wound.

“You will be okay in a few days if you keep it clean, Jud. Get Sadie to clean it for you. Tell her I said so. You don’t know the difference between clean and filthy.”

He extended his right hand to Galen. “It’s good you know how to handle yourself, Broussard. You will probably meet some other sorry louts before you reach your destination. Good to meet you. Have a good trip.”

Galen could hardly believe his good fortune. "Jim Harding," he muttered to himself, as he picked up the shotguns belonging to the Kreuger brothers. "I will remember that name." He placed the guns in the bed of the pickup as Harding tied the reins of the starving horses to the rear bumper.

The pickup moved slowly away with the horses walking at a comfortable pace behind it. Biddy began to curse the Kreuger brothers, blaming them for talking him into "this wild goose chase." Galen mounted his mule and left Biddy arguing with the uninjured Kreuger brother. The other one began to walk while holding his right arm against his body with his left hand. Finally, Biddy and the other brother began to walk as they continued to argue.

In spite of the heat, Galen urged Emma and Jack to a fast walk for a couple of miles. He just wanted to put some distance between him and those unworthy scoundrels. Somehow, he held out some hope for Slim. He was little more than a boy, and he had gotten off on the wrong foot in life. That he liked gospel singing was a good sign, and his Uncle Jim's influence just might make the difference in the young man's future. He mumbled a short prayer for him.

Galen's thoughts wandered as he rode, relaxed but alert. When his body adjusted to the heat, as it had over the past several days, he could tolerate it quite well. Such was his tolerance for the humid heat that he could actually enjoy his ride while reflecting on how he came to be riding to the Ozarks.

His mother's brother, who had raised his family in the Ozarks, had been the singing school teacher for several communities for many years. As a twelve-year-old boy, Galen spent a summer following his uncle from one singing school to another, each school lasting two weeks. By the end of the summer, he could look at a song he had never seen or heard, and within a few minutes, he could sing it proficiently.

The most important thing that happened, though, was his decision to make gospel music an important part of his life. He loved to sing with others who loved to sing. He liked to hear the bass leads, the alto leads, the tenor leads and the harmony of voices singing different parts. Sometimes he thought that it must be a little taste of Heaven.

The words of the songs spoke more of Heaven—and of Jesus, the way to Heaven—than of anything else. He always felt closer to his Master during and after a session of singing. And Heaven seemed more real.

His mother had thought that he needed to learn about life on shore and away from the river. She loved her life on the river boat, and she knew how Galen loved it as well. Even so, he needed to learn about life where people grew gardens, raised watermelons and peas, and took care of a barnyard.

As he grew up, his mother made sure that the family always had plenty of vegetables and fruit, although they did not grow any themselves. People on shore eagerly met them at several different locations to swap their produce for fresh fish. He gladly helped his mother shell peas and beans when they were in season. She trusted him to cut the watermelons into equal slices.

He didn't return to spend another summer with his uncle, because he had a younger sister and two younger brothers who wished to go. They each took their turns in succeeding years. When his turn came again, he had reached his sixteenth birthday, and he was earning money on the tugboats and barges.

In each city or town where he could go ashore, he asked questions about where he might attend a "singing." All up and down the rivers, especially the Ouachita River in Louisiana, people regularly gathered in churches to sing gospel songs. He frequently took advantage of shore leave to attend one of these singings. Often they lasted all day long, with dinner on the grounds. He had never found better eating.

By the time he turned nineteen, his disciplined habits had caught the attention of shipping managers, and he was recruited to work under cover to investigate and thwart thefts of barge cargos. Usually the thefts took place on shore before delivery to the individual purchasers, and sometimes supervisory employees were involved.

After spending five years in undercover work, his cover was lost in a major case in which he was compelled to testify. Jim Harding must have some inside knowledge of that case; otherwise, he was at a loss as to how Harding might have learned of his work on the river. Perhaps he had some acquaintance or connection with management of the shipping companies. He had no reason to suspect that Harding might be on the wrong side of the law.

Almost everyone up and down the river knew of his love for gospel singing. Shore leave to most of the men meant an opportunity to frequent a waterfront dive and the dubious pleasures to be found there. He sometimes endured some rough kidding, and even scoffing ridicule, about his preference for churches and singing.

He knew that his detective work could not last indefinitely, but the loss of his job at a time when one of every four men in the country was looking for a permanent decent-paying job, was tough. Fortunately, he had been paid well, and he had saved most of what he earned. Without a family to support, he lived frugally and saved his money with a view toward starting a family under decent circumstances.

As much as he loved the river, his childhood experience in the beautiful Ozarks made him wish to move to higher ground. The clear cool water that spilled over the rocks in the mountain streambeds, fascinated him no less now than when he was twelve years old. Long strenuous climbs up steep slopes were usually rewarded by a view across a mountain valley, often enhanced by moving and changing mists. There was fertile land to be found in those valleys, and free-flowing springs of sparkling water by which a home could be built.

He had been promised a substantial reward if he could locate the girl who had disappeared two years earlier from a small town in South Louisiana at the age of seven. There was strong reason to believe that she had been kidnapped by disgruntled family members on her father's side. The family, consisting of the father, mother and three daughters, lived in the Ozarks before

the mother fled with the three children to her parents'
home in South Louisiana.

She told of being treated badly by her husband and
her husband's mother. The ill treatment included being
physically beaten by her husband with the assistance
of his mother. Her husband and his mother consumed
whiskey of their own making on a regular basis, often
getting thoroughly intoxicated.

When she had first met her husband, he was a
handsome and polite young man who worked with his
father and grandfather in the jobbing business. They
traveled the river purchasing various products for
several different wholesale houses. As with so many
other businesses in the throes of the great depression,
their markets dried up to nothing. The imposition of
excise taxes by the federal government stifled any
movements toward economic recovery.

Her husband, Kelson Bean, talked his young wife into
moving with their three children to the Ozark farm of his
parents. "We can keep body and soul together until this
economic mess blows over," he assured her. It seemed
the logical thing to do, and she agreed.

He soon decided that he could make good money
brewing whiskey to sell along the river. His mother
already had one distillery going, and there were soon
three more, all of which used discarded automobile
radiators in the distilling process. Kelson and his
mother liked their make, and they drank significant
quantities of it every day.

The young wife noticed an undesirable change in
their personalities. They became ill-tempered and
difficult to live with. Then they progressed to being
demanding and cruel. Her efforts to get her husband to
quit drinking only angered him, sometimes prompting
him to strike her with his hand. His cruelty steadily
increased.

Deciding that the situation would never improve, but
would only get worse, she made the decision to
escape. She knew that neither he nor his mother would
ever voluntarily permit her and the children to leave.
She carefully made the necessary preparations for the

daunting challenge of escaping with three young children.

The arduous trip to Louisiana exposed her and the children to all sorts of dangers and hardships, but they made it with her husband in hot pursuit. Upon their arrival at her parents' home, the tables were turned. He and his cousin backed off quickly when met by a contingent of angry Cajuns. Over a year later the oldest daughter, Margaret, failed to return from picking huckleberries.

An older boy and girl who were also on the berry-picking trip, described two men they saw in the area minutes before Margaret's disappearance. The descriptions fit her father's cousin and his mother's brother. Shortly before, a Louisiana court had granted a legal separation to the mother and awarded custody of the children to her. A first-grade school picture of the girl was among Galen's belongings.

The kidnapped girl's family and friends had hired men at three different times to try to find and return little Margaret. Each effort had failed, although they readily located the father. He denied knowing anything about the disappearance of his daughter, but his smirking sarcastic responses to their visits left no doubt in their minds as to his guilt.

Local law enforcement officials showed no interest and refused to assist in the matter in any way. The suspected cousin had stated arrogantly, "The sheriff knows who he had better not cross." Neighbors, likewise, refused to discuss the kidnapping, although investigators came away with the feeling that they knew something about it.

The community in which the Bean family held sway had been one of those Galen visited as a twelve-year-old boy. He remembered several of the Beans as big and loud. He, himself, had been the butt of some of their raucous kidding, kidding that leaned heavily toward the raunchy side. There was one of them, however, who had been serious and kind. He had come to Galen's defense.

Carlton Bean, although among the younger of the Bean men, commanded the respect of all of them.

Even at the age of twelve, Galen could detect that the respect was given grudgingly by two or three of them, but they gave it, nevertheless. Carlton was especially interested in Galen's life on the river, and Galen learned that he had spent some time on the Mississippi tugboats.

Most significantly, Carlton Bean sang great tenor, and he loved the singings. He attended the singing school held in the Bean community and brought several others with him, encouraging as many as would to come. His lively and lovely wife, a native of Paducah, Kentucky, came separately with a group of teenage girls and her well-worn guitar.

The singing was taught a cappela, but a guitar was welcome if the guitarist could play it well. Laura Bean could play it well. She played several different styles very skillfully.

There was one church that had somehow managed to haul a piano over the rocky trails, but Galen's Uncle Louis hated it. Besides being virtually impossible to keep in tune, the lady who played it could play it only enough to be a hindrance. Louis Robinson was an exceedingly patient man who loved teaching others to sing, but Galen had seen his patience stretched to the limit over that piano.

In some of the churches, musical instruments were not permitted, based on the belief that they were inappropriate in worship services or in a building where worship services were held. Because there is no mention of a musical instrument being used in any of the churches of the New Testament, Primitive Baptists and some others forbade their presence in their places of worship.

Galen had been present when Uncle Louis persuaded a young man named "Stanley" to use his fiddle for the Lord. As a teenaged boy during the war in Europe, Stanley had walked the rugged roads and trails of the Ozarks, looking for opportunities to play his fiddle. People were always willing to give him food to eat and a place to sleep in order to hear him play.

If he could get someone to organize a dance, he would usually get a meaningful sum in hard cash. For a lad barely old enough to shave, he was making a pretty decent living. It all came to an end at a protracted meeting in a small hill-country church. As he listened to the preacher, he began to see the life he was living as shallow, misguided and worthless. When the invitation was given, he was the first one to walk the aisle to give his life to Christ.

Thinking of some of the really bad things that he had seen at some of the dances where whiskey was present, he began to think of his fiddle as the devil's instrument. It was his fiddle-playing that drew people to the place where bad things happened. He could not bring himself to part with his fiddle, but he quit playing it.

When Galen got acquainted with him, he had married and started a family. Neither his wife nor their two small children had ever heard him play the fiddle. Uncle Louis persuaded him that the fiddle was only an instrument, and that it could be used for the Lord as well as for the devil. He quickly adapted to the gospel music, and his playing made the singing school very special. His wife and young children literally bubbled with joy at hearing him play.

Galen recalled that as they rode away from that community, Uncle Louis told him, "Galen, the evil that Stanley was seeing at those dances came more from the whiskey than anything else. Young men and women get excited over one another, but they can usually control themselves pretty well if no whiskey is involved. When they start drinking, all kinds of bad things happen."

Those words had stayed with Galen down through the years, and the memory of them would run through his mind whenever he had an invitation to drink alcohol. Although he was not the only one on the river who did not drink, he was numbered among the few "odd-balls" who would not socialize with the others over a bottle. He and the other "odd-balls" lived daily with resentment from the majority of the drinkers because of their refusal to join them.

During the past winter, Galen had visited his uncle for the first time since his summer with him as a lad. He received word that Uncle Louis had developed some health problems, and he feared that he would leave this world before he thanked him properly for that summer. His uncle took advantage of his visit to persuade him to take over the singing schools that he had conducted for almost two decades.

The work was a labor of love—a love of both music and people—because there was very little monetary reward. There was even less now than there had been when his uncle first began the singing schools, as the entire nation suffered through an economic depression. The depression, however, had affected the Arkansas Ozarks less than most other parts of the country because the residents of the Ozarks had never enjoyed much cash flow anyway.

They had never had the opportunity to get their products to the city markets in any efficient way. As had the first settlers, they maintained a lifestyle that required very little cash, and they took pride in their ability to "make do" with what they derived from the land. Those who were unwilling to accept such an austere lifestyle, moved away. But many of them had now returned, finding that it was much better than living in a city without a job.

Uncle Louis and Aunt Mary had five children---three boys and two girls---all of whom were now adults with families of their own. Their children also loved gospel singing, and gladly supported Uncle Louis in his special passion. Between schools, he would make his way back home leading a pack mule loaded with all kinds of interesting things. Perhaps the most notable contribution came from a leather worker who noticed his worn and mended saddle. During the winter months he had made Uncle Louis horse a really nice new one.

Galen would work from the Robinson home, and whatever he was given by his students would be left with his aunt and uncle—almost all of it anyway. He would keep any cash, but he expected very little of that. If he could locate the kidnapped girl, he would make a good payday, but the personal satisfaction of helping alleviate that terrible situation would greatly outweigh any monetary compensation.

In the meantime he must ever be on the alert for such as the Kreuger brothers. There were scalawags out there who would murder him for his saddle and bridle. He had made some serious enemies on the river, men who were financially able to pay someone to hunt him down. And there was a plentiful supply of unscrupulous men—if they could be called "men"—who were willing to make a man disappear for a few measly bucks. Yet, in these hard times, was there such a thing as a "measly" buck?

After the trial and the consequent loss of his job, the free time thrust upon him prompted him to seriously consider things he had kept in the back of his mind. For years he had wanted an Ozark farm. He would find a place where he could somehow get his products to market. And there would surely be a market. The economy would recover.

Agriculture was changing, and he would continue to gather information--as he had for years—to ascertain what would be required to stay on the cutting edge of those changes. First, as much as he loved mules and horses, he knew their days were numbered. Even though he had never grown a crop or cared for a herd of cattle, he knew that new methods would be required in future years. More acres of land would be required.

He was one of the fortunate ones who had benefited from the monetary deflation because he had saved his money. It would buy more now than when he had saved it. When the banks failed, he had gone through a time when he feared that he would lose most of his savings. Things were more stable now, but he would feel better when the larger part of his money had been invested in land and a residence.

Galen had not dared think seriously about any particular young woman, although he dreamed of having a wife and family. He had enjoyed and appreciated his childhood on the houseboat, and he considered himself more privileged than children who grew up on land. But now he wanted to raise his children on a farm among domestic animals, crops, and garden produce.

The economy and society were changing, and he sought the best ways to adapt and position himself and his family for the future. The "hit-and-miss" schooling he received growing up would not be adequate for the next generation. His children would spend much more time learning in the classroom as he taught them to pay close attention to things outside the classroom.

First, the Lord would bless him with a good woman, one who he could cherish and respect, one who would be a true partner in life. He possessed that faith and confidence. Many capable young women had looked at him with fascination and interest, but they knew that he worked the tugboats. Even if they might be willing to accept the downside of being the wife of a riverboat man, their parents would not approve. He understood.

There was a restlessness within him. There came a time in life when young men and women wanted to mate—needed to mate—and produce offspring. He knew well the importance of patience in the crucial matters of life, and he understood the dangers of impatience, especially with regard to the choice of a mate. He had already asked God to give him a true mate, a real mate.

He wasn't asking for a perfect mate, because he knew that no such woman existed. Likewise, no such man existed, and it seemed that on a regular basis, circumstances reminded him of his own shortcomings. Although the restlessness within urged him to action, he determined not to permit it to push him into ill-considered decisions.

Would he devote more than one summer to the singing schools? That decision would come at some time after the completion of this round of singing schools. Perhaps another qualified man or woman could be found who would continue the tradition. Out of respect for Uncle Louis, and because of his own belief in the good that came from gospel singing, he would see to it that the singing schools continued.

Emma and Jack did not seem to tire if he didn't rush them, and he continued to travel until well after nightfall. He intended to make as many miles as reasonably possible each day until he reached the mountains, away from the mosquitos and high humidity. When he stopped at dusk at an attractive roadside home to refill his canteens and to water Emma and Jack, the nice couple invited him spend the night in a soft bed. He politely declined, having made a firm decision before beginning the trip to refuse such invitations for several reasons.

His spirits lifted several days later when he began the long climb into the mountains. He slowed the pace to spare his loyal equines undue strain from climbing the steep slopes. He checked their hooves regularly, for the rocky slopes were hard on them. The down slopes could sometimes be treacherous, and he proceeded slowly on them as well.

Always, he maintained a lookout for anything unusual or suspicious, for he knew the value of his animals and gear. It didn't take much to tempt some people. The bridle path, at one point, went by a free-flowing spring where he refilled his canteens with the best-tasting and coolest water he had drunk since his last trip to the Ozarks. Emma and Jack seemed to especially like the clean clear water. He began to enjoy the trip just for the trip itself.

Chapter Two

RENEWING CHILDHOOD ACQUAINTANCES

The day ended with a panoramic view of the wide valley in which Uncle Louis and Aunt Mary made their home. Galen topped out on a ridge facing the setting sun in the Northwest. The sun shone behind low-hanging clouds that hinted of rain tomorrow. Its rays produced flaming hues of orange, pink and crimson in the clouds. He dismounted so that he could stroll about, enjoy the soul-satisfying scene, and give his faithful animals a break from climbing the steep inclines.

He guessed that he would need another three to four hours to reach the Robinson residence. Emma and Jack had already put in a long and hard day climbing steep slopes, and he did not want to ask them to do more. He would greet Uncle Louis and Aunt Mary tomorrow morning. Anyway, he wanted to move leisurely through the valley during daytime hours in order to carefully observe all aspects of the countryside.

Another half hour took them to a spring branch from which Emma and Jack satisfied their thirst. Up the stream about two hundred yards he found a good place to make camp. Supper consisted of two boiled eggs and some cold bacon left over from his noon meal. Starlight filtered through the canopy of green leaves above as he concentrated on the night sounds and let his constantly wandering mind rest a bit.

He awoke refreshed and full of anticipation at seeing his Uncle and Aunt. He knew they would beam happily at his presence. Aunt Mary would hurry to the kitchen, restart the fire in the cook-stove, and begin to prepare a sumptuous meal. It was her way of saying, "I love you, and I am glad you are here."

As he rode through the valley, he wondered how long it would be before an access road would be built, over which a motor vehicle could travel. Within the valley itself, there would be little problem, but there lay miles upon miles of rough and rugged terrain between this tranquil valley and the nearest adequate road. A river ran through that rugged terrain, a river that often ran wild with dangerous white water carrying limbs and logs.

Sometimes dogs barked as he rode by. Women and children were busy with chores of one kind or another, including gathering vegetables from their gardens. They looked at him with curiosity, and even though they didn't know him, they waved a friendly greeting. They would soon know him as "the singing-school teacher," and that title carried definite status.

There were acres and acres of corn with the green leaves of the stalks moving enchantingly in the mountain breezes. A few of the corn fields—those planted earliest—were in full tassel, producing pollen to drift on the breezes to the green corn silks below. Just a few more good rains combined with warm sunshine would bring a bountiful harvest and a secure food supply for the winter days to come.

Corn fed both people and animals. Galen thought of the sounds made by mules, horses and hogs as they chewed the grains of dry corn off the cobs. Feeding corn to the chickens required more effort because the corn had to be shelled for them. Of course, the shucks had to be removed from the ears of corn in all cases, and they then became cattle feed.

At the lower end of the valley, located on a strongly running stream, a grist mill stayed busy both during and after the fall harvest as families put in stores of corn meal and grits for the year ahead. The mill was a favorite place for families to visit with one another and to get the latest news about how their neighbors were faring. Sometimes news from the outside world made it into the valley, prompting sometimes lengthy discussions at the mill.

Wheat and oats had already been harvested in May, and most of that acreage had been replanted in beans, cantaloupes, and watermelons. They would be ready for protracted meeting time in late July and early August. The wheat would soon be dry enough to grind into flour at the mill. Some of the oats would be cut into oatmeal in hand-turned grinders at home.

It was Tuesday. Yesterday had been wash day throughout the valley, and today women were making time between preparing meals and other chores, to iron and hang the clothes. Most of the men were busy in the fields, and they eyed Galen with curiosity while taking a break from their toil long enough to wave at him.

Aunt Mary concentrated on selecting green "snap beans" from "bean poles" about which the bean vines had wound themselves, always in the same direction. It was still early in the season, and only a few of the beans were mature enough to pick. The many white blooms promised green beans for many weeks to come.

Uncle Louis bent over among the potato vines, digging "Irish potatoes." His practiced eyes looked for the largest cracks in the soil that betrayed the presence of a well-formed potato beneath. From time to time he stood straight and then leaned backward, working his torso back and forth to relieve his painful back muscles.

"Snuffy," their snuff-colored cur, barked his warning at the approaching intruders, and the feisty squirrel dog, "Spunky," ran around the house to join him. Uncle Louis quieted them with a quick command as he and Aunt Mary hurried from the garden to meet Galen astride Emma. (Jack followed closely without benefit of a lead rope.) They left their woven white-oak baskets on the ground behind them.

His aunt hugged him tightly for long moments. Uncle Louis washed his gritty hands in a pan by the well, dried them on a towel hanging on a post, and then shook Galen's hand firmly as his left hand rested affectionately on Galen's right shoulder. After words of greeting, they returned to their unfinished jobs in the garden as Galen unloaded his packs on the front porch.

Galen led Emma and Jack to the mule lot and freed them from the tack. After they slaked their thirst from the water trough made of a hollow log split in half, they found a pair of dusty spots in which to roll. It was a special equine pleasure that they had been denied for many days.

Galen washed the potatoes and rubbed the thin tender skins off them while Uncle Louis sliced them. He declined to slice the smallest ones, but put them aside to add to the pot of snap beans. Uncle Louis then stirred the coals in the stove and got the fire going while Galen went to the porch and began to unpack.

When Uncle Louis came out of the house and saw the new Stamps-Baxter convention song books, he got excited, just as Galen knew he would. Galen had looked forward to that moment from the time he had purchased and packed the books. His mother's brother, who had a striking resemblance to his mother, took a seat in one of the rocking chairs and began to sound out various songs in the book.

Galen took great pleasure in watching him move his hand in the down, across, back and up motion used to count four-four time. Then when he sounded out a song written in three-four time, he moved his hand in a triangular motion—down, across and up, ready to start a new measure at the top of the motion.

Soon Aunt Mary joined them, also showing excitement over the new book. Within only a few minutes, as they each held a book, the three of them were singing new songs they had never heard before. Aunt Mary sang the lead while Uncle Louis sang tenor, and Galen sang bass. Aunt Mary sang soprano a bit lower than most women, and she could sing alto if it didn't go too low.

When they came to a song that gave the alto the lead throughout the chorus, Aunt Mary switched to alto and Uncle Louis, with his rich tenor voice, sang soprano. "That's a really good trio. You are sounding great on that new song. I like it." It was Cousin Barney with a hoe on his shoulder and a wood stave bucket in his left hand. The bucket had several inches of dark soil in the bottom.

Cousin Barney lived alone in a cabin near the grist mill, and he spent most of his time fishing. No one needed to ask what he had in his bucket. There would be enough night-crawlers to keep his hook baited until sundown. "Expecting a good shower later today," he said. "The fish should be biting for an hour or more before the rain."

"It's just real good to see you, G.W. I will put my fishing pole down long enough to attend your singing school. I love that good gospel singing."

"And it's good to see you, Barney. It will be a big help to have you leading the bass section."

He grinned broadly at Barney. "You see? I have a good memory. It has been twelve years since I heard you sing, but I remember. You haven't really changed much in those twelve years. You are looking hale and hearty."

Barney took time to examine the new convention book and sound out a couple of the new songs. Then he excused himself to get his fishing pole and head toward the creek. As Galen watched him go, wheels were turning in his brain. Cousin Barney just might be able to help him find the little girl.

A good meal of green beans, mashed potatoes, radishes, green onions, fried chicken and cornbread raised Galen's spirits. It had been so long since he had eaten a really good meal. "You are too lean, G.W., although there is good color in your cheeks," Aunt Mary commented. "You will leave here with a few more pounds on your frame. You will eat a lot of fried chicken and mashed potatoes, and there may be a fish fry or two."

"I know it takes a little extra effort to organize a fish fry," Galen answered. "I was sort of hoping that Barney might share some fish with us. I would be glad to clean them." It might give him an opportunity to talk privately with Barney about the kidnapped girl.

"I wouldn't be at all surprised if he brings us some fish this afternoon," Uncle Louis said. "He does that quite often. Barney likes Mary's cooking, and he loves to visit."

"There are several young widows in these hills who would be only too happy to make Barney a good wife," Aunt Mary volunteered, "but he says that when he lost Jennie, he knew he could never remarry. It wouldn't be fair to any other woman, because she could never mean to him what Jennie did. I know he gets really lonesome."

Galen knew the story. In the spring before that summer he visited Uncle Louis and Aunt Mary, Barney's wife of less than two years died while attempting to give birth to their first child. The child was lost also. During that summer Barney attended almost all the singing schools. He said that singing helped his troubled soul.

Now in his early thirties, Barney looked younger, but his boyish countenance sometimes betrayed a sadness that made him look like a tired old man. "G.W., there is no man who knows these hills like Barney does," Uncle Louis said. "He does a lot of wandering, gone for days at a time. If you want to know where to find wild turkeys or deer, what the squirrels are feeding on or whether there will be an increase in the fox population, he is the man to ask. He lives close to nature."

"The word will soon get out that you are here, and people will want to come by and visit." Aunt Mary was thinking out loud. "We are busy, and I don't have time to prepare food for all of them." It was the custom to offer food to visitors, usually a full meal. There were loafers who took advantage of that custom to avoid working. Good food on the table meant that someone—usually more than one—had expended considerable time and effort to put it there.

Aunt Mary continued after pausing for a moment while Galen and Uncle Louis waited for her next words. "I think I will talk to the women-folks and organize a greeting and singing at the meeting-house. Each family can bring some food, and we will just have a good time together."

"Good idea!" Uncle Louis dropped a closed fist on the table for emphasis. "People will look forward to getting a little break from the fields, and it won't take enough time to interfere with what they have to get done."

Uncle Louis began to chuckle, while Galen and Aunt Mary looked at him with quizzical expressions. "The people remember you as a twelve-year-old boy, except for the few who saw you during your short visit in January. They are going to be surprised."

"Surprised that I grew up?" Galen queried with a smile.

"Surprised that you became the impressive young man that you are," Aunt Mary answered very seriously. "I was surprised, and they will be surprised. You have your father's good looks, but the shoulders and height of your mother's brothers. The way you move, smoothly and easily, is like Louis moved before rheumatism got hold of him. But you move more quickly without trying to hurry at all."

Galen's face turned red from embarrassment. He didn't know how to respond. He knew that he was a blend of the characteristics of his slender agile French father with his strong angular jaw, and of his mother with her long legs, broad shoulders and long muscular arms. His mother stood an inch taller than his father, and her strong physique did not in any way detract from her femininity. She was quite feminine.

He had often marveled at how quickly his father could clean a fish, and he once saw him disarm a man who threatened him with a knife. He moved so quickly that Galen hardly saw him move. He had never seen anyone so surprised as the knife-wielder. His wide-open mouth showed his shock, as he held his bruised right wrist with his left hand and groaned from the pain.

Galen felt comfortable with his physical makeup and general appearance, but he saw no reason to take pride in it. He had worked among many men on the river who were taller, bigger and stronger. He knew that good judgment, discretion and vigilance were much more important. He had seen big bruisers get themselves into real trouble because they placed too much confidence in their physical prowess.

Galen arrived on Tuesday, and Saturday afternoon found him at the meeting house with almost two-hundred people. There were new-born babies, elderly people who needed assistance to walk, and all ages between. The log meeting-house served the people of the community as a church building on the first and third Sundays of each month and a schoolhouse during the months between harvesting and planting.

Aunt Mary had insisted that he permit her to press his white shirt and dark suit, even though it meant rekindling the fire in the stove in order to heat the heavy flat-irons. He put some fresh wax on his dress shoes, and took his first really good bath since he got off the boat. Uncle Louis trimmed his hair with the scissors. When fully dressed, he met the approval of his aunt and uncle. That was important to him.

Crops would be "laid by" at the end of July, and people would gather for a "protracted meeting" that would last from one Sunday through the next. There would be a visiting preacher, usually a different one each year, and services would be held both morning and afternoon. There would be fewer people at the morning services for various reasons, but in large part because of the lengthy ride many of them had to make to get there.

Galen's arrival aroused the interest of the residents of the valley, and they gladly adjusted their work routines to make room for the greeting and singing meeting. Repeatedly, childhood friends he had made during the summer following his twelfth birthday, introduced themselves to him. Some wanted to play the guessing game, seeing if Galen would recognize him or her as an adult. He appreciated those who didn't choose to test him in that way, but he fortunately remembered and recognized all who did.

They all addressed him as "G.W.," which felt perfectly natural because his family and friends had called him "G.W." since his earliest memory. He shared the same first name with his father, and his mother did not want to call him by his middle name, "Wilson." The initials had served him well, and he and his father knew which of the two of them his mother was calling when she needed one of them.

Ever since Jim Harding had recognized his name back in the delta country, he had considered reverting to his given name when introducing himself. He was beginning a new chapter in his life, and perhaps the time had come to abandon the initials. He had no shame where they were concerned. "G. W. Broussard" was a name that was respected on the river, but it had become a well-known name among the thieves and murderers that worked the river and its tributaries.

Galen remembered how he was able to use his youth, and the fact that he was not well known, to get information vital to breaking up the cabal of thieves and murderers. If they paid any attention to him at all, he was to them just a "working Joe" who could not be bullied—and someone who took religion too seriously. They regarded him as a man to leave alone, and they did so. Of course that changed when he took the witness stand in court and detailed their nefarious activities.

When Galen was given the opportunity to speak to the entire group gathered to greet him, he told them of his decision to begin using his given name in lieu of the initials. "I want to ask a big favor of all of you," he said at the conclusion of his remarks. "You know me as 'G.W.,' the name I have answered to my entire life. The initials stand for 'Galen Wilson.' My folks called me by the initials because my dad's first name is also 'Galen.' Now that I don't live in my father's shadow, I want to be known as 'Galen.' Will you do me that favor?"

There was conversation among many of the people, and then a distinguished-looking older man spoke in a booming voice. "Welcome to the valley, Galen! We will call you by whatever handle you like."

"Thank you, Sir! Thanks to all of you! My dad is a fine man, and I like the idea of being known by the same first name as his. Thank you."

"Hey, it's about time somebody said thanks to the Good Lord for the good food." It was another strong voice. "I'm ready to eat. And then I want to sing."

Cousin Barney was present, and Galen heard someone comment that he seemed happier than they had seen him since the death of his wife. The first singing school would begin the following week, and Galen expected Barney to be there. From personal experience, Galen believed strongly in the therapeutic powers of gospel singing, even though he had never suffered the sort of loss as that experienced by Barney.

Only one week after that first school closed, he would begin the singing school in a valley about twenty-five miles distant in which the Bean family held sway. According to information given to him by Uncle Louis, most of the Beans were fine people, but there were several who seemed quite prosperous while working very little. These often made two or three week trips out of the valley. The thrifty hard-working people of the valley gave them a wide berth, and those Beans seemed to like it that way.

Uncle Louis was persuaded that the people of that valley had at least some idea as to where Margaret Bean, the kidnapped girl, was being held. One man had hinted to him that any effort to rescue her might result in her being killed by her father or grandmother. Aunt Mary found it difficult to believe that she was being treated well, and she was certainly being denied an education.

Galen was pleased to see that the people looked to Louis Robinson for leadership, not only on matters related to singing, but on all kinds of other matters. The next day was not a scheduled day of worship, but several men came to him to ask if he would deliver a sermon the next day. "I would rather listen to him than the preacher," one man told Galen seriously.

After the Sunday worship service, in which Galen led the singing, Galen asked Barney to come by the Robinson residence that afternoon so he could talk with him. Hearing him make the request, Aunt Mary invited Barney to eat the noon meal with them. He quickly accepted. "I was going to eat some cold fish left from breakfast," he said.

"You eat fish for breakfast?" Aunt Mary responded. "I might have known. I am going to give you a basket of eggs this afternoon."

After a scrumptious Sunday dinner, Aunt Mary and Uncle Louis declared emphatically that Sunday afternoon was the time for naps that they looked forward to all week. "The dishes will wait until later," Aunt Mary declared.

Galen and Barney went to the back porch where they relaxed in comfortable rocking chairs made of tough hickory, with seats of woven white-oak strips. Accustomed to landscapes along the rivers, which had their own charms, Galen looked with special appreciation at the Ozark Mountain scene before him. He looked across a wide hollow with steep slopes to a mountain ridge beyond. As a twelve-year-old lad, he had wandered along the sometimes rapidly flowing creek at the bottom of the hollow.

There were many places where the water seemed to sing to him in soft tones as it tumbled over the rocks. Between those places there were tranquil pools where a fisherman like Barney could catch enough fish to share with neighbors. He still remembered the cool swims he had in one of those pools during his twelfth summer.

Closer to the porch, red hens scratched the ground and found something to eat that only their eyes could see. One hen sang a contented hum while another used her wings to stir dust into her feathers as she squatted on the ground. The big red rooster strutted around his harem in obvious pride and satisfaction.

Another red hen came from behind a shed followed by perhaps as many as ten chicks that had not yet shed their down for feathers. She stopped to scratch the ground, clucking to her brood all the while, and the chicks hurried to peck at something she had uncovered. There was something soothing about watching poultry on the yard.

"I am really glad that you decided to continue your uncle's singing schools," Barney told him. "It wasn't easy for Louis to give it up, but last summer was hard on him. I think it was the long rides that got to him more than anything else. The rheumatism in his back causes him a lot of pain on long rides."

"I don't know if I will do it for more than one year, Barney," Galen answered frankly, "but I will see to it that some capable person keeps them going. They are really important. That summer I spent here following Uncle Louis from one school to another has made a huge difference in my life. Good gospel singing is important in a lot of different ways. I know of people who found their Savior because they listened to gospel songs."

"Many people won't go to church to hear a preacher," Barney added. "And they won't take time to read the Bible. Some don't even own a Bible, but many of those same people will go listen to good singing. Then they get to thinking about the words in the songs."

Barney turned his head to look directly at Galen. "You say you may not do it for more than this one year?" he questioned. "Do you have plans that might interfere? I know there is not much money in it, and we all have to make a living somehow."

"Barney I am watching for a good buy on a farm. If I continued to work on the river, I would probably be murdered sooner or later. That's just the reality of things. The thieves won't forget, and there may be a contract out on me now."

"Do you know anything about farming?" Barney asked.

"I know there is no substitute for practical experience, but I have done a lot of reading. I ask questions of good farmers when I have the opportunity. Even if there was no problem with staying on the river, I would want a farm anyway. I want a family, and I want to be at home with them."

Barney continued probing. "You were raised on a houseboat. Your father apparently made a pretty good living selling fish."

"He did, and he does. I am glad that I grew up on a houseboat. My sister and brothers feel the same way, and my mother likes it. But times are changing. I want children, and I want them to have the best opportunities to get a good education."

He paused, and Barney looked at him with interest, expecting him to say more. "I want a farm in the Ozarks, but I want to have access to flatland markets. I have to decide what I'm going to produce and sell. Right now I'm thinking about cattle. Just thinking. Nothing definite."

Barney grinned mischievously. It did Barney good to see him grin that way. The smile seemed to erase the ever-present sadness in his eyes. "Got a particular woman in mind? You would have to think about what she might want. Gotta keep mama happy if you have a good life."

The question startled Galen. He had given it no thought. After a few moments while Barney waited patiently for an answer, Galen replied. "I guess it's a good thing you asked me that question. Looks as if I have been overlooking one of the most important things. I just assumed that the woman I find would be glad to go along with whatever I planned."

"Assumptions are dangerous things. Especially that one."

"Well, Barney," he grinned, "the first thing is to find a good woman who likes me. That may be a tall order."

Barney looked at him seriously, but with a twinkle in his eye. "I can see I had better take you under my wing. You are a bit slow on some of the basics of life. You don't find the woman. She finds you. And if she likes you, you have had it! Over! Done with!" He gestured with his hands, palms up, to indicate the futility of resistance.

"I respect your opinions and I don't take your advice lightly, Barney, but when it comes to a wife, I won't seek any advice."

"Well, don't say you weren't warned when you find yourself hogtied with all your freedom gone. You've been a free spirit, going your own way without having to answer to anyone. You go where you want and come back whenever it suits you. Nobody to answer to but yourself."

"Sounds like you are against marriage, Cousin. And it looks like you practice what you preach." When he added the second sentence, he immediately regretted it. All the jocular bantering light left Barney's eyes, and Galen knew that he had touched a deep sore spot within him. Neither of them said anything for a long time.

Finally, Barney spoke in steady, solemn tones. "I'm a lonely man, Galen. A very lonely man. I don't know why Jennie and our little boy had to die, but what I do know is that she gave me the happiest days of my life. I hope you find a good woman who will give you that kind of happiness."

Then the twinkle returned to his eye. "Or rather, that she will find you."

Galen started to say something, but Barney interrupted him. He was not through talking. "I have been doing some thinking lately, G.W.—uh—Galen. I really don't think Jennie would be pleased with the way I am frittering my life away. I know she would understand that I couldn't get it all together for a year or two. But twelve years? I'm just marking time and amounting to nothing."

Galen took a chance. "Every man needs a mate, Barney. The Bible teaches that in the second chapter of Genesis."

"Yes, I know that. 'It is not good that the man should be alone,'" he quoted. "I have stood out under the stars and talked to Jennie. And our son as well. Did she hear me? Maybe not, but maybe the angels told her what I said. I apologized for not being a better man since she has been gone, and I told her that I hoped I could get another woman just half as good as she was."

"Well we both know," Galen answered seriously, "that life is a special gift. We have an obligation to our Maker to make the best use of it. And we have just one—just one life."

They both remained silent for several minutes. Barney took a stick from one pocket and his pocket knife from another. The stick had a well-done fish head already carved on one end, and he began to carefully take off more wood, while leaving enough for a dorsal fin behind the head.

Noticing Galen's interest in what he was doing, he said, "I carve all kinds of little animals. I like to give them to children. Sometimes an adult will want me to do one for them, but I do them only for children. There is always a waiting list."

Changing the subject, he said, "You wanted to talk with me about something." He waited expectantly.

Galen looked at him somberly. "I was enjoying our visit, and I didn't want to get into something unpleasant. This is not a pleasant subject." He jumped directly into the subject. "A kidnapped little girl."

Barney's head came up quickly, and he quit whittling. "I'm sure I know where you are going with this. So teaching the singing schools is not your primary job." It was a statement, not a question.

Galen quickly objected. "Yes. Conducting the singing schools is my primary job, and the people will not be shorted. They will get my best effort. Three men came to see me when they heard I would be going to this area to teach singing schools. They knew of my work as an investigator on the rivers, and they thought that I might be a fit for this investigative job."

"The little Bean girl? That's who it is, right?"

Galen nodded his head. "I had never heard of the case until the men came to me. One of them was the sheriff of the parish where her mother and her mother's folks live. What really has them on edge is the fear that any attempt to rescue the girl will result in her being killed. It seems that the last man who tried to find her was told pretty directly that she would be killed if there was another attempt to free her."

"Yeah, that's the word that is out around the mountain valleys. It's a matter people don't talk about. Not safe to do so."

"So everyone is aware of the situation, then?"

"Not everyone, but most people are. There is a lot of worry about the little girl. It's a huge shadow that hangs over the whole area."

"Barney, one way or the other, I intend to get her back to her mother. And I don't intend to endanger her in the process. I just need to know where she is. I need to be able to scout the place and all the ways in and out without being detected."

"And that is where I come in, I suppose. I know where she is being held, but she may be afraid to cooperate in a rescue effort. Her grandmother has made a servant out of her."

"It's hard to believe that any grandmother could do her granddaughter that way," Barney responded, "but I am told that she would beat the child's mother in the face while her son held her. I understand that she has scars from it. Their drinking bad liquor may be a large part of the reason for their cruelty."

"It's likely that the little girl is receiving similar treatment." Barney said. "Yeah, something has to be done. If we don't rescue her, they may kill her anyway. Count me in. I will do what I can. It may help make up for all the years I have frittered away wandering the woods."

"Well, I don't know that those years were completely wasted, Barney. First of all, you had to go through a healing process. And there is something about nature that does that. Helps get your head on straight and feeds something deep inside that needs feeding. There must be a lot of children out there who will never forget that you whittled something worthwhile for them."

CHAPTER THREE
MARGARET'S ORDEAL

Margaret squatted beside the cool waters of the spring and repeatedly lifted a wet hand to her left cheek. The water cooled and soothed the raw skin where Grandma Bean had repeatedly struck her with a wood paddle carved and shaped to work butter. She knew that her grandmother was going to be striking her when she spoke the words that were on her heart and mind. But those words had to come out. She absolutely had to speak them.

"My daddy is mean and evil!" she had said in a steady and forceful voice, a voice that sounded years older than her nine years. "He has no right to bring Yvonne here. Y'all just want to work her and hit her the way you do me. A daddy is supposed to love his children. And Grandmas are supposed to love their grandchildren. Not be mean to them."

"You have a smart mouth just like your sorry, good-for-nothing mother." As she spoke the words, she was spinning to attack Margaret with the butter paddle she held in her hand. She had pulled down Margaret's protective arms to expose her face to the blows. "I am going to beat you in the face until you are so ugly nobody will want to look at you."

Margaret's father had left that morning with his brother and cousin to go to Louisiana. The last words he spoke upon leaving was to Margaret. With an evil sneer on his face he asked, "Now won't you be glad to see your little sister? She's eight years old now. Plenty big enough to work. Ma needs more help around here, and you are so stubborn that we can't beat you enough to get you to work the way you need to. But I have an idea about that. We are going to try it when we get Yvonne here."

Glancing at her grandma, she had seen a smug smile as her grandma looked at her. She remembered her mother telling her on the way to Louisiana as they fled from her father, "Margaret, I don't want my daughters growing up with hate in your hearts. Don't hate your daddy and your grandmother. We just need to get away from them."

Even after she was forcibly brought back to the mountains, she tried to put her mother's words into practice. She thought that if she worked really hard and obeyed her grandma, things would somehow work out. But in spite of all her efforts, she began to really hate her daddy and grandma. She didn't want to grow up with that hate in her heart, so, like her mother, she made up her mind to get away.

She concealed some corn meal and some dried salt pork near the spring when she went to fetch the water. It would take several weeks for them to get back with Yvonne, and she intended to be gone well before that time. They would surely mistreat Yvonne when they wanted her, Margaret, to work harder and longer. And after a while they might decide to kill one or both of them.

Her conclusions were largely based on conversations between her daddy and her grandmother that were not intended for her ears. She had heard her grandmother suggest that Yvonne should be brought to the mountains, and how she could play one of the girls against the other.

By piecing together comments she had heard throughout the past two years, she knew that her grandfather had been poisoned by her grandmother. Difficulties between her father and her grandfather had become so intense that her grandma decided to help her son by getting rid of him. His tortuous death happened several months before their escape to Louisiana.

She remembered her grandfather as a kind man who quarreled with her father over his bootlegging activities.

He tried to get his wife and son to quit drinking the whiskey they were making. She remembered well his saying, "You are not the same people you were before you started drinking that stuff. It has changed you into cruel, hardhearted people."

Grasping the stiff rope bail of the wood bucket in her right hand, she laboriously made her way up the trail to the house with the water, leaning sharply to her left to offset the weight. By keeping the bucket behind her right leg and shortening her steps with that leg, she managed the weight that was much more than a nine-year-old girl should be carrying. She recalled the blows that always rained down across her shoulders if she lightened the load by carrying less water.

Struggling up the steps with the water, she heard the harsh words she expected. "Well you shore took long enough. You lazy whelp! Now get out there and hoe that grass out of the beans. And you better not leave even one blade of grass if you know what's good for you."

Margaret actually looked forward to getting the grass out of the bean rows because it took her out of the presence of her grandma. It also gave her an opportunity to think. She had to think through her plan to escape. She knew she had to have help from adults, and she didn't want one or more of them to simply bring her back.

If she could get out of the immediate community and into another valley, her chances of getting help would increase. She had heard her daddy and his friends talk about a nearby county that they avoided. She did not understand what a "county" was, but she concluded from their conversations that it was large piece of land. Also, that each county had its own sheriff.

The sheriff of the county in which she lived was not likely to help her because he was afraid of her daddy and his friends. At least, according to them, he was. She had learned that sheriffs were elected by a vote of the people, and they would be concerned about who would vote for or against them. She wanted to get to where her father and his friends had no influence.

The county they avoided lay toward the south if she understood them correctly, and Louisiana lay toward the south. She remembered well the route taken by her mother when they fled three years ago, and she remembered the location of a family who had been especially kind to them. She believed that it was in the county her daddy and his friends avoided.

As she used the hoe that was much too large for her, with a long handle that protruded behind her, she pondered various things that would likely come into play as she made her escape. She knew who her grandma would call on to find her, and their brutal natures made her shiver when she thought about them.

She would travel at night. The moon would be full within a couple of nights, and there was no indication of rain. She would find a place to sleep and rest during the day that was far from any trail or road. The two men who she believed would be searching for her, would not venture far from the well-traveled ways, and they were unlikely to search at night.

Upon hearing an argument between her father and one of the men who ran with him, she had chanced to acquire a small .32 caliber revolver. The man complained of losing the pistol and her father berated him for being so careless. Remembering that the man had come from the spring, Margaret easily located the gun where it had slipped from his pocket when he was getting water to drink.

Possession of the pistol gave her a measure of comfort, but her main concern was food. That, and durable footwear. She had no shoes. Having outgrown her worn-out shoes, her requests for new shoes had been ignored. She had cut leather from a discarded saddle and pieced together two makeshift moccasins that helped her get through the winter. Since late April she had been going barefoot.

She understood that she must travel light and move fast. She would need thick leather under the soles of her feet to protect her from the sharp edges of the many rocks. When her father left to go to Louisiana, he left the leather pouches he always used on his bootlegging forays. When her grandmother went into her drunken sleep that night, she would have time to cut and fit the leather around her feet, using the leather strings attached to the pouches to secure them.

From what she had overheard, her father had much less need for the money pouches now. Some eighteenth amendment had been repealed, and beginning the past December, liquor was legal again if produced by companies licensed by the government. Those companies were quickly taking the market her father had developed for his "white lightning."

Her father left his thicker hunting knife in favor of a long slender knife that he could easily conceal. He kept his knives sharp, and the knife could be worn on a belt around her waist, a belt that had belonged to her grandfather. Her grandfather's oversize socks would protect her feet within the makeshift leather moccasins and prevent the formation of blisters.

She had only two changes of clothing, all of which she had laboriously cut and sewn from shirts left by her deceased grandfather. She was grateful for the warm weather. She would be comfortable both day and night with just one layer of clothing. At night she would be walking rapidly, and if the night got a bit cool she would still be okay because of her physical exertion.

The day went slowly by and she tried to conserve her strength for the night's journey, risking blows from her grandmother for not working more productively. As the day wore on, her grandmother would become less active and more churlish until she eventually flopped onto her unkempt bed. Margaret thought through each move that she would make at that point in order to hasten her departure.

On her last trip outside, Grandma directed her to gather the eggs and come inside to clean the kitchen. Grandma went unsteadily back through the door, reaching for the door jamb the second time before she found it and steadied herself. When Margaret got inside she was already in her bed and oblivious to all that was going on around her.

Margaret moved quickly with intense excitement. She had to make her escape successful not only for herself, but for the rest of her family, especially Yvonne. She hoped to send word ahead to warn her mother of what her father was attempting. Although she felt strong enough to withstand the abuse foisted upon her, she could not bear the thought of Yvonne being subjected to the same abuse.

There was barely a year's difference in their ages, and some people thought they were twins because of their close similarity in appearance. Although younger, Yvonne was only a fraction of an inch shorter and three pounds lighter. At least that was their relative size when she was snatched from her family. She wondered if the long hours of hard work and limited food might have stunted her growth.

Margaret had found a piece of a broken mirror under the back porch, and she used it to look at her face and hair when she had the opportunity. There was no mirror in the small storage room attached to the kitchen which served as her bedroom. She was not permitted to enter her grandma's bedroom, although she was required to keep her father's bedroom clean.

Access to her father's bedroom, where there was likewise no mirror, enabled her to see things that helped explain her father's activities. She knew that he owned a .32 caliber pistol similar to the one his friend had lost. He concealed it in his clothing when he traveled while wearing a larger pistol in a holster on his hip.

Margaret hurried to her father's bedroom and opened a box made of wood that contained ammunition for the smaller pistol. She remembered when he brought the box into the house from his horse. It had aroused her curiosity because the manner in which he carried it indicated that it was quite heavy for its small size.

A few days later while he was gone and her grandmother had stepped outside, she opened it. She gained particular satisfaction at what she saw because it would provide additional ammunition for the pistol she had found. Now the time had come to take advantage of her discovery, and she filled an empty leather coin purse with a handful of the cartridges.

Her mother's father, a proud descendant of the first Swiss settlers in the German Coast area of Louisiana, carefully taught her and Yvonne how to use a pistol during the months they lived with him. His purported concern was the snakes that were plentiful in the marsh country of Louisiana, but Margaret had wondered if his real concern had been his fear of what her father would do.

She had carelessly left that pistol behind the day she was snatched by Uncle Clem and Cousin Joe. She could have stood them off if she had brought the pistol with her, and she had promised herself that she would never make that kind of mistake again. She knew the time would come that she would escape, but she had to make careful plans so that she would not be caught and returned.

Grand Pere Favre emphasized that the snakes should be shot in their heads, and he taught them to draw the front sight down to just the right level. After she and Yvonne had learned to hit a small stationary target, they then began to hunt snakes. They learned that they had to get close, but not too close. They learned to adjust to the movements of the snakes' heads and to squeeze the trigger at just the right moment.

When he was satisfied with their abilities, he told them very gravely, "Some human beings are the very worst kinds of snakes, and you may have to shoot one of them. When and if you do, the shot should go right between the eyes. That's the only place that you can shoot to make sure he won't keep coming, and you are no match for a grownup. That pistol will likely be your only chance to protect yourself."

Her father had two canvas bags in which he packed his clothes and personal items for his trips, a large one and a small one. Margaret had learned to judge how long he would be gone by which of the two bags he would take. If he took both bags it would be a very long trip. On this trip he took two large bags, one of which was Grandpa's old bag. She felt a little thrill of satisfaction when she saw that he left the small bag.

That answered her question of how she was going to carry everything.

She had to consider very carefully each item. The bag must not weigh enough to tire her and slow her down; yet, she could not afford to be without essential items. In the barn she had found a discarded tin pan in which she could cook. It didn't weigh much. She also found a light piece of canvas sufficient to protect her from any rain shower. It would cover a bed of cedar boughs on which she would sleep.

Soon she was on her way, the bag in her right hand, the pistol in the pocket of her makeshift dress and a long stick in her left hand. The stick had been used to manage the cows, and she picked it up at the barn as she left. She felt sure she would need it for neighborhood dogs, which were her greatest fear as she started her journey.

Then she thought about another item in the barn that had special meaning to her. It had no practical value, but it was neither large nor heavy. From under some old corn shucks she pulled an intricately carved and painted Blue Bird. It had been carved by a fisherman who she saw from time to time on the creek behind the cow pasture.

He would sometimes sit with two poles with lines in the water while he whittled. He was too far beyond the fence for her to talk with him, and the one time he tried to approach her she ran away. She ran away because she was afraid it might get him in trouble. Her father and grandmother had strictly forbidden her to ever talk with anyone, and they had promised some really bad things for both her and the person she dared talk with.

Noticing her interest in his whittling, he held it up so that she could see that it was a bird. Then one afternoon when she was driving the cows to the barn, she saw him almost one hundred steps ahead of her down the fence line. He held up the bird for her to see and then set it on a flat spot on the top rail of the fence. He didn't tarry, but faded into the woods.

She caught glimpses of him twice after that, but she knew he was respecting her desire that they not talk with one another. She wondered who he was and how much he might know about her captivity. She dared not hope that he would help free her. She must act on her own.

She walked rapidly in the moonlight, and it was probably more than an hour before she was compelled to pass near a house built near the road. No lamplight showed, indicating that the occupants had probably gone to bed. She moved as quietly as she could manage, hoping that she would not catch the attention of the dogs they surely had.

Thinking that she was safely past, she began to stride more quickly. A burst of barking from at least two dogs made her heart begin to pound. They rushed toward her as she turned to face them. When they were close she showed them her stick, and they were duly impressed. Apparently a stick had been used on them before.

As she stood them off their barking subsided, and they seemed to become just quietly curious. She talked to them very softly while watching the house for possible activity. Finally she picked up her bag and began walking slowly away while looking back over her shoulder. God had given her a way with animals, especially dogs, and she breathed a short prayer of thanks as they just sat on their haunches and watched her go.

Twice during the night she had similar experiences with dogs, both of which worked out well. Shortly before daybreak she came to a small stream that ran sprightly over the rocks. When she saw the stream, she knew that it was time to make camp. She had walked through a wooded area for quite a while, gradually climbing out of the valley. There were ups and downs, but more up slopes. And the up slopes were steeper than those that inclined down.

Excited to be on her way and wishing to get out of the valley as soon as possible, she had not felt tired. But now she was feeling the effects of working all day and then walking all night. More than just fatigue, it was a feeling of weakness. She was reaching the limits of her strength.

She left the road by wading in the stream, carefully taking each step on the slippery rocks. She would leave no trace of having left the road for either a person or a dog to follow. Fortunately there were no deep pools, and she didn't leave the stream until she was well beyond earshot from the road. She found a rock ledge, still farther along, on which she could cook and make her bed.

Building a fire to cook presented a real danger of discovery, but it was a necessary danger. She must have food in order to keep going. She hoped that this would be the only time she had to build a fire before she reached the kind family where her mother had found help for them more than three years earlier.

She had fourteen eggs that she would boil. Fried salt pork would last almost indefinitely without spoiling. She had a bag of pecans which she was not permitted to eat in her grandma's house. They were strictly for grandma. She would be angry beyond words when she found that Margaret had taken a goodly portion of them.

If there was anything that would make her even angrier, it was the fact that Margaret had taken five of the Baby Ruth candy bars from her private stash. She seemed to enjoy eating them in front of her granddaughter while telling her that she was not worthy of a candy bar. Margaret knew that she could not live off candy bars alone.

She took matches from a tin used by her grandfather when he wanted to light his pipe. He had made the tin by cutting away most of a Prince Albert tobacco can, removing the bottom from the larger discarded part, and then affixing the bottom to the shortened part of the can. That gave him a drastically shortened can that was perfect for carrying matches.

There were dry sticks scattered about that she could readily see in the early dawn. She gathered those she could use without breaking because she didn't want anyone to hear her breaking sticks. She soon had a small but adequate fire going. From sticks she had piled nearby she could add fuel as needed.

While she was eating two scrambled eggs with fried salt pork, she boiled six of the twelve eggs remaining. When they were done she boiled the remaining six, her pan being the right size for six. Not wanting to create any more fire odor than absolutely necessary, she covered the remains of the fire with dirt. Then she poured water on the dirt.

The sharp knife, neatly contained in a scabbard belted to her side, enabled her to cut cedar boughs very quietly. She spread them carefully on the ledge. She had no more than stretched out on the canvas that covered them, than she was sound asleep. She awoke several times during the day for short times. The second time she awoke she ate a candy bar.

When dusk came, she felt well rested and eager to be on her way, but she forced herself to wait until an hour after dark. There would be less likelihood of travelers on the road later. She had no concern about being able to avoid the people she might meet, but she worried that their dogs or horses might alert them to her presence.

While she waited, she peeled and ate two eggs together with some pecans. She muffled the sound of the pecans cracking by putting them into a hole and cracking them gently with a fist-sized rock. Beginning her escape brought back vivid memories of coming this same way with her mother and sisters. Strong feelings of love and sympathy for her mother overwhelmed her as she considered how that she was making the trip with no responsibility for anyone but herself.

Her mother had three young daughters with her, ages six, five and three. She and Yvonne helped her with their younger sister, Lynette. She and Yvonne each carried a pack that contained food and other essentials. It was in the early spring, and the nights were cool.

When she went to sleep the following morning she believed that she had made it out of the valley where the Bean family held sway, but she did not know if she had made it into the next county. Careful not to eat too much of her food, she felt confident that she could make it to the home of the friendly family before it was gone. So much depended on that family still being there.

She was awakened from a deep sleep by a very unpleasant raspy voice. She looked up to see cruel eyes above a sneering grin. "Well, if you ain't a fine one? Smart, you are. Slick. But not so slick that old Peck couldn't catch you. Klepto gave up on you and quit, so I'm going to get this reward all by myself."

Then he laughed, an eerie unpleasant laugh. "Don't look so shocked. Get yourself up and get out of that ugly dress. I'm gonna have some fun with you before I take you back."

Margaret got up slowly and fumbled with her dress as if obeying. He grunted his approval. Then she sprang back and Peck found himself looking into the barrel of her pistol. "Oh, you got a little popgun, have you? Give that to me before you hurt yourself with it." He leaped toward her.

Margaret had taken aim on the bridge of his nose between his eyes. As he leaped, he lowered his head enough that the bullet entered his scalp on the top of his head and made a large bloody spot on the back of his head where it exited. Margaret stood looking at him, ready to squeeze the trigger again. He was unconscious, but breathing. As he had hit the ground he rolled onto his back.

For long moments Margaret held the pistol's front sight on the bridge of his nose, but she could not bring herself to do it. He was no longer an immediate threat to her, and she was not a murderer. As she watched him she dug a cartridge from the pocket where she kept the pistol and replaced the spent round.

Quickly she folded and packed her canvas, grasped her bag and stick and carefully worked her way back to the road. She looked at the sun. It was early afternoon and she had enjoyed several hours of restful sleep. She felt the need to put distance between her and that evil man. He might regain consciousness and pursue her. She would have to accept the risks of traveling during the day.

She knew that if anyone saw her, her appearance would capture their attention and prompt action that might spoil everything. She absolutely must stay from anyone's sight until she was among people who would help her. She succeeded in doing so until sundown.

The sun was setting behind a cloud bank, creating an especially beautiful sunset while warning of the likelihood of rain. She could feel moisture in the air, and even though she withstood heat quite well, she felt unpleasantly warm. There was no need to worry. She had her canvas to keep her dry, although rain would interfere with her rest.

While admiring the sunset, she noticed some blackberry plants located about 200 feet from the road along the edge of a corn field. As much as she wanted some of the berries, she hesitated. She had been able to avoid ticks and chiggers on her trip, but she would surely get some if she went to those brambles. She had decided that the berries would not be worth it and was ready to move on when she heard a kind female voice.

She turned to see an attractive young woman sitting on a large rock behind her, on the opposite side of the road from the corn field and berry plants. She had not seen her because a large white oak tree hid her from sight as she approached. "You would like to have some of those berries, wouldn't you? You look as if you may be hungry."

Margaret waited for her to make some remark about her poor state of dress or the prominent bruise on the left side of her face, the side that had been turned toward her. Margaret knew how obvious the bruise was because she had brought with her the broken piece of mirror. It matched her broken piece of comb that she used to keep the tangles out of her hair.

Caught off guard, she could only answer simply, "I don't want to get chiggers and ticks. I have been lucky so far not to get any."

"You look as if you are on a journey. Let me share some of my berries with you." She reached behind her and produced a large basket of succulent blackberries. "Some energy for the road."

"Oh, I couldn't do that," Margaret protested. "You must have picked them to make a cobbler."

"I have plenty for the cobbler and plenty to spare. The vines are loaded with them."

Trying to remember what her mother and Grand Mere Favre had taught her about being polite and gracious, she smiled and said, "Merci, tres' beaucoup. They look delicious." She walked toward the young lady with the basket. She had not intended to utter the French phrase. It just came out.

As Margaret ate some of the berries, trying not to let her hunger make her greedy, the young woman initiated light conversation. "I sat down here so that I could watch the sunset. God is such an accomplished artist. I noticed that you were admiring it too. That says something good about you, that you can appreciate the beauty of the world in which we live."

She continued, "We have to go into the brambles and chiggers to get these berries, but can you think of anything more satisfying to the palate? We are in the middle of a great economic depression, but if we look around us in these beautiful Ozarks, we can find all kinds of good things for which we need no money at all."

"Why don't we just walk along together? I live with my parents just a short distance up the road. I teach school in the next county south of here, and in the summer months I help my parents on the farm. I have four older brothers who are all married with families. They live on their farms nearby. I am the only daughter, and I think my parents would like for me to find a young farmer to marry. They fear that I may marry a city man and move far away."

Margaret felt that she could trust this young school teacher, but she didn't know how to respond to the friendly remarks she was making. She appreciated the fact that she was not asking questions. The bruises on her face and the makeshift clothing spoke volumes without the need for questions, but at the same time they raised questions.

They walked along in silence for a while, and then the teacher broke the silence. "My name is Janet," she said. She waited for Margaret to respond. Margaret was glad that she didn't give her surname, because that would have put pressure on her to do likewise.

"My name is Margaret," she answered. "I appreciate your kindness, Miss Janet."

"I was hoping you might spend the night with us. It looks as if rain may come before daybreak."

Margaret didn't hesitate. She had to trust someone, and it looked as if God had smiled on her by putting Miss Janet on that boulder by the road. "Thank you very much. I was hoping to find someone who would be kind enough to give me a place to sleep. I will help you do anything that needs to be done."

Janet's mother came from the kitchen with a wooden spoon in her hand when she heard Janet talking with Margaret. She stopped in mid-step when she saw Margaret, but quickly recovered and carefully avoided showing consternation at her appearance. Looking at Margaret she said in the kind tone that Margaret had been hearing from Janet, "Well, my daughter has brought a guest to our humble home. Welcome! Make yourself comfortable. I am preparing something for us to eat, and it is almost ready."

She spied the basket of blackberries. "Oh, just look at those berries! Tomorrow we will enjoy a large tasty cobbler." She raised her nose a bit, obviously sniffing.

"You had better change your clothes right away, Janet, and hang those on the line outside. The kerosene you used to keep off the chiggers and ticks will soon smell up the house."

"I will hang them on the back porch," Janet answered as she took quick steps toward a side room. "I believe a thunderstorm will develop by midnight or shortly thereafter."

Margaret was left with Janet's mother and found herself feeling very comfortable with her. "My name is Margaret, and I have had some problems. I am taking a trip to try to get them worked out." Then she added, "For others as well as myself."

Showing pleasant surprise in her face, she answered her. "Well, you certainly seem to be self-possessed and well-spoken. I hope we can be of help in some way. My name is Mamie. My husband, Jeff, will be coming through the door any minute with a big pail of milk. Our surname is Williams. You are in the Williams household."

The expression on her face changed as she thought of her cooking. "Margaret, come into the kitchen with me. We can talk in there. I've got to stir the stew before it sticks to the bottom of the pot."

Soon Janet was back in a pretty flowing dress suitable to wear in and around the house. Then her father came through the back door with a full pail of milk with foam on top. Without thinking, Margaret went to take the milk from him and, although surprised, he permitted her to do so. Her action was simply from force of habit. "What do you strain it into?" she asked.

Intrigued, they all watched as she strained the milk into two gallon-sized jugs and then placed the straining cloth into the dishpan for washing. As she poured the milk, Jeff Williams looked at her bruised face and frowned. When she finished he smiled at her and said, "You seem to be a right handy and capable young lass. I haven't had the pleasure of making your acquaintance."

"This is Margaret, Jeff. She has had some problems, and she is making a trip to try to get them straightened out. We will have the pleasure of having her spend the night with us. As soon as you wash the barnyard off your hands, we will eat this stew I have cooked."

CHAPTER FOUR
SINGING SCHOOL FOR MARGARET

Margaret's shiny black hair, trimmed and held in place by two curved reddish-brown combs, contrasted nicely with her red-trimmed white dress as she walked erectly into the large log meeting house. Her alert brown eyes quickly surveyed the happy scene before her, and she smiled. Janet Williams escorted her protectively toward a group of adolescent and pre-adolescent singing school students who were visiting with one another while awaiting the arrival of the singing school teacher.

Upon seeing the unfamiliar face of Margaret their lively conversation ceased, and they focused their attention on the new girl. A new face in the community occurred rarely. Janet explained that Margaret would be present only until men arrived to take her back to Louisiana where she would be reunited with her mother and two younger sisters.

She and Galen had agreed with one another that the entire community needed to be made aware of the circumstances surrounding her unwilling presence in the Ozarks. When Janet introduced Margaret she did not shy away from using the term, "kidnapped." Only two years had passed since public outrage over the kidnapping and killing of the son of Charles Lindbergh, followed by the passage of the "Lindbergh Laws." The word evoked strong emotions.

The faces of the children reflected their understanding of the ugliness of the word, "kidnapped," and they made sympathetic sounds in response to Janet's description of the situation. Although none of the children had been her students, they knew her well and respected the fact that she was a "schoolmarm." Her words carried authority.

The adults had ceased their conversations when they espied Margaret, and they heard all that was said. Some began to express indignation to one another in low tones. When Galen walked through the door Margaret brightened in recognition, for he was the one who had told her that two FBI agents were on their way to take her back to her family. When he had related to her the efforts made by her family to rescue her, she had cried long and softly.

Galen allayed her deep concern for Yvonne, telling her that she was still with her family, and that law enforcement officials in Ascension Parish and surrounding parishes were on the alert for men fitting the descriptions she had furnished. The beginning of the singing school had been delayed so that Galen could get to a telephone and make all the necessary contacts. Only now did the people begin to understand the reason for the delay.

Barney was riding to meet the FBI agents in order to quickly guide them to the Williams household. Jeff Williams called upon two neighbors, both with teenage sons, to see that a sentry was posted at the house twenty-four hours a day. People who knew Margaret's Grandma Bean believed that she would likely attempt to grab the child or have her killed.

From Margaret's memory of the family who had assisted her mother and the three young daughters in their flight, Mr. and Mrs. Williams were able to identify them. They had moved to another community to a larger and better farm, and the house Margaret was trying to reach stood vacant. Her meeting with Janet had been fortuitous indeed.

Upon receiving word of her presence, that entire family came to visit with Margaret, a trip that required special efforts. There was not a decent wagon road between the two valleys, and they arrived on two horses and three mules. One mule and one horse had been borrowed. Margaret's spirits were lifted by a two-day visit with the mother and father and five children.

They were saddened by Margaret's ordeal, but gladdened by her escape.

The singing school instruction got under way, and Margaret gave Galen her complete attention. He explained the staff, the key signature, the timing and the notes of the songs. The shapes of the notes fascinated her, and soon she could readily sound the different pitches as indicated by the different shapes of the notes and their locations on the lines and spaces of the staff.

She learned the difference between eighth notes, quarter notes and half notes, and how to count the time as she gave each note its respective length. The first exercises contained only quarter notes, and when after a couple of days, eighth notes were mixed with the quarter notes, she really enjoyed the life they added to the music. She learned to hold a half note, or even a whole note, for its full length instead of letting her voice trail off.

Several days passed before they sang a song containing sixteenth notes, and her youthful exuberance came through in full force when they did. Galen told her that although she had a soprano voice, it was deeper than average for her age. He felt sure she would develop an alto voice, and he wanted her to learn to sing harmony on the second line of notes when they didn't get too low.

Singing harmony presented a special challenge and an intriguing one for Margaret. It added even more pleasure to her singing school experience. As much as she eagerly put herself into the singing school experience, she could not wait to see her family. She knew from past experience that it was a very long trip to Louisiana, but it would go much faster when they got to the river.

Galen and Janet couldn't have been more pleased with her participation in the singing school and the delight that she derived from it. Yet, during the inevitable pauses and slow times, they would notice a faraway haunted look overtake her facial features. They knew that despite her remarkable strength and courage, her mistreatment would always be a part of who she was.

There was no adult present who was possessed of more stalwart stoicism than she, a stoicism that seemed to contradict itself with a burning determination that always emanated from her very being. She related well to the other children, but she did not permit herself the careless buoyancy that was so much a part of all of them. And they seemed to understand. That they were her loyal supporters, was plain to see.

After being sorely deprived and abused for two years, a virtual eternity for a pre-adolescent child, Margaret threw herself into the music and the affectionate interactions with both children and adults. Janet, drawing on her schoolmarm experience with children, thrilled at seeing the day-to-day progress Margaret was making. She searched her mind for everything she could think of that might encourage the child to make the most of her new life.

Margaret's longing to see her mother, sisters and grandparents added an immeasurable dimension to her gladness at being free. Her emotions stirred relentlessly within her, but only a person with special insight, such as Janet, could detect the power of those feelings. No one needed to tell her that Margaret carefully controlled her outward demeanor in order to prevent those emotions from spinning out of control.

Margaret had questions and hopes that she did not share, even with Janet. She understood that two or more men would come to escort her to her family in Louisiana. Wouldn't it be nice, she thought, if her mother came with the two men? But that was impossible. Those two men were being dispatched from Memphis, and her mother would have go to Memphis from several days downriver.

She had heard from some of the children that "Barney," who was meeting and guiding the two "federal agents," carved little wood animals and gave them to children. She looked forward to seeing him, for surely he was the fisherman who had carved and painted the bird for her. She would mention it to no one until she saw him.

The singing school teacher, a nice man who seemed very alert and capable, had met with her and Janet at the Williams home before the singing school opened. He showed her a picture of herself made at her Louisiana school shortly before she was kidnapped. At the same meeting, he showed her a copy of some official looking papers containing her name and those of Yvonne and Lynette.

Although she had attended only one year of school, she had a clear memory of what she had learned. She readily recognized her name and those of her sisters. Mr. Galen explained that the funny looking black paper with white letters was a photocopy of an order of a Louisiana judge. It granted legal custody of her and her sisters to their mother. He pointed out the name of her mother, and Margaret quickly recognized it.

One day in the middle of a song, the side door burst open, and three men wearing stars on their shirts strode arrogantly into the meeting house. The larger and older of the three announced that he was the sheriff in the adjoining county, and that he had come to arrest Margaret Bean. Galen stepped quickly in front of the man, blocking his path. The sheriff indignantly thundered, "Get out of my way. Where's that girl?"

"There she is!" one of them said, as he reached to draw his pistol from the holster.

Janet was suddenly beside him with a fire poker in her hand. She had quickly seized it from where it hung on a post by the nearby wood heater. "If you draw that pistol Harry Rutland, I will break your arm. You have no business bursting in here this way. And to think that you would draw a pistol in the middle of a crowd of people, most of whom are children."

"You can turn around and walk back out that door, sheriff," Galen said evenly. "That girl is in the custody of federal agents, who will arrive here at any time to return her to her family in Louisiana. She was kidnapped two years ago, and she is going back home."

The sheriff seemed stunned by the news that federal agents were on their way, but he quickly recovered.

"I'm arresting her for attempted murder. That overrides anything else. She is going with me."

"Sheriff, if you took custody of this girl, you would be participating in a kidnapping. I don't believe you want to do that. You know how the entire nation feels about kidnapping since the Lindbergh case. This move you are trying is not only bad for the girl. It is foolish and dangerous for you."

"I am not taking any advice from a singing school teacher on how to do my job. Move aside before I arrest you too."

"You are trying my patience, sheriff. You are outside your jurisdiction, and you are telling me that you are going to arrest a nine-year-old girl as if she were an adult. But I will bear with you long enough to ask you, who did she attempt to murder? And how?"

"She shot Howard Peckham in the head. A miracle she didn't kill him. Now hand her over."

Galen had no knowledge of any such thing happening, but Margaret had shared her experience with Janet after Janet discovered that she possessed a pistol. Janet responded to the sheriff's assertion.

"Yes, she shot him after he told her to take off her dress so that he could have some fun with her. That is self-defense, Sheriff! Not attempted murder."

Several voices spoke at once. The loudest one said, "Peck? That sorry piece of scum? Killing him would be a service to mankind."

Twenty or more children of all ages had made a protective circle around Margaret, and that fact was not lost on the sheriff. He decided that he should produce his service weapon. As he withdrew it from the holster, he yelled in pain. More quickly than he could have imagined Galen grasped his right wrist with his left hand in a grip so tight that the pistol fell from his fingers.

With his right hand, Galen caught the pistol as it fell, while moving behind the sheriff and pushing his wrist up to his shoulder blades. A fourth man with the sheriff tried to come to the sheriff's rescue. He had come in from a different door, one of the two front doors. He now stood just inside the door with his pistol drawn. Most people had not seen him.

"Everybody freeze! Freeze, or I start shooting!" No sooner had he spoken the words than strong arms wrapped around him from behind while a different pair of hands grasped his arm. His arm went down, and the pistol was pulled from his grasp. In a fit of temper he squeezed the trigger, but the gun did not fire. Puzzled, he immediately saw the answer. The thumb of the hand that took the pistol had kept the hammer from falling on the firing pin.

"You are interfering with officers of the law!" he bellowed. "You will pay for this!"

A low voice growled in his ear. "I am an officer of the law. FBI. Take it easy." After a few long moments, the agent released him from the tight pressure around his chest, and he almost fell to the floor. He was ready to pass out from lack of oxygen."

The protective crowd around Margaret turned to see what was happening at the front door. They parted enough for Margaret to see. She saw the fisherman who had left the wood-carved bird. She knew now that they called him "Barney." He held the pistol he had just taken from the hapless victim of the federal agent's strong encircling arms. That frustrated victim was one of her father's friends, a man her father called "Jake."

Jake came by often to get some whiskey. She had never seen him wear a star, but he had one pinned to his shirt now. He rode with her father often to deliver whiskey shipments to the flatland country.

One of the FBI agents took charge of the situation. He pulled a badge from his clothing for everyone to see. As he gestured toward the other agent he said, "We are FBI agents, assigned mostly to kidnapping cases. Margaret Bean was kidnapped two years ago in Louisiana, and we will return her to her family there. Other agents are following close behind us to investigate and apprehend those responsible for her kidnapping. Any information any of you can give will be appreciated."

He walked forward to where Galen still held the sheriff in an arm-lock. Addressing Galen, he said, "I believe you are G. W. Broussard?"

"That is correct," Galen answered.

When the agent uttered the name, "G. W. Broussard," Jake's bowed head snapped up, and he stared at Galen. The color fled from the sheriff's face, and Rutland's mouth dropped open as he stared stupidly at Galen.

The agent turned his attention to the sheriff. "Sheriff, we are going to overlook—for now—the fact that you tried to aid this little girl's kidnappers. As you know, since the passage of the Lindbergh Laws, any assistance given to kidnappers is a very serious federal offense."

He looked at the sheriff very pointedly. "I am advising you that we overheard what you and your deputies discussed before you entered." He paused long enough for the significance of those words to sink in.

Then he explained, "We arrived before you did, and we did not wish to interrupt the singing school. You are skating on very thin ice, Sheriff, and you would be well advised to cooperate fully with the agents who are following us. If you think to cause them any problems, there are still more federal agents who can and will be made readily available. Your distance from the more populated areas will afford you no protection at all."

Sullenly, the sheriff turned to leave. Galen spoke to him. "Hold on, Sheriff." The sheriff turned fearfully, expecting more bad news. When he saw Galen extending to him his pistol, he grunted his thanks and walked out the door as he thrust it into the holster.

Overjoyed at the words spoken by the agent, Margaret pushed her way out of the circle and ran to Barney. She wrapped her arms around him and hugged him tightly. Surprised and pleased beyond words, Barney returned the hug. His efforts to show his concern had been successful. She had, indeed, been encouraged.

She stepped back and looked up at him. "I brought the Blue Bird with me when I left. You did such a great job. Tres bien! Merci tres beaucoup!" The French words flowed from the excitement she felt. She did not realize she had used them until Barney responded in French.

"Vous parlez Francais!" she exclaimed.

"Very little," he said. "I spent four winters near Breaux Bridge. I'm torn between the mossy oaks and bayous of South Louisiana and the clear streams and valleys of the Ozarks."

"Are you coming with us to meet my mother?" she blurted. "I want her to meet you."

Barney was taken aback. "If you want me to meet your mother, I will be there. The FBI agents know the way back, but it won't hurt to have someone familiar with these mountains go with them."

Margaret didn't need to ask Barney if he had a family. Janet, when she saw the Blue Bird he had made, told her Barney's story and Margaret's heart reached out to him. Her separation from her family enabled her to empathize with him.

Janet had noticed Jake's head abruptly come up when the federal agent mentioned the name, "G. W. Broussard." She was still standing beside Harry Rutland, and Jake's reaction made her look at Rutland to see if he reacted to the name, only to see him staring at Galen with his mouth hanging open. She then noticed that all the color had drained from the sheriff's face.

Janet knew Galen only by his first and last names, and her curiosity suddenly expanded exponentially. She did not accept him at face value from their very first meeting. There was more to this man than teaching singing schools. How did it happen that he was trusted to locate and rescue a kidnapped child?

He possessed ample musical talent, a rich baritone voice and an obvious love for teaching others to sing. Yet, there was more to this man. Now the crooked sheriff and his lackeys betrayed their knowledge and fear of him when his name was varied by the use of his initials.

He had not hesitated to take the play from the sheriff when the sheriff barged into the meeting house, obviously expecting timid compliance with his demands. She didn't see the movement of Galen's left hand when he took the pistol from the sheriff. As quick as a wink he went from confronting the sheriff in front of him to standing behind him with the sheriff's right hand between his shoulder blades. He deftly caught the falling pistol with his own right hand.

Galen's voice caught her attention. He was speaking to everyone. "Tomorrow we will begin with the song we were singing when we were rudely interrupted. School is dismissed for today, but I know that you will want to say good bye to Margaret. You will want to wish her well as she begins her long trip back to her family."

Although their acquaintance had been quite brief, Margaret's imminent departure evoked the free flow of many tears. Several times girls near her age begged her to find a way to come back for a visit. Margaret hugged each one as tears ran down her own cheeks.

Mules had been hitched to the wagons, cinch straps had been tightened on the saddle horses, and other preparations had been made for the trips home. Then all eyes shifted to the arrival of two fast-moving horses. Carlton Bean and his oldest son, Robert, rode as if they were on a mission. They wished to speak to all the people at the school.

When he had everyone's attention, including the two FBI agents, Carlton began. "Robert and I didn't know what we could do, but we overheard Margaret's grandmother Bean giving the sheriff a bad time about letting Margaret get away. She declared repeatedly that she wanted her dead. She threatened the sheriff with the loss of his job if he didn't do her bidding. Shortly after that conversation, we saw the sheriff and three men ride away. We noticed that Jake Latham, a well-known bootlegger was wearing a star. They headed in this direction."

He paused and searched the people's faces as if gauging whether they understood what he was saying. "I didn't know what Robert and I could do, but I knew we had to do something. We had heard that Margaret was attending Galen's singing school here, and they were headed in this direction. We thought our best chance of rescuing Margaret would be to intercept them as they left here. We found a likely place about a mile down the road and set up."

Margaret listened intently, and she was not surprised that her grandmother demanded that she be killed. Even so, it hurt deeply. The thought hurt. She had tried to love her grandmother. Her mother had told her not to hate, and she had tried. After all the wrong her grandmother had done, first to her mother and then to her, she was not surprised. Nevertheless, it hurt.

This man, who somebody said was Carlton Bean, was willing to risk his life and that of his son to rescue her. It helped her feelings to know that there were good Beans out there. She remembered when her father had been a good man, and she remembered when her grandma Bean had treated her kindly. She believed that the whiskey they drank had made them cruel.

Carlton Bean continued. "When they reached the point where we had set up for them, it became obvious Margaret was not with them. That scared us. We were afraid they had already killed her. They stopped, and we wondered why. They had stopped to talk. I was at a point where I could not understand what they were saying, but Robert could hear them clearly. He will tell you what they said."

Robert's horse was restless and would not stand still. Robert had dismounted and he stood in front of his horse while holding a tight rein. "Oh they were angry! They were fit to be tied. The sheriff said, 'He's as good as dead. He's gonna die. It will be sweet to collect some hard cash for doing it. But cash or no cash, he's gonna die. No man can do me that way and live. He's gonna die.'"

His father dismounted and walked over to take the reins of Robert's horse. Carlton's horse shook his head at Robert's horse as if to rebuke him. It seemed to work. The horse settled down.

"Jake Latham seemed to calm down some. He said, 'I just want my cut of that mob money. You have a grudge fight going with him because he threw you off that deck into the water, where the port police found you and arrested you. But you don't know for sure that it was him. It was dark.'"

The sheriff said, "Oh I know for sure now that it was him. After he made that move on me today, I know it was him. No doubt about it. And everybody knew that G. W. Broussard was crazy about gospel singing."

Janet was listening thoughtfully. She was learning more about Galen Broussard.

"Harry Rutland was of a different mind. He said, 'It don't take much money for me to live. I'm plenty sore about what happened back there, but I'm gonna leave this new deal alone. This ain't local stuff where we can control things. I don't want them federal agents breathing down my neck. I got kinfolk in Missouri, and I may go visit them for a while.'"

"The sheriff said, 'Okay, so you are out. That's more money for the rest of us.'"

"'If you collect,'" Harry said. "' There ain't no guarantee you will ever see a dime of that contract money.' The sheriff gave him a cussing, and they rode on. Bill Pritchard brought up the rear and he seemed to be thinking things over. He had not had anything to say."

Galen stepped forward to speak to the group. Horses and mules were eager to be moving, so he would make it short.

"I have been known for most of my life as 'G.W. Broussard.' That was the name by which I was known when I worked on the river. I prefer now to go by my first name instead of the initials." He gestured at the FBI agent who had verified his name within the hearing of everyone.

"When this federal agent called my name by my initials, I noticed the sheriff stiffen, and I saw two others take notice. Word is circulating that the mob that works the riverboats and ports has put out a contract on G. W. Broussard."

In spite of the restlessness of the animals, he had their attention. He would make it short. "I won't go into the reasons why they put out a contract on me, except to say that I worked as an undercover agent on the river until I had to testify against some of them in court."

One man spoke up. "Sounds like that crooked sheriff is gonna try to gun you down wherever he can find you. And there may be others comin' after you. I would like to help you, but I don't want my wife and kids to be caught in the middle of a shootout. We won't be comin' back to singing school."

His children began to protest, but he silenced them with a stern look. Other adults began to express the same concern, and Galen could see the logic in what they were saying.

"Okay, so I guess we need to cancel the remainder of the singing school. I don't want to endanger any of you."

"Look Galen," one man said. "I will circle around in the community tomorrow and take up a collection for you to show our appreciation. Just tell me privately where I can find you when I get it together. Looks like you can't let it be known where you are gonna be or the route you are gonna take to get there. We people will be pulling for you and speaking a word to the Master on your behalf."

Carlton Bean had been talking intensely with his son, Robert. He turned and spoke loudly. "Hold on, everybody. I want to ask Galen a question. Give me your honest answer, Galen, without sparing my feelings or my son's feelings. Would Robert qualify to teach the rest of this singing school?"

"As sure as a bird can fly!" Galen answered enthusiastically. "The most important thing is being able to communicate and make singing interesting and fun. Robert can do it. His wife can be a lot of help if she is willing."

Galen had just finished a singing school in the Bean community, and he had especially appreciated the help that Robert had given him. In that community Galen had enjoyed one of the best tenor sections he had ever heard, and Robert Bean was largely responsible for it.

"I don't want to overload you, Robert, but I have two more singing schools scheduled following this one. I surely would like to get someone to take those. Don't make the decision now, but think about it."

The man who had first announced that he would not be bringing his family back spoke up again. "Well that was a quick solution to the problem. I'll be bringing my wife and kids back tomorrow." His children began to jump up and down and pump their arms in gladness.

"Galen, all of us will be looking for any way we can help you," he added. "Who knows? We may find a way. But you shore better be looking out for yourself."

Galen noticed Janet standing at his side, waiting to get his attention. "I am making the trip with Margaret until she is reunited with her mother. She needs a woman to go along with her. I want you to go with us."

As Galen paused for a moment to consider her request, she realized that she had not given a reason for wanting him to come along. She quickly added, "There is safety in numbers. That sheriff has not given up. He will be coming for Margaret as well as for you."

Several considerations ran through Galen's mind. The sheriff would probably give priority to the mob contract money, and his presence with Margaret would draw him and his lackeys to her. How would the federal agents feel about his presence? And what about the return trip for Janet?

"Let's discuss it with the federal agents," he answered.

From different directions people were calling to Galen, thanking him and wishing him well. One of the women mentioned his Uncle Louis and Aunt Mary, and her words reminded him that he would need to send a message to them. Everything was happening fast, but he had learned that life was often that way. Dull routine would suddenly become pandemonium. It was not a new thought at all.

Nature taught so much, and offered so many parallels to the ups and downs of life. He thought of how calm, pleasant weather would often precede violent storms. He thought of the Ozark streams in which a placid flow of water would lead to rapids that could overturn and ruin a boat. He thought of how a seemingly minor decision would sometimes alter the course of a person's life.

Why did he have thoughts like these in the middle of active interaction? It had always been thus with him. Conflict and multiple considerations prompted mental activity. And suddenly he knew that, one way or another, he would actively protect Janet and Margaret. His own safety was secondary.

CHAPTER FIVE
VIGILANT TRAVEL

"How did you manage to acquire such a good mule and donkey?" Cliff asked Galen. Cliff was the older of the two agents, probably in his middle forties. The horse he rode was good on level ground, but he quite obviously did not like sloping rocky ground. When stones slipped beneath his feet on an incline, he abruptly jostled his rider. Cliff noticed that the mule and donkey carefully placed their feet, seemingly knowing where to step without even looking.

When, inevitably, a sloping surface did slip underneath their feet, Emma and Jack seemed to just soak it up without jerking or jumping. Both agents, especially the older one, suffered from saddle soreness. Having become accustomed to riding in automobiles, this trip into rough Ozark hill country challenged them more than they had anticipated.

Margaret controlled with remarkable skill the gentle pony selected for her. When one of the agents commented on it, she explained that her father had taught her to ride when she was only four years old. "That was when he was still a good father," she said. "It was before he began to drink so much."

"Have you ever seen the still he used to make the whiskey?" Galen asked her.

"Yes Sir. He has four of them," she answered. "I have worked at all of them."

"Do you know what a car radiator looks like?" he continued.

She answered in the affirmative. "He uses one at each of the stills. The whiskey drips out of the bottom of them." The three adults looked at one another knowingly.

"That explains it," Janet said. "Horrible consequences. So sad."

Margaret looked from one to the other. "Explains what?" she asked. "What does it explain?"

Janet answered her question. "Margaret, for some reason, whiskey that is distilled through an automobile radiator causes people to develop mental problems if they drink enough of it for long enough. They become very difficult to get along with and do some really bad things."

"Grandpa tried to get Grandma and Daddy to quit drinking the stuff. He said it was making them mean. They wouldn't listen to him."

"The car radiators have a lot of lead in them, and that lead gets mixed into the whiskey just a little at the time," Cliff volunteered. "It is believed that the lead is what makes people get sort of crazy. But I think it is more than just the lead. Briar-patch booze just does bad things to a person."

Margaret continued to listen closely as she turned the bacon in the skillet. She had insisted that she would be the camp cook. "All of you are going to a lot of trouble just for me," she had said. "I will do the cooking." All of them had gotten to know her well enough to know that arguing about it would be futile. They could not have found a better cook.

"I am not really hungry yet," Galen said. "I will relieve Barney. I noticed that he didn't eat much lunch." The sun had just descended below the tree line of the mountain ridge lying west-northwest of them, and dusk was coming on rapidly. It would be a likely time for an attack. Although he trusted Barney's vigilance, he just wanted to be out there watching and listening with his own eyes and ears.

He had not seen or heard anything worth mentioning to the rest, but he had a strong feeling that they had been scouted by unfriendly forces. The sheriff, with several of his toadies, had made the decision to return to their old criminal operations along the Mississippi River. The federal agents, Cliff and Walter, had overheard enough to deduce their plans when the sheriff arrived at the singing school to abscond with Margaret.

"Just another two or three months," he had said to his deputies. "I want to leave here on good terms so I can come back if I want to. The liquor business has been good while it lasted, but we gotta find a new game now. We gotta get rid of this girl to keep the Beans happy. That old woman's gonna cause us some real problems if we don't, and the girl's daddy knows too much about our operations on the river."

Galen had been piecing together bits of information in his mind since the agents shared with him what they had overheard outside the singing school. It had never occurred to him that the sheriff of the county in which the Beans lived had any connection with the river. There was something vaguely familiar about the sheriff, and he had jerked spasmodically when the federal agent addressed Galen as "G. W." at the singing school.

On the river everyone knew him by his initials. Almost no one knew that his first name was "Galen." Something kept gnawing at the back of his mind, something he could not quite bring to a conscious level. The drastic effect that the sound of the initials had on the sheriff must mean that the sheriff knew about him from the river.

Having relieved Barney and sent him to chow, he pondered as he watched and listened. What was there about the sheriff that seemed familiar? He must have encountered him somewhere on the river, and he had a keen memory for all the men he met there. Remembering them and recognizing them had been a matter of life and death. The fact that he could not place the sheriff gnawed at him, worrying him endlessly.

Some sense of caution had prompted him to lead Emma and Jack to a secluded cul-de-sac. There was a small patch of lush green grass there and a pool of fresh water from a freely flowing spring. The federal agents were glad to see him separate Jack because he intimidated their horses.

Finally he pushed the sheriff from his mind as dusk turned to dark. The still and humid evening was changing. A breeze from the southwest grew cooler and stronger. It was going to rain. Then he saw distant flashes of lightning in the direction from which the breeze blew. He felt himself growing intensely alert, as if ready for quick action, although he could give no reason for the feeling.

It was a feeling he had experienced often while doing his investigative work on the river, and he had learned to trust the feeling. It had saved his life on several occasions. Another brighter flash of lightning illuminated the dim figure of a man at a higher point, where he could look into their camp. Flashes of memory caused a lightning surge of energy to course through his entire body.

He had seen that vague image on a barge on the river. The man, tall and well-built with agile movements, had attacked him with a knife. As he came toward him, the knife held low in his right hand, Galen could see the knife clearly as a gleam from a port light shined on it between stacks of freight. He quickly grabbed the threatening wrist and thrust it between the man's shoulder blades as he shoved him overboard.

The knife clattered to the deck and Galen retrieved it. The fixed-blade knife with a bone handle was of top quality, and Galen still retained it in his luggage. As quick as the flash of lightning, his mind made the connection. That dim figure looking into the camp and the vague image on the barge were the same. It was the sheriff who had come to the singing school to get Margaret.

Was the sheriff really the same as the elusive and cruel "Nighthawk?" Galen now had no doubt that it was the sheriff he had pushed off the barge that dark night. Nighthawk ran a theft ring that targeted the barges and docks, and law enforcement officers captured him when Galen pushed him into the drink. Within twenty-four hours he had escaped with the aid of a threatened and bribed jail guard.

Known for his cruelty to anyone who got in his way, his exact identity had never been established. The body of one of his own men had been dropped at the door of port police headquarters in New Orleans, showing signs of horrible torture. He was an informant who had been carefully groomed by the police.

Nighthawk had been a sheriff in the Ozarks for more than ten years. That explained his ability to drop out of sight for long periods of time. The revealing flash of lightning told Galen that they were in greater danger than he had imagined. The attack by the Mississippi River criminals would surely come before they switched from the horses to vehicle transportation. Their aim would most certainly be to destroy them without a trace to be found.

Galen knew that Nighthawk would love to get him under his control, not just for the reward the mob offered, but for his own satisfaction. Did he know that Galen was the one who threw him off the barge that dark night? Yes, he had probably guessed that.

Now that he knew for sure that they were under surveillance, and he knew the nature of those who sought their demise, he would seek them out. He would not merely wait for them to attack. He would necessarily operate alone, for Barney and the FBI agents knew their duty to stay close to Margaret.

If he had correctly sized up Janet, she would fight like a quick and smooth-moving panther protecting her young. From the beginning of the trip she had stuck close to Margaret while searching the surrounding landscape with her eyes and ears. Margaret, in spite of her strong streak of independence, stayed close to Janet and accepted her care and guidance.

Galen found himself thinking of how lucky a man would be to win Janet's hand in marriage. What a terrific wife and mother she would be. But this was not the time to be having thoughts like that. Without close attention to their surroundings, none of them were likely to live another forty-eight hours.

When Barney relieved him on watch, he told Barney what he had seen in that illuminating flash of lightning. He gave Barney a brief summation of what he knew of "Nighthawk."

"We will talk later," Barney said. "What you know fits with some things that I have learned about the sheriff."

When Galen finished his meal, served to him by Margaret, he talked in low tones with Cliff and Walter. Their faces turned grim when they realized the danger the party faced. Cliff walked to his pack and took up the rifle he had propped against it.

Their conversation, the grim expressions on the agents' faces and Cliff's action in taking his firearm in hand, were noticed by Janet and Margaret.

"Margaret is wise and strong well beyond her years," Janet said to the men. "You need to share with us the danger you are discussing. We need to know. Margaret can handle it."

When Galen explained their situation, Janet said, "We may be outnumbered, and they have the advantage of choosing the time and place, but evil always suffers a disadvantage. Evil men abound with false confidence, and we serve a just God who knows their dark hearts."

"I can stand watch," Margaret said. "I can see and hear real well. I know how to sit still and move quietly."

All were amazed at the girl's quick grasp of the situation, and they were not surprised in the least that she sought ways to help. Nor did they doubt that she would do a good job at whatever assignment she was given.

"We need to move our camp to that ridge over there," she suggested. "They may attack when it begins to rain, and they know where we are now. From that ridge we can see in all directions."

In the failing light of the dying campfire the adults looked at one another, silently overwhelmed by the sagacity and unflinching courage of this nine-year-old child. "I will check out the ridge," Galen said. "They may be up there now. Walter, would you let Barney know what's going on?"

What seemed like a long wait was only a few minutes. Galen spoke in low tones from the darkness to the group he could now barely see near the newly extinguished campfire. "Let's see how quietly we can move the animals. I have found a narrow trail and a decent place to bed down. It's defensible."

"There is a campfire about a mile or a mile and a quarter ahead of us. It was built in a place where it was unlikely to be seen, and I almost failed to see it."

In the meanwhile, Nighthawk and his four men gathered about that campfire were filling their bellies in anticipation of a short night of work. According to Nighthawk there were three men, a woman and the girl. "That singing school teacher has cut out for some reason. He may be still hanging around, so be on the alert for him. He's a slick one, but I will get him sooner or later, one way or the other."

All the sheriff's lackeys knew the plan. The sheriff knew of a narrow and deep ravine nearby that could be accessed from only one direction, and that open end had recently been blocked by a large treetop that had toppled into it. Apparently a windstorm had been too much for the old tree that grew against the mountainside with poor root depth and with all the limbs on one side extending over the ravine.

They would take the bodies of the men, the woman and the girl and drop them into the narrow depths of the ravine about two hundred yards up the ravine from the treetop. It was unlikely that they would ever be discovered. Despite Nighthawk's nonchalant remark about "that singing school teacher," the inability to locate G. W. Broussard caused him deep anxiety. The man had a way of appearing from nowhere at the most inopportune times.

"They are relaxed, enjoying themselves and not expecting anything," Nighthawk told them. "We just move in quietly after they have gone to sleep and knock them in the head with a club. The rain may keep one or more of them awake, but it will cover any noise we may make. Don't fire your pistol unless you have to, but if you need to, don't hesitate."

Jake Latham had been thinking of what Harry Rutland had said before he left for Missouri. Harry had said he didn't like the idea of tangling with federal agents, but the sheriff scoffed at him. "I have tangled with federal agents on the river for years. They put on their britches the same way everybody else does. One leg at a time."

The sheriff had stressed the importance of killing the two federal agents who had heard them talking about their river operations at the singing school. That worried Jake. The FBI would not take lightly the disappearance of two of their agents. They would look under every stone, and the clues would lead straight to the sheriff's office.

Margaret's daddy, Kelson Bean, would be a suspect, even if he could prove he was in another state. They would quickly check out anyone who had ever been associated with him, anyone who might be doing his dirty work. Any way Jake looked at it, he could see himself having to answer questions from grim and determined FBI agents. He didn't like that thought.

The one thing that had brought him along was the hope of collecting a nice share of the contract money for killing Broussard. Now the sheriff had said that Broussard had cut out, but might still be around somewhere. At the outset he had not given a second thought to taking that little girl from the singing school and then killing her. As the days passed, it seemed that he was developing a conscience, and the thought of killing an innocent child ate at something deep inside him.

If that little girl disappeared, Broussard would be investigating. Despite the sheriff's confidence that he would get him, Broussard would not be easy to kill. He had earned that reputation on the river. Maybe the sheriff was trying to cut the rest of them out and collect all the contract money himself. The more Jake thought about it, the more he felt sure that the sheriff would do that very thing.

"I don't like climbing over that ridge on foot," the sheriff said. "If we did, someone would have to walk back to get the horses to carry the bodies. When the rain starts, we can get close on the horses without making any noise they would hear. Just be sure not to let your horse talk to their horses."

For several minutes, the murderous crew could hear the rain coming across the ridge they must cross to commit their dirty deed. As it came closer, they saddled their horses and donned slickers. The reluctant horses made their way up the mountainside while the blustery wind drove the slanting, driving drops into the faces of the riders. No matter how much they hunched forward, the rain ran down their collars and wet their chests.

The physical discomfort particularly irked Jake Latham because he had decided that he wanted no part of this dirty deed. It was not that he was ready to mend his ways, but common sense told him that this was several steps too far. He never had any intention of getting in this deep.

And that little girl seemed to nag at him. He had seen the ill treatment to which she had been subjected by her own father and grandmother, and that had rubbed him the wrong way at the time. He had dismissed it by telling himself that it was none of his business. That was the way he had gone through his short life, just minding his own business and being careful not to expose his nose to anyone who might want to punch it.

Although he had not intended it, he had somehow taken the rear position in the single file of horses and riders. His reluctance, together with his preoccupation with his own thoughts, had served to open a considerable distance between him and the rider ahead of him. The decision was purely spur-of-the-moment when a flash of lightning illuminated a well-traveled intersecting trail to his right.

Jake gently reined his horse to the right and permitted him to continue to plod methodically in the rain. Instead of showing reluctance to leave the other horses, a reaction Jake was watching for, his horse seemed glad to turn his side to the driving storm. Jake, himself, felt considerable relief, relief that increased with each step his horse made. He, too, had relatives in Missouri. They would feed him until he could get something going.

Nighthawk saw what seemed to be the figure of a man on the trail ahead of him. His heart beat faster, his muscles tensed, and he reined in his horse. The three riders who remained behind him stacked up behind him one by one, perplexed by the halt. They watched while they waited for an explanation.

The explanation came from the strong voice of a man ahead of them. "It seems strange that men would be riding these hills in a rain storm at this hour. Could it be that there is evil afoot?"

A flash of lightning revealed a man stepping behind a tree. Nighthawk was the only one who had his pistol in hand, and he fired a quick shot at the moving figure. Galen was moving to his left to gain the protection of the tree, rifle in his right hand, when a blow to his right leg caused him to crumple and fall.

From his prone position, without aiming, he returned two quick shots in the direction of the riders. Galen had spoken no more than three words before Nighthawk recognized his voice. Fear exploded within him, and the shot he fired was more a desperate move than a calculated act. G. W. Broussard had again appeared unexpectedly out of nowhere.

He reined his horse hard. The horse was a cutting horse that had made his way into the Ozarks from an Oklahoma ranch. He turned so quickly that he unseated his rider, and the sheriff spilled onto the sharp corners of the rocks on the trail. Panicking, he ignored his pain and scrambled to his feet. Running blindly down the trail, he ran hard into the side of his horse.

In the confusion, horses and riders pushed against one another. No more shots came in their direction, but they wanted to get away. They saved their curse words for later, not wanting to make themselves a target. They had seen one man, but they didn't know how many there were.

No one missed Jake until they were gathering their camp gear. His ground blanket and saddle pack were still where he had left them, and they guessed that one of those two shots must have hit him. Was he wounded or dead? No one seem inclined to investigate.

The sheriff was sore in more ways than one. His entire right side hurt where he had hit the rocks on the trail, and once more that cursed Broussard had appeared when least expected. The other three would-be murderers thought they had ridden into an ambush by several men, but the sheriff felt sure G. W. Broussard was alone. That was just the way he operated. He chose not to share his opinion with the others.

When one of his men suggested to the sheriff that they abandon their unworthy quest, he declared ominously, "I didn't get to where I am by quitting when some pipsqueak challenged me. We are going to do what we came to do, and you are with me. Get that? If you are not with me, say so. We will take care of it here and now."

There was a hurried response by the one who had suggested that they quit. "We are with you. You can count on us."

After a short pause the sheriff said, "Good! Now let's get out of here while this rain will cover our tracks."

In the meantime, Galen was painfully making his way to Emma and Jack. The bone on the outside of his knee had a groove in it made by a bullet. His leg was working, but he had some painful days ahead. He hoped the bone was not shattered or fractured.

Tomorrow Janet would gladly clean and bandage the wound. That thought gave him comfort, a special kind of comfort. He would not take the chance of drawing trouble to them tonight. The three shots would have alerted them to trouble afoot, and they would take precautions. Neither he nor they would get much rest tonight, but they would all live to see another sunrise.

He rigged a shelter from the rain by tying his tarp to two low-hanging limbs barely within the reach of Emma's tether rope. Emma was protective of him, and she would alert him to an intruder. He took two aspirin tablets from his pack, swallowed them with gulps of water from his canteen and tried to make himself comfortable on his hard but dry bed. Maybe the pain would subside enough for him to get some sleep.

During a restless sleep, he was awakened by Emma pawing the ground near his head. The rain had ceased, and light from the night sky enabled him to see Emma sink her teeth into the neck of what looked like a dog or wolf. She threw it into the adjoining area where Jack was tethered. Jack's front hooves came down on the animal sharply as it howled in fear and pain. Suddenly it hurtled beneath Jack's belly and between his back legs.

Quickly repositioning himself, Jack's back legs kicked out and sent the intruder flying through the air. Joined by three or more canine companions, it went yelping out the open end of the cul-de-sac. Galen concluded that they were wild dogs attracted by the smell of blood from his wound. He knew that feral dogs could be more dangerous than wolves. Usually, they did not have the same fear of humans as did wolves.

Galen was pleased to notice that the rain had ceased and the clouds were moving farther away in a northeasterly direction. He could see distant flashes of lightning and could hear faint rumbles of thunder. Overhead and toward the southwest the sky was clear, and within it pinpoints of light sparkled as if to reassure earth-dwellers that all was well.

"Thank you, Emma. Thank you, Jack." Emma walked to him and nuzzled him with her nose. Jack began to graze on the lush grass as if nothing had happened. Galen drifted off to sleep again until the first light of dawn penetrated their little natural paradise. Soon he rode Emma into camp, while Jack followed without the necessity of a lead rope.

Janet seemed especially glad to see him. "Thank God you are safe. We heard those shots and were worried sick for you. Oh, you have been injured! Your leg is bloody!" She ran to him.

She peeled away the bloody strips of torn towel with which Galen had wrapped his knee, not waiting for him to dismount. "That is a bullet wound!" she exclaimed.

Regaining her usual composure, she took the reins from Galen's hand. "Go ahead and dismount. We must get that knee cleaned and sterilized."

Margaret stepped forward to help. She produced a small knife from the pocket of her dress and removed it from its leather sheath. As she began to pick at the cuff of the right pants leg, she said, "We will cut the threads along the seam to expose that knee. That is a good pair of pants, and when we sew the seam back and close the bullet hole, they will be as good as ever."

Walter looked at Cliff knowingly and just shook his head. Margaret never ceased to amaze them. Janet caught their looks and smiled at them. She said to Margaret, "While you do that, I will get some water boiling."

While Janet cleaned and sterilized his wound under Margaret's watchful eye, Galen told them of his encounter with the sheriff. He concluded the explanation of the previous night's events with a warning. "You gotta be vigilant every mile of the way. Nighthawk is a ruthless operator not accustomed to defeat. He will be back. Now he knows we have been alerted, and he will just change his tactics."

Cliff looked thoughtful, and Barney was searching the countryside with his eyes. Their vantage point enabled them to see for miles on three sides. Galen had chosen a campsite where they blended with a grove of trees on the other side so they could not be readily seen. Jagged terrain and steep slopes beyond the trees would make it difficult for an enemy to approach them from that direction.

"Looking at it from his viewpoint," Cliff said to Galen, "he's gotta make sure he takes us out of the picture now, if he expects to continue to live openly. It's either that or go underground. We know too much about him, and he knows that we know it. He has figured by this time that you know who he is, and that you have told us. He can't let us get to a telephone."

"This was supposed to be an easy assignment," Walter said. "Just escort a little girl to Memphis where her mother would meet her with two agents to escort them back to Ascension Parish in Louisiana."

After pausing he added philosophically, "Nothing in life is as simple as it seems. You have to be ready for anything."

Soon Margaret and Janet served the four men a good breakfast of bacon and eggs with biscuits and gravy. Barney poured steaming coffee, which he had made, for all except Margaret. "I like the smell of coffee," she had said, "and I may acquire a taste for it when I am older. For now, I don't really care for it, but I'm going back to Louisiana where they keep a pot of coffee hot all day long."

When the horses were saddled and Jack had accepted the pack that was larger and heavier than he had been accustomed to carrying, Galen told the others, "I am going to ride ahead and keep an eye out for any sign of Nighthawk. I will also double back and watch the rear at key points. You need to study the terrain all around for points that might conceal a sniper. They may try to put you in a crossfire from all sides."

"All of you take notice of what Galen is wearing," Cliff said. "We don't want to fire on him, but we don't want to wait too long to pull the trigger on anyone who is attacking us."

"I hope some innocent stranger doesn't happen into the middle of a firefight," Janet observed. "We have to keep that in mind."

"This is the way it's going to be for at least five days," Barney said. "We will pass homes and settlements, but it will be that long before we can get to a telephone. There may be a last-ditch effort to keep us from getting to a phone. And that doesn't mean that we are in the clear when we make those telephone calls."

When Galen rode off on Emma, Jack began to protest by braying loudly. That was one thing none of them had anticipated. If Nighthawk was within hearing distance, he would be able to add two and two. He would know that Galen had ridden off on Emma, and he would be on the lookout for him.

In fact, the Mississippi River outlaw did hear Jack, and he did draw that conclusion. What Galen could not guess was how he felt about it. G. W. Broussard had taken on superhuman qualities in his warped criminal mind, and the braying of the donkey ignited fear in him. Almost always a cool and calculating operator, this young man with the French last name had shaken his confidence to the core.

On several occasions, he had managed to thwart their theft operations without ever showing his face. Nighthawk had hidden among pallets of freight that night in an effort to bring an end to the repeated interference Galen caused them, although he, at that point in time, had no clue to as to Galen's identity. It was only when Galen had testified against several of his best men that he gained that information.

Sure that he was going to bring a quick end to the interference from that shadowy figure, he moved stealthily in the dark for a quick kill. Suddenly, an unimaginably tight grip on his wrist caused his custom-made knife to fall from his hand, and the hand that had wielded the knife was quickly thrust between his shoulder blades. The pain caused him to cry out in spite of himself, as a hand on his belt propelled him toward the edge of the barge.

His cry of pain and the splashing sound as he hit the water drew the attention of the harbor police, who had already been alerted to the theft operation. He didn't know a man could move so quickly, and how Broussard had become aware of his presence puzzled him. More particularly, how could he have seen the hand that held the knife? The night had been pitch black except for dim harbor lights that gave just enough light to see vague shapes.

He dared not show his face at the trial lest he somehow bring attention to himself. People would wonder why a mountain country sheriff had an interest in such a trial, and one of his men might inadvertently spill the beans. Although his women on the river missed him and the money he spent on them, he forced himself to stay close to his law enforcement duties in the mountain valleys. He mentally patted himself on the back for being smart enough to wear a badge. It was the perfect cover.

Now that man might be behind any tree, or even in a treetop, a ridiculous thought as to any other man. Riding confidently in a pouring rain to kill sleeping victims, suddenly a voice had spoken from the darkness only a few feet ahead of them. Except for the brief light furnished by the lightning there would have been no more than just the voice. He had snapped a shot at the figure of a man as he stepped behind a tree. Two blasts of return fire came from the barrel of a rifle with almost no interval of time between the two.

Those shots had been close. One put a hole in his hat brim and the other in the loose folds of his slicker. How could Broussard have known they were coming? Was anyone else with him? Probably not. Did he need anyone else? Probably not.

After all, he must have gotten Jake Latham. But how did he manage to do that without creating enough stir to alert the rest of them? A big part of him wanted to just hightail it out of the country. But what about his men? He had always had men around him doing his bidding, and he liked to live that way. But, on the other hand, they could quickly become a real liability when he had to dodge the Feds.

Then there were those who were higher up in the ranks of the mob. He desperately needed to maintain good standing with them. Killing Broussard would assure that standing, but taking out two federal agents at the same time worried him. That would create a big stir, and those suit-and-tie types who nobody associated with the mob, would not like that. Nevertheless, those agents knew things about him that absolutely required their destruction.

Two of his men were scouting ahead for a good ambush location, but Broussard wandering about alone threatened to mess up that plan. With all those thoughts flooding his mind, he sat still on his horse for a long time. As he was pondering what kind of plan he could come up with to deal with Broussard alone, he saw something move on the opposite side of the narrow mountain pass he had been watching.

With only casual interest, thinking that it was perhaps a deer, he continued to watch, although the movement had ceased. Then there it was again, a few feet farther to the right, and this time he saw something that quickened his pulse. "Mule's ears! Those were the brown ears of a mule." But a mule at that location? How could a mule get up there?

Then his heart began to beat faster. There was a man astride that mule, just sitting there listening and looking around. The sheriff carefully pulled his rifle from the saddle boot and dismounted ever so slowly. A limb protruded from a small tree at just the right height to afford the perfect rest for his rifle.

Broussard's head showed clearly with no obstruction, and the crooked lawman had confidence that he could make a perfect head shot. He had proved many times that he was one of the best with a rifle. He had to get that shot off before he moved. He could not hope for another such perfect opportunity.

Galen squinted his eyes as he looked toward the morning sun. Something had moved across the pass. Yes, that was a horse. It shook its head and flicked its ears as if to ward off a pesky fly. But there was no rider in the saddle. Galen's eyes began to water from the strain of looking toward the sun, and he blinked to clear his vision while dropping his chin to his chest. That was the last he remembered.

The sheriff saw Broussard fall and knew that he would not get up. He knew that he had hit his target. He must get across the pass quickly to retrieve something he could use to claim the reward. Broussard would have official identification on him, and he would cut a lock of his hair. His bloody hat would help convince any doubters.

Quickly he made his way down, across and up, leaving his horse on the trail below. The climb was difficult. How in tarnation had that cursed mule gotten up there? But that "cursed mule" greeted his arrival with clicking teeth and front hooves that pounded the rock-filled turf. He pulled his revolver from the holster, but before he could bring the barrel up, she charged him. She knocked him down the hillside, and his pistol was left lying somewhere in the leaves.

Painfully, he worked his way back down the hillside toward his rifle. His right shoulder hurt, and his left knee was bleeding where his trousers had a long tear. Both elbows hurt, and one was bleeding. As he reached for his rifle, he heard the unmistakable steps of a horse on the trail over a rise and around a curve. It was a walking horse, not in a hurry, but he had to get away.

Not content to let Galen do all the scouting, Barney had left Margaret and Janet in the protection of the agents to do some scouting of his own. He had studied Janet closely enough to know that she was very alert, closely attentive to her surroundings, and capable of looking out for herself and Margaret. She said she could shoot, and he believed her. Moreover, there was very little that escaped Margaret's attention.

When he heard the rifle shot, he did not have a good feeling about it. He had picked up Galen's trail and knew that he had gone in that direction. Although anxious to arrive at the location of the shot, he did not hurry. He rode loose in the saddle with his rifle across his saddlebow. As he approached the place where he had calculated the shot was fired, he heard a horse begin a fast lope.

There had been no sound at all, and then a fast-moving horse began to go in the opposite direction. Yes, that was very suspicious. No, he would not ride around that curve. Securing his horse to a tree well off the trail, he moved quietly forward, using all the cover that was available.

Then he saw where a heavy animal had moved along the hillside. Getting closer he found one clear hoof print, and he quickly recognized it as Emma's. Apprehension gripped him. Galen had ridden under the sights of a sniper, and his approach had caused the sniper to ride on. Maybe he had not killed Galen and had been stalking him to finish him off.

In any event it would not help Galen if he, himself, walked into a trap. And he didn't want Galen to mistake him for the enemy. Using the skills he had acquired from many years of wandering the woods, he moved slowly forward. Eventually he saw Emma. She alternated between looking around and looking down. Fearing the worst, he closed the distance between them a little at the time, and then Emma spotted him.

It took her little time to recognize him, and she whinnied a welcome. Barney watched her nuzzle Galen's body with her nose. Was he alive? Before moving farther forward, Barney waited for a couple of minutes as he listened and looked. Emma became impatient and whinnied again as if to say, "Come on!"

Galen breathed evenly as if sleeping peacefully. There was a nasty gash in his hair at the place where older men often had a bald spot. He would live. In fact, he was showing signs of coming out of the darkness to which the fast-moving piece of lead had consigned him. Barney got the canteen from Emma's saddle and with his handkerchief he wet Galen's brow, being careful to let none of the water flow into his hair toward the wound.

"Are you about ready to wake up, Cuz? Looks like you fell off your mule for some reason. You've got Emma all worried about you. You don't want to worry your mule. That's a good mule."

Galen tried to sit up, but Barney restrained him. "Just take it easy for a little bit. Looks like you got a bad blow to your head. Just lie there 'til you know everything that is happening around you."

"Where did you come from? How did you find me? I was looking at a horse on the other side of the trail."

"You were dry-gulched, Galen. He almost got you. By the looks of things, Emma protected you when the killer came to finish the job. There's a pistol downslope in the leaves where he tumbled. That killer is probably bruised up some."

"It's all real clear in my mind, but it seems like it happened yesterday. He would have gotten me if I had not put my chin on my chest to clear my eyes. They had begun to water from looking into the sun trying to see him."

Barney picked up Galen's felt hat and brushed the trash off. "Do you have spare money for another hat? This one has a pair of holes in it where the bullet went in and came out. I will bet Janet and Margaret could figure a way to repair it so that it would still look neat."

"It's getting too hot to wear it now. I was wearing it because of the rain, and it's not so easy for someone to see in the woods as is my summer hat. Sure hate to have to buy a new hat this fall, but better the hat than holes in my head."

"Well, you do have a pretty good hole in your head, but it won't be fatal." He grinned. "Looks like you will do just about anything to get Janet to fuss over you."

Then Barney raised his hand for silence. They both listened to gunfire in the distance. After a burst of fire, sporadic gunfire continued. "We gotta get there to help them!" Galen declared. He started to rise, and his head began to spin.

He gripped a bush near him and waited for the spinning to subside. "I don't know if you are up to it," Barney said. "I will go on ahead. You take your time and stay alert. Don't get that bleeding started again. You still have to think about that hip wound, too."

With that he worked his way quickly back to his horse. Emma nuzzled Galen as if to encourage him to get up. The spinning had ceased, and he rose very slowly, hoping not to cause it to begin again. The pain on the back of his head intensified with his movements, but he began to work his way down the steep slope. Emma followed close behind.

His eyes caught the glint of the pistol Barney had mentioned. The grip was covered by leaves with only a part of the revolving chambers and barrel exposed. He struggled along a steep precipice to reach the pistol as Barney rode by on the trail below. "Take it easy," Barney said.

When he pulled the pistol from the leaves, he recognized unusual etching on the walnut grip. He had noticed that etching when he picked up the sheriff's pistol from the floor at the singing school, but he lacked the time or inclination to examine it then. Now the distinctively shaped head of a nighthawk leaped out at him. It identified his assailant and told him that the dry-gulching sheriff took pride in his nickname.

The nighthawk was a bird about which most people had good feelings, and it seemed somehow odd that he felt more resentment over the murderous sheriff's misappropriation of the name than the sneaky scoundrel's attempt to kill him. "Maybe that blow to my skull by a piece of fast-flying lead has messed with my brain," he thought.

In spite of a splitting headache and a painful hip, he felt strong. As soon as he reached the trail, with Emma following close behind, he tucked the incriminating revolver in the saddlebag and mounted. He heard another shot, and after a short pause, two more shots. The first and last shots sounded like rifle fire, but the one between sounded like a small pistol. Janet—or possibly even Margaret—had gotten into the action.

The only sense he could make of what he had heard was that an ambush had failed, and Janet, Margaret and the agents were pinned down, but making a fight of it. Barney should be making his presence known soon.

CHAPTER SIX
UNDER ATTACK

It was Janet's alertness and keen eyesight that had kept them from being wiped out in a fusillade of flying lead. Always fascinated by the habits and quick movements of squirrels, she spied one sitting on his haunches and stretched to his full height, rigid and still. It was obviously watching and listening to something that had captured its attention. Then it turned and scurried away in the opposite direction.

She reined her horse to a stop and assumed the same attitude as that of the squirrel before it had run away. Margaret and Cliff, who were following close behind, did likewise upon seeing her action. Then she saw it. The barrel of a rifle came into view over the top of a boulder, and she could see a man's hat behind it.

"Quick! Over there! Take cover!" She spoke just loud enough for Margaret and Cliff to hear. Walter had ridden around a huge boulder and was out of sight. She had to warn him.

"Walter! Gunman on the hill to your left," she shouted. No sooner had she spoken the words than a rifle spoke, but it was to the right. Then the one she had seen on the left spat fire. As a glancing bullet whined by them after its encounter with the huge boulder, they heard Walter grunt. They also heard his rifle speaking.

Janet and Cliff both sent bullets into the space just above the rock over which they had seen the rifle barrel. Then a third rifleman behind them and to their right put a bullet through the loose fold of Margaret's dress underneath her left arm as she moved to better cover.

"You evil fiend!" Janet yelled. "Trying to kill a little girl! You evil fiend!"

The words actually touched the sheriff. He had enjoyed a measure of dignity and respectability in the years that he had served as sheriff, and to be called an evil fiend who would kill a little girl evoked a surge of shame. It was one thing to steal goods from barges and docks, and to kill any unfortunate laborer who got in the way. It was quite another to shoot and kill a little girl in order to pacify a deranged old woman who knew some things about him that he wished she didn't.

Yet, he couldn't turn back now. Quite satisfied at having killed G. W. Broussard, he had to now get these FBI agents who also knew too much about him. He would soon throw their dead bodies into an inaccessible pit. It made him feel a bit queasy to think that the woman and the girl would have to go along with them, but it was just necessary.

It was Jeff Williams' daughter who had somehow detected their presence and tipped off the others. She was a school teacher and quite a looker. It had always been in the back of his mind that one day he would find a decent woman like her and retire from the river. He admired decent people and liked to be in their company, to be counted as one of them. It was just that the honest life was too confining.

He began to consider how to finish them off quickly before some innocent traveler heard the shots and investigated. He had planned to get them all in one fusillade of gunfire. Except for that Williams girl, that school teacher, it would have happened.

A startling question ran through his mind. Where was Barney, the guy who roamed the woods all the time? He had been with them. He knew where the two federal agents were, but where was Barney? They just had to get Barney. Where was he?

It was almost as if Barney had read his mind. "Wondering where I am Sheriff? This is Barney, and I have you in my gun sights. I would just go ahead and pull the trigger, but I need you to call off your three men."

Then in a much louder voice he commanded, "Now! Do it now before another shot is fired. If another shot is fired, I am going to pull this trigger."

"Hold your fire! Pull back!" The sheriff shouted. Then he leaped behind a boulder to his right, and he dropped into a crevice that cut into the hillside. He ran up it to his horse that was tied just over the rise. Gasping for breath, he mounted and kicked his horse in the flanks. Quickly finding the trail, he galloped back in the direction from which he had come.

His mind was racing as well. That cursed Barney. That wandering no-good waster. He had ruined everything. Who would have thought it? He would now go directly to the river where he could live and prosper as "Nighthawk." The sheriff thing had worked well for as long as it had lasted, but this was the end of all that.

Suddenly there was a mule in the middle of the road. It was as if a jolt of lightning coursed through his body. It couldn't be. "No! It can't be! No! No!" He was screaming the words. G.W. Broussard had done it again. He had appeared from nowhere. He sat so nonchalantly on that mule, the cursed mule that had attacked him.

"You're dead! I didn't miss! I saw you fall!" Suddenly he sprang from the saddle, leaving his rifle behind, and he began to scramble up the hillside.

Galen had been waiting for Nighthawk to bring his rifle into action, and he, Galen, would shoot first. He could not shoot a fleeing and unarmed man, no matter how evil. He comprehended that Nighthawk's sighting his nemesis, who he believed he had killed, had temporarily robbed him of his sanity. Galen knew that to call upon him to halt and surrender would be futile.

He considered putting two or three bullets alongside him as he fled, but he decided against it. At this moment he was insane, and there was no way to shock him into reality. He wanted to check on Margaret, Janet, and the others. Nighthawk's abandoned horse waited placidly, his sides heaving as he sucked in oxygen to recover from the galloping flight of his rider. Galen grasped the reins and led him alongside Emma at a fast walk.

Galen had heard no shots since shortly before he heard the pounding of the hooves of Nighthawk's horse coming in his direction. The brigand was obviously fleeing, a sure indication that their ambush had failed. Barney's arrival on the scene had probably turned the tables against the killers.

He spied Barney's horse tethered to a tree limb, and he cautiously tethered Emma and the sheriff's horse nearby. His head throbbed with pain and his injured knee ached fiercely, but he had to ascertain whether Janet and Margaret had been injured. He must find a position where he could assess the situation and bring his rifle into play if necessary.

Although he was certainly concerned for the wellbeing of Barney, Cliff and Walter, Janet and Margaret were the ones for whom he felt responsible. Margaret was the reason for the trip, and he could not imagine a more worthwhile reason. Her mother was coming up the Mississippi to meet her at Memphis, and would probably be there awaiting them well before their arrival.

Margaret's chance encounter with Janet Williams was so fortuitous that it simply had to be more than mere chance. Galen had learned to see the hand of providence during the many close calls he had experienced on the barges and docks. He had learned to give close attention to vague—and sometimes not so vague—feelings that warned him of danger. And now, something deep within him told him that he had to be there for Janet.

On the one hand, Janet seemed highly capable of looking out for herself, but, on the other hand, her obviously superior abilities would motivate self-important people to seek her destruction. At this point it was just a feeling, but a strong one nevertheless.

Even as he, through his physical pain, wrestled with his thoughts and feelings, trying to put them into some kind of sensible framework, Chug Worley, a brawny bulk of muscle—of the head as well as body—was talking with the other two thugs who had pulled back from the ambush at Nighthawk's order. Chug was the one who Janet had spotted after seeing the squirrel scurry to safety, and he heard her shout the warning of impending attack.

"That ##### woman messed us up," he fumed. A string of expletives flowed from his mouth. They were his cover for his limited mental abilities. During his decade of adulthood, he had encountered only two men who were able to compete with him in terms of physical strength. He had bested both of them. He challenged others at every opportunity.

There was one intense fear that he kept carefully concealed. He feared a quick-moving man with a knife. Nighthawk was such a man, and he carefully avoided irritating him for that reason. He grudgingly respected Nighthawk's ability to consistently line up well-paying heists.

He didn't like to admit to himself that there were people who were smarter, and when he encountered someone who was obviously of greater intelligence, he searched for ways to trip that person up. He especially disliked intelligent women who spoke their minds.

He knew that Nighthawk was smarter, but he had worked for him for years because the money were really good. Nighthawk assigned him to jobs that called for brutal strength, and he liked that too. It fed his ego. All the while, he studied Nighthawk for any weakness with the thought of edging him out and taking his place.

He especially liked forcing women to do his bidding. The greater their intelligence and good breeding, the more he liked it. Those who were alert enough to avoid him, stirred within him a deep frustration. That frustration rendered him miserable and dangerous virtually every day and under all circumstances.

"Where is Nighthawk?" one of the men asked. "He should be here by now. I don't like just waiting around. Somebody may be slipping up on us."

The third man voiced another fear. "All that shooting may have caught the ears of some traveler or hunter. I think I will go up on that knoll and keep a lookout."

"Just be sure you don't get any ideas of lighting a shuck," Chug growled. "Nighthawk wouldn't like that, and I wouldn't either. Our business ain't finished. That ##### woman is gonna learn that."

The third man winced inside because "lighting a shuck" was exactly what he had in mind. He didn't want problems with Chug or Nighthawk, but he didn't want to find himself in the sights of the FBI. Their ambush had failed, and they were not likely to get a second chance. Hanging around now would get them nothing but trouble.

Barney, having determined that the ambushers had indeed pulled back, turned his attention to Margaret, Janet, Cliff and Walter. He found Janet and Margaret dressing a bullet wound located near Walter's navel. His solid brass belt buckle deflected most of the bullet, but a bit of it had splintered off and sliced like a knife. Cliff moved to and fro with his rifle at ready, looking and listening as he paced and turned.

"You will have a bad bruise from the blow to the belt buckle," Janet told Walter. "The soreness from that blow may bother you more than the cut. We just have to make sure the cut made by the splintered bullet doesn't get infected."

Galen found a position from which he could keep watch over his friends while keeping an eye on the area where Emma and the horses were located. He steeled himself against the pain in his head and knee, avoiding any movements that intensified his suffering. Barney soon resumed his scouting, unaware of Galen's whereabouts.

Galen had chosen a position where he could see in all directions, but an exceptionally sharp eye would be required to distinguish him from the limbs and vegetation around him. He waited for his pain to subside while the warm breeze seemed to bathe his body with soft palliative strokes.

As the sun sank lower in the western sky behind him, he began to feel stronger. As his strength returned, he noticed a slow-burning anger within him. Still, he did not move from his position. He would wait and watch there a while longer. Then he detected movement to his left, almost two hundred yards away. Perhaps it was Barney, but something told him that it was not.

Chug Worley was much more at home in the Mississippi delta country. The steep rocky slopes irritated him. Other things irritated him at this time. Nighthawk had not returned to camp, and the man who he had warned not to leave had ignored the warning. He was gone.

But most of all, that woman irritated him—gnawed at him. Her voice kept ringing in his ears. "Walter! Gunman on the hill on your left," she had shouted. He had been drawing a bead on the federal agent behind her when she shouted the warning.

Now he was back at the ambush site. They were still there, and he would demonstrate what he could do alone. He had told the other man to stay behind, and he had seemed only too glad to do so. He was probably gone now. Good riddance. He would just be a hindrance. Nighthawk had often trusted him to handle tough jobs alone, and he liked it that way.

As Galen watched, the movement continued, and he soon saw clearly the bulk of a thick-bodied muscular man inching his way toward their temporary stopping place. The ambushers, thankfully, could have chosen a much better place for their ambush where no cover was readily available. Chug was the one who had chosen the location, partially from over-confidence and partially from simple laziness.

He expected the first fusillade of bullets to take them out, affording them no opportunity to take cover. He accepted no blame for the failure, but focused all his ire on "that ##### woman." Even if he failed to get anyone else, he would leave with the satisfaction of having gotten her. "There she is," he exulted. "I will have a perfect shot from that rock over there."

"Put your rifle on the ground and move away from it." Galen's voice jolted Chug like a charge of electricity. He wheeled and fired two quick shots in the general direction of the voice while desperately trying to locate his antagonist with his eyes. As his finger tightened on the trigger for the third time, a searing pain enveloped his chest.

Having fired the third shot, he attempted to work the lever to inject another round into the firing chamber as the searing pain spread and intensified. He tried again and again, but his right hand would not do his bidding. Then the rifle fell to the ground. Realization began to flicker in Chug's dull brain as he lost the strength to stand erect.

As terrible as the pain was, it was the loss of his physical strength that panicked Chug. He tried to scream, but he only gurgled as blood filled his mouth. He was on the ground, and he could not raise himself. The searing pain was subsiding, but the day was quickly growing dark. His last conscious thought was: "That ##### woman!"

Galen did not move from the position he had held for the past two or three hours as he looked about and listened. Were there others? Was there another would-be murderer lurking about? Again and again his eyes searched every cranny and any likely place where a stalker might find concealment. All was silent except for the sounds made by the warm gentle breeze, undisturbed by the conflicts of mankind.

Finally, Galen yelled to those in the camp, who were apprehensively awaiting further developments. "One of the thugs came back and was trying to get a shot into the camp. I took him out. He is a tough guy I remember from the river. They called him 'Chug.' Stay alert, but I don't see any other threats. I will be coming in now."

Barney spoke from a place that Galen had scanned repeatedly without seeing any indication that anyone was present there. "From all I can find, we are in the clear for now, but we must stay alert. I will come in a little later. We will need to move out before sundown. I have located a secure campsite."

CHAPTER SEVEN
SLIM'S MISSION

Jim Harding spoke to his nephew in the direct, no-nonsense, voice he used with everyone, but Slim detected a slightly softer tone than usual. He especially appreciated the softer tone after having suffered the full force of his uncle's displeasure over the past several weeks. Over that span of time, his uncle's disappointment at finding him on a criminal errand with Biddy and the Kreuger brothers, had gradually transferred into his own breast. He had become sorely disappointed with himself.

There was something about that singing school teacher that had touched him deep inside, as well. The thought kept returning to him that Broussard had encouraged him to attend gospel singings. That a complete stranger could generate that much personal interest in him on the spur of the moment under those circumstances, amazed him.

He had responded to that encouragement, and he had attended several singings. The singing had done him good, as Broussard had promised, and he discovered that he especially liked the people who gathered to sing about Jesus and that land of promise. One young man, only slightly older than he, had taken an interest in helping him learn to sing. The more he learned, the more fascinated he became with the idea of reading music.

"You said you wanted to do something to prove yourself to me, Slim. You don't just do something to prove yourself. Life is a marathon, and you don't prove yourself in a day or a week. I do have a job for you, though, that will be a step in the right direction if you do it well."

He gave Uncle Jim his full attention, but his only answer was, "Yes Sir!"

"First, let me tell you a little more about that singing school teacher who Biddy and the Kreuger boys woefully misjudged. I hope you learned not to accept their evaluation of anything. They almost got you killed."

"Yes Sir. I know."

"He worked undercover for several years for shipping companies in which I own an interest, and he was able to drastically reduce the losses we were suffering from thieves. He had to testify in a major court case, and that blew his cover. That cost him his job. With the country going through this depression, it was a bad time to lose his job. I'm working with the other owners to pay him a nice bonus. He doesn't know about that."

"Something else has come up that he may or may not know about. The mob has put out a sizable contract on him, and two men were overheard in one of the local dives last night planning to collect on that contract."

"You mean kill him?"

"Yes, that's what it means in the criminal world to 'put out a contract' on someone. Criminal activity is not some high-spirited fun thing." He looked long and hard at his nephew. Slim felt his cheeks burning.

But it sounded as if his uncle was ready to trust him with something really important, and that encouraged him. "What do you want me to do?"

Jim Harding raised his right hand, palm toward his nephew. "Hold on. Don't rush me. Just listen carefully."

"There is a man on the way up the river who we hired after Broussard had to come out from under cover to testify. He's had years of experience fighting mob activity, beginning ten years ago in Missouri when the illegal whiskey operations were beginning to really gain steam across the country. He has organized a whole network of undercover agents to combat criminal activity all the way up to the mob bosses."

The information overwhelmed Slim. First, he had no idea that Uncle Jim was so involved with operations on the river, although he knew vaguely that he held investments in certain businesses connected to river commerce. Second, that his uncle would share this inside information with him both thrilled and scared him. He must have been doing something right over the past several weeks. With God as his helper, he wouldn't let his uncle down.

"This man's name is Stephen Weber, but he is better known as 'Patrick,' a nickname he acquired while fighting in France during the big war. He and his parents conduct a large beekeeping operation scattered across central and southeast Missouri, and they ship many barrels of honey on the river."

Jim Harding saw his nephew's eyes getting big and his mouth hanging open. "First, you must learn to conceal your emotions better than that. Your goggle eyes and hanging jaw enable me to read you like a book. I'm glad that you grasp the import of what I'm telling you, but don't let it be so obvious."

Unknown to Slim, Jim Harding had been chiding himself since discovering his nephew with Biddy and the Kreuger brothers. Nine years had passed since Slim's father, Jim's brother, had died in a logging accident. The twelve-year-old Slim, the youngest of five children which included two older brothers already out of the house and on their own, had been devastated by the loss of his father.

The two teenage daughters remained at home with their mother and younger brother, and Jim had seen to it that they suffered no need for material necessities. Slim's two older brothers found good jobs miles away from home, and the entire family was happy for them, in spite of the disadvantages associated with the distance.

The father and the older brothers had played a huge role in Slim's upbringing, and then, in short order, they were all gone. Jim's own family and business interests occupied his days, and Slim was left to cast about on his own to find male companionship and influence. Jim realized in looking back that he had neglected his nephew in that vital area on his path to manhood. He vowed to do all he could to make amends for that failure.

"Also coming up the river is a mother accompanied by two FBI agents. She is to meet her nine-year-old daughter who is being returned to her after having been kidnapped two years ago. That nine-year-old girl is on her way out of the Ozarks in the company of two FBI agents, a woman and two other men. One of those men is Broussard, the singing school teacher."

Slim grinned. "Well I'm trying to keep my eyes from getting big and my mouth from hanging open, but all this information is just bowling me over. I'm trying to absorb and remember it all."

"You will repeat it back to me to be sure you have it straight," his uncle answered patiently. "And yes, it's important that you remember every detail. Now, here is the crux of the matter:"

"All these people, plus several different brands of malefactors, are converging on Memphis. Things could get out of control very quickly. The girl and those with her have already fought off attacks by scoundrels wanting to kill them all for different reasons, including the contract money. Broussard and one of the FBI agents were injured, but not disabled."

Jim Harding's expression hardened, and Slim waited for him to say something that would help explain that change of countenance. "There was a man called 'Chug Worley' who gave us no end of trouble on the docks. He was unbelievably strong and cruel. He loved to abuse those who were physically weaker, and that included almost everyone. He made the mistake of getting into a gunfight with Broussard a few days ago, and he won't bother us anymore. But he has a younger brother who is almost as bad."

"'Tag,' so called because he used to tag along after his older brother, will be looking for revenge. He will surely be one of those causing problems. Like his brother, he has more brawn than brains, and he is likely to do any crazy thing. He is average height, dark hair, thick build and very muscular. Be on the alert for him."

"Weber has a younger brother, Lance, who is going to give you a ride to Helena. Weber's boat will make a stop there, and you will go on board. Your passage from there to Memphis is paid. Weber's brother will drop you off, and you will be on your own. I will give you a password and my code name. You must remember them. Nothing can be written down, and you must make no notes."

A question loomed in Slim's mind. "Will I have time to get to Helena before the boat arrives? Is the boat that far down the river?"

An amused expression captured Harding's face, and his eyes twinkled. "You told me two or three years ago that you wanted to ride in an airplane, and I intended to make that happen. It takes more than good intentions to make something happen, and time slips by while attention is turned to other things. Now that ride will be more than just a pleasure trip.

"Lance Weber is a pilot?"

"More than that. He is an aeronautical engineer. He designs planes. You will ride in a plane that is different from any you have seen, and it is faster than most. When he drops you off at the airstrip, you will be left to your own devices to get into town and to the dock."

"Also coming up the river, in all likelihood, is the father of the little girl. He arranged to have her kidnapped over two years ago after custody was awarded to the mother in South Louisiana, and he and his mother held her as a servant girl in a remote area of the Ozarks. According to the little girl, whose name is Margaret, he and a cousin went to Louisiana a few weeks ago to kidnap one of her two younger sisters. They planned to make that girl, Yvonne, a servant girl also."

"Margaret, prompted by concern for her younger sister, escaped so that she could send a warning to the family in Louisiana. She made contact with people who were willing to help her, and the singing school teacher kept her from being recaptured by a crooked sheriff acting on behalf of the father and his mother. The family in South Louisiana got the warning about the effort to kidnap Yvonne just in time to prevent it, although the father and cousin got away."

"The crooked sheriff happens to be a longtime member of the mob operating on the river where he became known as 'Nighthawk.' He is the one who led the attack on those escorting the little girl, and it is certain that the FBI will not rest until he is apprehended or killed. The father will also receive their full attention."

Slim shivered in spite of himself. "What kind of man could do that to his own daughters?"

"An evil man. You must keep in mind the kind of people involved here. The world is full of evil people. They seek one another's company and tend to run in packs. A man who will do that to his own daughters won't think twice about killing someone who gets in his way."

"I am to go on board and make contact with Stephen Weber?"

"That's right. He needs to know that these various evildoers are converging on Memphis. Anything can happen. There may be more than one attempt on the life of our singing school teacher. The FBI now has too much information on Nighthawk for him to return to his home county as sheriff, and he will surely return to the river like a wounded wolf to his den. You will probably be able to identify Tag Worley, and you should pay close attention to anyone you see in his company, especially anyone who interacts with him without seeming to do so."

"Patrick needs to know all the things I have told you and other things I am about to tell you. We trust him to know what to do with the information. The only safe way to get that information to him is by personal emissary. You are that emissary. I am making you available to him to be used in any way he may see fit."

"We have quite a bit of information, but there is more that we don't have. Keep your eyes and ears open to gain any additional information. Think. Add two and two and read between the lines. Fill in the blanks, but don't jump to conclusions."

Jim was pleased that his nephew was paying very close attention. "What is Margaret's last name?" he asked. "What is her father's name?"

"Their family name is 'Bean,' spelled the same way as beans that come out of the garden. I don't know either the father's first name, or the name of his cousin. I can't give you any suggestions as to how you might recognize them, and they will surely not be using their real names."

"That means I must be alert to any clue." Slim, whose real name was 'Michael,' was warming to the task ahead of him. Jim Harding was pleased to see it.

Although, much to his regret, Jim had not taken much time with his nephew, he had seen to it that he received certain advantages to prepare him for manhood. He paid for a gym membership where Slim learned self-defense and fought several amateur boxing bouts. He hired a veteran from the big war to teach him about firearms and the use of weapons.

Knowing that any young man needed to do responsible work with responsible adults, he sent him on several trips downriver on the barges and arranged for him to do some work on the docks. Reports from foremen and fellow laborers were unanimous in agreement that the young man had acquitted himself well.

Then his nephew's behavior went in the wrong direction. He didn't want to take another job that took him away from home, and there was simply no work available at home. For every job at home there were at least two men seeking it, most of whom were capable, conscientious family men.

Puzzled and disappointed, Jim Harding eventually discovered the problem. Her name was "Eula Mae Bulger." She was playing Slim against an irresponsible "ne'er-do-well," several years older than Slim, who had access to family funds and did not work. She pressured Slim to stay close to home while she played her games with the older man. Taunting Slim with the free-spending habits of the other man, she persuaded him to spend money on her that went well beyond his means.

He had become satisfied over the past weeks that Slim had overcome his infatuation, having come to see Eula Mae in the clear light of day for who and what she really was. Slim showed severe shame for what he had permitted that infatuation to do to him. Jim was confident that he had learned a lasting lesson.

Harding was also confident that his nephew was equal to the task he had assigned him. Knowing that he was sending him into danger, he also knew that one of the worst things he could do would be to shield him from the many and varied dangers of an avaricious world. Simply doing right virtually guaranteed that challenges would come, and a real man did not shrink from those challenges.

Jim took the long view, well aware that character and personal integrity grow out of repeated challenges and struggles. He believed that at this point in Slim's development as a man, he genuinely needed to be challenged. He needed to be tested. He believed that his nephew would pass the test and learn from it.

Lance Weber bade his passenger farewell and wished him well. "My brother can be a bit brusque at times," he cautioned. "Don't misread that or let it bother you. He has a heart as big as the whole outdoors. Give him my best regards."

Amazed at how quickly he had arrived at his destination, and fascinated at the aircraft that had brought him there, Slim watched the plane increase its speed on the runway. He listened to the roar of the engine as it lifted from the ground at the last moment

- -

and soared above the treetops directly ahead. "I want to learn to fly," he muttered to himself.

Thinking of the flight and how the landscape looked below, his vigilance failed him. He should have seen the two men coming while they were still many paces away. Suddenly they were within ten feet, and his startled reaction caused them to laugh. Their laughter, sneering and contemptuous, alerted him to danger.

They were unkempt with ragged beards and dirty clothing. Their unpleasant body odor assaulted his nostrils. Where had they come from? There was no place of concealment nearby. Then he saw it. Their packs lay just outside the entrance to a crawl space underneath a platform on which a wind sock was mounted. They must have spent the night and early daylight hours there.

One was quite tall, taller than Slim who stood well over six feet. Wild eyes stared at Slim from his gaunt face, creased by a smile that was not at all pleasant. "Now ain't you a pretty one? A man who gets off a fancy looking plane like that, wearing nice new duds and carrying expensive luggage can surely cough up a few dollars to help a couple of good men who are down on their luck."

The other man echoed his words. "A man who is prosperous in these hard times ought to help the less fortunate. He ought to do it without dallying around."

"Well, gentlemen…" Slim began, before being interrupted by their harsh ridicule.

"Gentlemen? Gentlemen? Gentlemen? Gentlemen?" they snorted, repeating after one another.

"Look here, pretty boy!" the taller one said menacingly. "We ain't gentlemen. Get that straight. And we don't have any notion of trying to act like gentlemen. You give us a nice road stake, or we will just take all you have and leave you for the buzzards."

The shorter of the two began a step toward Slim while beginning to raise an approximately eighteen-inch length of lead pipe that Slim had noticed from the outset. He had only begun to move when Slim's tightly closed left fist struck his mouth at the end of a stiff left jab. A straight right followed the left, and the pipe-wielder crumpled.

Wheeling to face the other miscreant, Slim produced a .38 caliber revolver furnished to him by his uncle. The taller man had gone into a crouch with a slender-bladed knife in his hand, point turned upward and outward. When he saw the pistol, he straightened up and backed away. Frustration etched his face with lines of vicious malice.

Slim circled away from the crumpled figure on the ground while steadily holding his pistol on the other. A glance at the one on the ground told Slim that he was probably unconscious for the moment and might have a broken jaw. He continued to circle to his valise and gripped the handles with his left hand.

The sound of a quick-moving vehicle coming closer caught the attention of them both. Without warning, the knife-wielder turned and ran toward a nearby wooded area. Slim watched him while holstering his pistol. The man on the ground began to stir as Slim walked briskly away. He correctly surmised that the approaching vehicle was the airport shuttle Lance Weber had told him to expect.

"Was sort of expecting someone older," the affable driver said. "No particular reason except that most of my pickups are middle-aged men. I was making change to a customer when I heard the plane. I yelled for my wife to take over at the counter, and I hurried out to get you. How was the weather on your way here?"

"The weather was perfect all the way. It was my first ride in an airplane, and I really enjoyed it."

"I noticed you had a couple of unfriendly greeters when you got off the plane. It's not the first time we have had that problem. It looks like you handled them pretty well. A man has to be prepared to take care of his own. Law enforcement officers can cover only so much territory. In these hard times, there are a lot of people trying to get along by taking what belongs to someone else."

As he skillfully maneuvered the 1932 Model 18, with a rear tailgate and side-mounted spare, he told Slim that the boat had not yet docked. "You are welcome to wait at my store, and you can get a bite to eat at the café across the street if you are hungry. It won't take me long to get you to the dock when we hear the boat whistle."

Slim estimated the man to be in his fifties. He had a neatly cropped white mustache and perched on his head at a jaunty angle was a well-worn felt fedora, notwithstanding the warm temperatures. Slim guessed that he wore it throughout the year in order to be always prepared for a cloudburst while he was handling luggage for passengers.

He had just finished a good breakfast of sausage, eggs, grits and biscuits with may-haw jelly when he heard a boat whistle. Would that be his boat? The storekeeper, Mr. Telford, would know. He paid for his meal, left a generous tip, and walked back across the street while keeping his eyes open and moving. That encounter at the airstrip had served to make him more alert and cautious.

Telford's friendly voice greeted him as he walked through the door. "That was your boat whistle," he said. "It will take me just a few minutes to finish waiting on Mrs. Jennings, and we will get you there in plenty of time."

On the way to the dock, he questioned Slim about the men who had tried to rob him. "Would you give me all the information you can about the men who tried to rob you after you landed? They will still be around trying to rob someone else."

"Their grip was by the platform on which the wind sock is mounted," Slim answered. "I am guessing that they spent the night there. They had a knife and a lead pipe. I had a pistol. That was the difference. By their appearance and their smell they haven't had a bath or a change of clothes for quite a while." Slim gave him a good physical description of each of them.

"Sounds like the tall one would stand out in a crowd. If the shorter has a broken jaw, we can certainly identify him. Thanks for telling me. I will have some deputies go out there and check it out. And I will be more careful when I go out there. I will take my pistol with me."

- -

Weber looked him up and down. Slim had never had anyone to so obviously size him up. It was as if he was not only looking at him, but also looking into him to see what he was made of. After long moments, a look of satisfaction crossed his face. "So fill me in on what you came to tell me. Take your time, talk slowly, and cover every detail. I want to know everything that you know."

Remembering that admonition, Slim included the account of the attempted robbery. "Just might be the father of the little girl and his cousin," Weber commented.

"That had not occurred to me," Slim said.

"Gotta consider all the possibilities. When you are thinking of what might be, it keeps you on your toes. Makes it less likely you will get a rude surprise. You can't get paranoid and let a might be become a probably or a certainty. It's just a matter of being alert to all the possibilities."

"I have a pretty good picture of them in my mind. If there was some way to check with someone who knows what they look like, we could either eliminate that possibility or raise it to a probability. That could be important for the safety of the little girl's mother. I'm wondering how close she is to Memphis."

Patrick studied Slim with a new measure of respect in his eyes. "Write the descriptions so that we can study them and pass them around. As to the mother, she is on this boat, and she can tell us whether the descriptions fit. Even if your would-be robbers are not the Beans, they may become a part of the picture somehow. Desperate men can be expected to do desperate things."

He looked at the three of his men who were in the room with them. "The description of the taller man could fit Nighthawk, but it is hard to imagine that he could have made it to Helena by now. We have learned the hard way, though, not to put anything past Nighthawk."

- -

When Nighthawk came face to face with Galen, after having satisfied himself that he had killed his nemesis with a perfectly placed rifle shot, something snapped in his mind. He could react only as a feral animal surprised by its most feared enemy. He fled. He fled with all the vigor that his adrenaline-flushed muscles could provide.

Hours passed before a measure of sanity returned to his tortured, misguided mind. He didn't know how much distance he had covered during his wild flight. He began to feel the pain from falls, scratches and overtaxed muscles and ligaments.

Slowly, in sporadic glimmers of understanding, he considered his plight. He had no food, no horse, no gun, no camping equipment and no clear idea of where he was. He was exhausted. Every step required maximum effort. Hearing the sound of running water, he realized that he was desperately thirsty.

After slaking his thirst from the clear water flowing over a bed of rocks, he found a place where an earlier overflow had deposited a bed of leaves. Anticipating their softness, he flopped his overtaxed body onto them. Ordinarily, he would have been concerned that a copperhead was embedded in them, but his mind was not functioning at that level.

Dusk had arrived and the failing light meshed with his extreme fatigue to lull him into a deep and troubled sleep. In his dreams he repeatedly killed his enemies, only to have each one rise from the dead to confront him again. Those scattered rays of the rising sun that found openings in the canopy of leaves awakened him.

Pain accompanied each move that he made. He began to evaluate his physical condition by moving first one arm and then the other. He moved his head from side to side. Then he drew up his right leg, followed by the other. As he moved his left leg, he felt a sharp pain just above his boot top.

He saw the small copperhead coil for a second strike. Frantically he rolled away from the snake and struggled to his feet. He possessed sufficient presence of mind to immediately reach for his pocket knife. With the small blade that he kept razor sharp he cut a slit between the two fang marks. Gripping his flesh well behind the cut and the fang marks, he squeezed out blood for long minutes.

Knowing that he would need it soon, he cut a bush of appropriate size and fashioned a crude walking stick. At some time during its growth the top had been broken off, and growth had continued through a limb set at the right angle and height to use as a handle. Painfully he began to walk, looking for a trail or road.

As the burning pain increased below the knee of his left leg, he hobbled toward a trail he had seen when he paused at the crest of a low knoll. The trail showed evidence of regular use, and it seemed to lead into a small valley. He walked hopefully in search of a residence, because it was in the valleys that people found tillable land where they could establish a home.

He easily and quickly concocted a story that would explain his poor condition. He knew how to play on the good nature of his Ozark people. He would find help. He stopped long enough to remove the star from his shirt, and he tossed it into the leaves beside the trail. He would never need it again, and surely the federal agents would soon be looking for a "renegade sheriff."

Through his pain and distress, he felt a pang of sadness at the thought of leaving these hills and its charitable people. He had to get away as soon and as quietly as possible, and he could never return. Born and raised in the Ozarks, they were home to him. He enjoyed the abundant raw pleasures on the big river, but he had always hoped to spend the last years of his life soaking up the familiar scenes of his boyhood days.

His spirits lifted when he heard a farmer talking to his mule. "Haw. Haw around here. Get up now." He was coming into a small valley with tillable land, and none too soon. The swelling and increasing pain in his lower left leg was going to compel him to stop. Although he had not eaten for twenty-four hours, he was feeling nauseous. With a feeling of satisfaction, he thought of how his condition would elicit sympathy from his victims.

He had no qualms in thinking of them as victims even before he had met them. He hoped it would be an older couple who had little interaction with their neighbors. They would nurse him back to health, and then he would take supplies for the road, at least two of their firearms and a horse if they had one. Of course, they would have to die so that they couldn't put anyone on his trail.

Then he saw the mule coming out of a grove of trees. It was pulling a slide loaded with cuts of heart pine, commonly called "lightwood" or "lighterd." The resinous heart of a long dead pine tree that was left after all the sap wood had rotted away, made ideal kindling. Almost all the homes had a stack of it close at hand for regular use.

Walking behind the slide with wagon reins in his hands, was a young man of perhaps seventeen years of age. Glad for the help he knew he would get, he felt disappointment. The young man probably had a mother and father and siblings at home. That complicated matters.

"Young man, I have a story to tell when I feel better. Right now I have a bad leg and injuries from a fall off my horse. I need help."

The clean-shaven young man, short blonde locks of hair showing beneath his straw hat, had already unhooked the trace chains from the slide and hung them on the hames. "Looks like yuh been through a tough time. I'll help yuh onto Dick's back and you can hold onto the hames. He's a gentle old mule, and I will lead him in a slow walk. Is your leg broke?"

"No. A copperhead bit me this morning, and it's swelled. I should have had better sense than to lay on that pile of drifted leaves, but I was exhausted. I couldn't have walked much farther. It gave me hope when I heard you talking to your mule."

"My name's Kit, Kit Treadway. Named after Kit Carson." Kit noticed that his beleaguered guest didn't politely respond by giving his own name. Maybe he was too distressed by his pain to be polite.

For his part, the conniving sheriff had forgotten a key part of his cover story. He had forgotten to choose an alias to use while he was making his way to the river. To conceal his failure to respond with his own name, he groaned. And he, indeed, had reason to groan, for his foot and lower leg were swelled tightly within his boot, even though he had split it with his pocket knife.

"It makes no difference to Dick which side you mount him on. Get on his right side, and I will help you lift that bad left leg and lift you onto his back." Nighthawk was duly impressed by the ease with which Kit lifted him to the mule's back. Once mounted, he suffered a dizzy spell and held to the harness tightly to keep from falling. Kit steadied him.

"We got just a little over a mile to go Mister. Can you hang on that long?" The unsteady rider nodded his head.

As they approached the residence constructed of logs skillfully shaped and fitted at the corners, the fleeing sheriff saw a teenage girl and boy of about ten years on the porch. A boy of about fourteen years walked around the corner from the back of the house. Rooms had been added to each end of the house, and the steep-pitched roof indicated cold-weather sleeping space above the main fireplace room.

The eyes of the dishonest sheriff looked past the children and the house to the barn lot at the side and back of the house. A beautifully built bay gelding, watching their arrival, stood in a pose that would stir the pulse of anyone with any appreciation for good horseflesh. That horse could carry him quickly to a larger town where he could lose himself in the crowds.

What he could not know was that the four-year old gelding had been raised from a foal by Kit, and he was very much a one-man horse. That was a fact respected by Kit's father and every member of the family. There was a bond between Kit and "Blaze" (so named for the white blaze between his eyes) that fascinated family and friends. No one dared intrude on that relationship.

Nighthawk was soon made as comfortable as possible on a cot that Kit slept on each night. The tall broad-shouldered father, Milton Treadway, arrived with a milk cow and an unsteady newly-dropped calf. The cow's udder, stretched to its limit, gave promise of fresh milk and butter during the coming months. Treadway had found her and the calf in the same place that she had hidden when she gave birth to her previous calf.

The patient represented himself as a man going back to his home in Memphis after visiting his family in the county in which he was raised. So that he could accurately answer any questions, he gave the name of the county in which he was still the duly elected sheriff. The fictitious name he chose was that of a man who he knew from firsthand knowledge had left the county some twelve years earlier and then died in a carefully arranged accident on the river. The man's family had continued through the years since to search for an answer to his disappearance.

He attributed his appearance without a horse, camping equipment or personal belongings to having ridden a young and half-broken horse that was spooked by something that ran across the trail in front of him shortly after dark. The horse reared up and he attempted to dismount because of his fear that the horse would fall backward onto him. His left foot hung in the stirrup and he was dragged through brush and bushes for a hundred yards or more.

Unable to trail his horse the next morning, he had resigned himself to walking forward until he could get help. He walked rapidly all day long, and at dusk, exhausted and thirsty, he drank from a flowing stream and then slept on a pile of drifted leaves. When he awakened the next morning and began to get up, he was bitten by a copperhead that at some point had crawled into the leaves.

The Treadway family seemed satisfied with the contrived explanation, and the conniving sheriff congratulated himself when he saw their looks of sympathy. Their care given him reflected their concern for his distress. It could hardly have been better. He was furnished clean clothes that belonged to the father, and his clothes were washed and ironed.

The Treadway family ate well. Mrs. Treadway and her sixteen-year-old daughter cooked tasty food from the garden and patches, as well as meat from the forest and fields that Kit and the other two boys brought home almost every day. Nighthawk quickly came to respect their hunting abilities, including their skill with firearms.

There was one thing that irritated him. Each evening they devoted a half hour or more to Bible study. He had long since rejected the admonitions contained in The Bible, and he did not want to hear them again. He had worked at persuading himself that the "Good Book" was just a collection of fairy tales, because the clear condemnation contained in its pages for his kind of life, worried him.

There was so much in The Bible that made good sense, but he didn't let anyone, even God, tell him what to do. He could not imagine any man having the ability to write the way Jesus spoke; therefore, the gospel accounts must be authentic. He had resolved the inner conflict by putting it all out of mind, and it distressed him to be reminded. In fact it made him really angry. He struggled to control that anger.

As his leg healed, he walked outside quite a bit, testing and exercising it. He stared long moments at the big bay gelding, admiring everything about it. There seemed to be a special relationship between the horse and Kit Treadway. In fact, he saw no other family member even get close to the horse.

Each day Kit saddled the horse and rode him for an hour or more. The two of them were poetry in motion in all they did together. But Nighthawk could see himself in that saddle. He knew of a place on the river where he could leave the horse with no questions asked, and where he could come and go as he wished. Even in this age of fast automobiles, a good horse would sometimes be quite handy. There were so many places a motor vehicle couldn't go.

Kit had something else that the devious sheriff intended to make his own. From time to time, Kit strapped on a custom-made holster with a snugly fitting Smith & Wesson .45 caliber revolver in it. The young man wore the gun in a relaxed and natural way, indicating long experience with it.

A panther had been prowling around the pig pen at night, and Kit responded to the panther's visits by wandering around the homestead at odd hours. His large left hand gripped a double-barreled shotgun by his left side while his right hand remained free to draw the pistol from the holster on his right side. The sheriff envied the sure and alert movements of the young man.

Then came the night when three very rapidly fired shots from the pistol were followed, after a short pause, by the booming sound of the shotgun. Soon the entire family gathered around the dead panther that Kit had dragged to the front step. In the light of the kerosene lamp the tawny coat showed a healthy sheen over a well-developed feline body. The dogs circled the dead cat warily, poised to spring away if it moved.

"He was set for me," Kit said. "He must have gotten tired of me interfering with him getting a pig. He was on that big limb of the red oak near the pen, and I heard him just as he sprang from the limb. I was able to jump back and draw my pistol. The first two shots didn't stop him, but the third one must have broken his left shoulder. If that one hadn't stopped him, he would have gotten his teeth and claws into me."

Mrs. Treadway shivered and sucked in her breath audibly, as the fingers of her right hand touched her chest at the base of her throat. "Kit, I was worried about you. Do you think there may be another one?"

"He may have been taking meat back to a mate with young ones," the elder Treadway answered. "If so, she will now be desperate and may hunt in the daytime. She will be looking for something quick and easy. We will all have to be careful. The chickens on the yard would probably be her first prey."

Their ungrateful guest made a quick calculation and changed his plans. His departure with the gelding, guns and all provisions for the trail would not be as easy as he had thought. The family would not be as easy to kill as he had imagined. But how? He still wanted that horse, and he really needed that forty-five. It was very important to have a rifle also.

Nighthawk became concerned the next day when he saw the teenage daughter pause as she ironed his shirt. She frowned while looking at the left pocket. Immediately the sheriff realized that she was looking at the holes he had made by repeatedly pinning the star to the pocket. She continued ironing the shirt, but she was obviously thoughtful.

He went outside and began to walk about the homestead, as had become his habit. A few minutes later he saw the daughter talking with her father in the yard as he repaired a wagon wheel. He saw the frown that wrinkled Milton Treadway's forehead and narrowed his eyes as he listened.

Treadway had come back two days earlier from a visit with their nearest neighbor, who lived four miles away, with news of a nearby ambush by a renegade sheriff and henchmen that wounded an FBI agent. Two agents were escorting a nine-year-old girl who had been kidnapped and held in the county of the crooked sheriff. Nighthawk tried to show just the right amount of interest in what he said—neither too much nor too little.

The word was that the sheriff had been left afoot, and area residents should exercise caution. Nighthawk asked only one question: "I guess the little girl is okay?" Insofar as he could discern, there was no thought on their part that he might be the sheriff who had been set afoot.

He immediately began to finalize his plans for leaving. More than anyone else, he feared young Treadway. The father would stay with his family, but the seventeen-year-old son would trail him to hell and back to find his horse. Nevertheless, he had to have that horse. That big bay gelding had gotten into his blood, and he stubbornly refused to give up the desire to make him his own.

Perhaps he could set an ambush for Kit as he trailed the horse, but he wanted to move fast. He didn't want to take the time for that. He didn't want to admit to himself that the chance of a direct confrontation with Kit scared him to his core. If somehow Kit detected his presence, as he had the presence of the panther, he could not strike him down from hiding. That thought brought tremulous feelings to his midsection.

He saw family members begin to surreptitiously talk with one another while furtively casting sidelong glances at him. He knew the time had come. He had to move before they did. He walked casually to a chair on the front porch which he had used often during his recovery. Seating himself, he pulled up his pants leg and eyed his lower left leg. The discoloration had paled, and the leg felt almost normal. He was ready to travel.

His position in the chair placed him only one quick step from the double-barreled shotgun that leaned against the door jamb inside. It stayed there when not in use so as to be ready for quick action against predators. He had furtively watched Milton load it with OO buckshot.

Mrs. Treadway came around the house from the back, the ten-year-old son came from the garden, and they joined the older daughter and the father at the wagon. Where was the fourteen-year-old boy? As they talked with one another, they kept looking up the road in the direction Kit had gone astride his big gelding. Although feeling nervous and on edge, Nighthawk sagged in his chair and pretended to sleep.

Shortly, the sounds of the gelding's hooves cut the still afternoon air, making a sort of music for anyone who appreciated the movement of a good horse. The fourteen-year-old came around the corner of the house from the back yard. The sheriff pretended only casual interest in Kit's arrival, even as all the Treadway family manifested intense interest. As soon as he dismounted, his father began to talk with him as the others listened closely.

The sheriff arose from the chair in a slow casual way and stepped nonchalantly into the house. He immediately stepped back out the door with the shotgun aimed at the Treadways. "It's nice of all of you to gather in a bunch so that I can get all of you under my gunsights at one time," he announced loudly.

"Yes, I am the sheriff they are looking for. A lying singing school teacher together with a few others falsely accused me and set federal agents on me. They ambushed me a few miles back and I believe they killed two of my deputies. If I surrender to them I won't get a fair trial, so please understand, I am a desperate man."

He paused to see how they would react to his lies, and he took satisfaction when he saw the doubt written on their faces. That was all he had hoped to achieve. Any uncertainty would produce a bit of hesitation.

"I am a kind and reasonable man, but I am desperate. I will not go to prison. I will not be taken alive, and I have confidence that I won't be taken at all. But you must understand me. I am desperate. I will kill any one of you or all of you if you try to stop me. Don't make a fatal mistake."

He paused again to let his words register in their minds. "It's a matter of life and death that you follow my instructions to the letter."

After a long hard stare in which he looked from one to the other, giving special attention to the father, he pointed the shotgun at the teenage daughter. "Jenny, step into the house and pack two changes of clothes and a sack of grub. Any false move by anybody, and Jenny will die. Kit, unbuckle your gun belt and bring it to the edge of the porch."

The outlaw sheriff stood in the doorway where he could watch while she packed clothes and provisions for him, a position that enabled him to keep an eye on everyone. When she stepped out onto the porch with them, he moved to where Kit had placed his gun-belt with pistol in the holster and picked them up.

"Now, Travis," he instructed the fourteen-year-old, "tie my stuff behind the saddle of the horse and lead him over here."

Jenny looked at him incredulously. "Mister, there is something you don't understand. The only person who does anything at all with that horse is Kit. Travis can't lead him anywhere, and you can't ride him."

Nighthawk could go from an altogether calm demeanor to fiery and vicious anger in a moment's time, and this was one of those times. "Don't mess with me!" he shouted. "I will leave all of you bleeding and dead here on the ground. Kit, bring me that horse." Kit shrugged his shoulders and complied with the command.

As the big bay followed his owner, Nighthawk leaned the shotgun against the wall long enough to buckle on Kit's gun-belt. Picking up the shotgun again, he instructed, "Kit, tie my provisions to the saddle. I am watching you, and if you don't do a good job of it, you get a full charge of buckshot in your chest."

"Now that's a good job, Kit," he declared with satisfaction. "You're a smart boy. Hand me the reins and back away." He pointed with the barrel of the shotgun at the place where he wanted Kit to go.

The big gelding followed his master with his eyes as if to ask, "Why are you doing this?" He continued to watch his master while Nighthawk mounted. Nighthawk reined him around as the entire family watched in disbelief. Was he really going to let this interloper ride him?

When Nighthawk had the bay headed in the direction he wanted him to go, he did something to him that Kit had never done. Never had the big horse been kicked in the flanks. He reacted violently and Nighthawk hit the ground hard on his left shoulder. Desperately, he grabbed the shotgun with his left hand and checked the holster with his right hand.

His face twisted with pain and hate, he pointed the shotgun toward Jenny. The Treadway family watched silently with deep satisfaction etched on their faces. They realized, however, that they were probably now in their greatest danger. Milton Treadway stood poised to jump in front of Jenny while Kit eyed the big monkey wrench laying on the ground by the wagon wheel.

The tense moments passed, and Nighthawk instructed Kit to remove his pack from behind the saddle. "Lay it on the ground and then back away. Then go put the saddle on the mule. Lead him here. Bring a lead-rope for the gelding."

In short order, he was mounted on the mule with his pack of clothes and provisions secured behind the saddle. A cotton plow-line secured the gelding to the saddle horn. Even Mark, the ten-year-old, knew that was a bad idea.

The plow-line, made of three cotton cords twisted together, was strong enough for the purpose for which it was made—to rein a plowing mule in one direction or another. The gelding would easily break the line with a sudden jerk. If he just pulled instead of jerking, the rope might not break, but the errant sheriff would likely find himself on the ground again.

"This gelding goes with me for a few miles, just for insurance." Looking directly at Kit, he said, "I know how much you think of the horse, Kit, so if you and Milton will just cool your heels here at the house until I have put a few miles between us, I will release him. He will make his way back home in short order, but I will be miles away."

He was lying, of course. Every member of the Treadway family could see the lie in his face and hear the oily deceit in his voice. They had watched him eyeing the big bay from day to day, and Milton had warned his son that avarice was written in those long looks. Neither of them had worried then because they knew Blaze would not go with him.

For that same reason, they were worried now. What would he do when Blaze pulled away? "Go along, Blaze," Kit said. "Go with Dick. Follow Dick."

He felt confidence that Blaze would obey for at least long enough to get the family to safety. That would leave Blaze in dire danger, however. The family depended heavily on Dick for food on the table. The other mule, a young mule, was still being broken to plow. They had lost half of a team three months earlier when Dick's partner, Tom, broke a leg. It was beyond mending, and the faithful mule had to be put down.

There was no way Kit would permit either Blaze or Dick to be lost. The family could do without Blaze, but the loss of Dick would produce real hardship. Before Nighthawk had gone ten feet with the two animals, Kit was thinking of ways to recover them.

And that pistol: It had a history. His father had received it as a gift from a dying officer in France during the big war. Kit was born while he was fighting on the other side of the big water, and Milton took special satisfaction in seeing his son develop exceptional skill in its use.

"Walk slowly toward the house," Milton directed. "If you make any quick moves it may upset Blaze."

"I will hang back so he can see me," Kit said. "It may bother him when we are all out of sight." As Kit watched, Blaze swung his head to the side several times to see that he was still there. Apparently satisfied that he was doing what Kit wanted him to do, he continued to follow Dick as they went out of sight around the curve.

Kit listened to the steps of Blaze and Dick until they moved beyond hearing distance. The outlaw sheriff held a steady pace. "He must feel that he has things under control and going his way." Kit muttered to himself. Of course, Dick would be almost too rough to ride if he moved faster than a walk.

Kit did not mention to his father that he intended to pursue and regain the firearms. His father would forbid it. He expected Blaze to return soon. He would follow only so far, and then he would break loose. He feared that their ungrateful guest might shoot him when he pulled away, and he whispered a little prayer for the safety of his beloved equine companion.

As he expected, he heard Blaze's steady canter just before dusk. The sound of the hoof-beats played in his ears like beautiful music. He had waited outside in eager anticipation, and the rhythmic sounds melted the anxiety he had been feeling.

The twisted cords of the cotton plow-line had unraveled from the point where they had broken, and they dangled from the bridle. Fortunately, the break had occurred close enough to the bridle to keep the cords above the ground where the gelding's hooves would have stepped on them. He ran directly to Kit and nuzzled him in the chest as Kit stroked his head.

Kit led him to the barn where he rubbed burlap sacks over his sweat-drenched body before putting some oat hay, with grain heads attached, into his feed trough. "Rest up big boy," he said. "You and I are going after that scoundrel two or three hours from now. We need that pistol and shotgun."

Every member of the family had worked hard all day, and with full stomachs from a table set with good food, they were soon sound asleep. Kit walked quietly out, knowing that if one of them awakened, they would not think anything of his going outside. They would assume that he was just keeping watch on everything as he often did during the night hours.

Their living was dependent upon their animals and their crops. Varmints of different kinds often tried to find a way to get into the chicken house. The mate of the panther he had killed might come to get a pig. Raccoons liked to ravage the corn, leaving a pitiful looking area of broken stalks and half-eaten ears. Twenty-four hour vigilance was the only answer.

Kit counted on being able to locate Nighthawk and to quietly approach him while he slept. He left the twenty-two caliber rifle and the old single-shot shotgun on their pegs above the fireplace. His father might need them while he was gone. There was no way of knowing when a predator might cause a commotion.

The only saddle was with Nighthawk and Dick. Kit and Milton habitually shook out the burlap feed sacks, stacked them neatly near the door of the feed room and covered them with a canvas sheet to keep dust from settling on them. They found varied uses for them.

Kit removed the canvas and took three of them. Holding them in his hand he led Blaze slowly out the back gate, down through the pasture and then through the gate at the back of the pasture. Only then did he mount him after first placing the burlap bags of the gelding's back. He had probably ridden the horse more with burlap bags in lieu of a saddle, than with the saddle.

It was not easy to acquire a good saddle, and he had performed long hours of hard labor for a saddle maker to earn the top quality saddle now in the sheriff's possession. Even after acquiring it, he still rode often with only the burlap sacks in order to keep the saddle new. He kept it clean and well oiled.

He calculated how many miles the sheriff would ride Dick before making camp. The night was a dark one beneath thick clouds, and it was likely the sheriff would sleep a few hours while waiting for the cloud cover to move out. The clouds moved steadily north, although the gentle wind at ground level blew toward the east.

An open expanse of almost an acre bordered a stream that made a moderately deep pool immediately downstream from shallow rapids where wagons crossed. Several area churches used the pool to baptize. The baptisms offered an excuse to have a social gathering with dinner on the grounds. That area would be too attractive for the sheriff to pass when he reached it at dusk.

Kit tethered Blaze to a tree limb well off the wagon road before they got close enough for the sheriff to hear the horse's metal shoes as he dropped them sharply against the rocky roadway. After speaking a few reassuring words to the gelding, he walked parallel to the stream for about three hundred yards to a haul road used by the farmer who owned the land. He was quite familiar with the land because the owner permitted him to hunt there.

The road led to the stream and then alongside it in both directions among an abundance of White Oak and Hickory trees. The White Oaks and Hickories were useful for various purposes, including fence rails, firewood and handles for tools.

Having walked quietly to the stream, he stopped and listened. Dick would probably move his feet occasionally or blow through his nostrils. Having heard the sheriff sleep on his bed night after night while he, himself, slept on a quilt pallet across the room, he knew that he breathed heavily when he slept. He didn't snore, but he breathed heavily.

The night was so dark he could barely see his hands when he held them in front of him, even though his eyes had become accustomed to the dark. From hunting and working with others at night, he knew that his night vision was good in comparison. Having spent much time stirring around the farm at night, he had developed a certain indescribable awareness of his surroundings.

Of course, he could be mistaken about the sheriff stopping at the crossing. He might have gone to the farmer's house to get a horse. He might have killed him and his wife, and be now resting in the comfort of their bed. In any event, it was most unlikely that he had gone farther than the crossing used for baptizing.

He began to move upstream one slow and deliberate step at a time, pausing for long moments after each step. He carried in his hand his only weapon, a pick handle that his father had made during cold and rainy weather the previous winter. When he got the burlap bags, he had retrieved it from the rafters above.

His father, a very deliberate thinking man, had taught him patience. Although he didn't talk much about his wartime experiences, he told Kit on numerous occasions that he had come back home alive because he had learned and exercised patience.

"When you know the enemy is probably close, but you don't know where, you keep your head down and listen. You don't go blundering around making a lot of noise," he had said. "You gotta be patient! You have to stay alert, never completely relaxing. Just looking and listening. Listening more than looking. In order to look, you have to stick your head up, and an enemy may have his rifle lined up on your position waiting for that very move."

Before each step he felt ahead with his free hand and advancing foot. The breeze gently stirred the leaves, making little sound. Tree frogs and crickets made their presence known. An owl hooted and the sporadic hopping of a rabbit stirred the leaves.

After countless slow steps and what seemed an endless amount of time, he heard what he had been listening for. Dick blew through his nostrils, and he was close. Very close. He was downwind of Dick, so Dick was unlikely to alert the sheriff to his presence. He stood completely still and listened for the heavy breathing of his fleeing guest.

He must have tethered Dick some distance from where he chose to sleep. That would make sense. If a curious passerby heard the mule and investigated, he would not be discovered until he chose to reveal himself. He would be considering the possibility that Kit or Milton Treadway, or both of them, would trail him.

The clouds were beginning to thin, and starlight was peeking through. Moving in a direction that would not put him downwind from Dick, he continued to take one very slow step at a time. He feared that a vagrant breeze might take his scent to Dick, causing Dick to bray. That mule liked to bray. If while grazing in the pasture he happened to see Kit hunting in a wooded area nearby, he would bray. His bray would ring across the countryside, almost loud enough to wake the dead.

Then he heard a shuffling sound that he was unable to identify. Waiting very still, he peered in the direction from which it had come, which was near the edge of the clearing where people gathered for baptisms. Then he moved ever so slowly in that direction, careful to stay in the shadows, for enough light was now coming through the clouds to enable a person to see vague images.

The shuffling noise came again and with it Kit detected movement. The sheriff had made his bed on the long hard table that had been erected for potluck dinners at the baptismal services. Kit had often eaten from a long line of tasty dishes set on that table. The sorry scalawag's presence on the table seemed a desecration of something almost sacred.

Perhaps he was taking special precautions to avoid being bitten again by a copperhead. In so many ways the sheriff, himself, was a poisonous snake. He was not asleep. It was as if he lay there coiled and ready to strike. Kit could see the holster with pistol laying on the table near his head. Leaning against the table within easy reach was the double-barreled shotgun.

Suddenly the air was split by Dick's resonant bray. Mules possessed much better night vision than humans, and the starlight coming through the clouds had enabled Dick to see and recognize him. Kit had learned in school that the volume of a sound was measured in decibels. He had sometimes wondered how many decibels Dick's sonorous bray generated, for he could be heard throughout the countryside.

Kit raced toward Nighthawk as the startled outlaw jerked erect and reached for the pistol. As his left hand grasped the holster a swinging pick handle struck his left forearm. The sound of the breaking bone registered in Kit's sharp ears. As he skidded to a halt small rocks rolled underneath his feet and he almost fell.

Ready to strike the sheriff again, he barely comprehended that the sheriff was screaming with pain as he ran across the open ground toward the main road. He ran awkwardly because he was reaching across his body with his right hand to hold his left arm. He splashed across the ford and disappeared from sight around the curve.

When Kit arrived home, lamplight shined through the open front door of the house and his father stood in the yard where he had been pacing back and forth. His mother stood on the front porch. Bracing for a tongue-lashing, he swung out of the saddle that he had transferred from Dick to Blaze. He attempted to hand the shotgun to his father, but he found himself in his father's bear hug.

His mother was there too, and through relieved and happy sobs, she scolded him. His father added his words. "If I wasn't so glad to see you, Son, I would skin your head."

His mother backed away and looked him over good. "You don't look like you got hurt any kind of way, and you went unarmed," she said.

"Well, not exactly," he replied. He walked to the trusty mule and retrieved the pick handle.

Milton Treadway grimaced and grunted. "Yeah, that is a pretty mean weapon alright."

"He was trying to rest on the potluck table at the baptismal crossing," Kit explained. "Dick recognized me as I sneaked up on him and that mule began to bray. Before the dirty rascal knew what was happening, he reached for the pistol near his head with his left hand. I'm pretty sure I heard the bone break in his forearm when the heavy end of this handle hit it. He splashed across the ford while he screamed and held his left arm with his right hand."

Milton Treadway put his right arm around his son's broad shoulders. "I gotta admit, Son. I'm proud of you! But I gotta say this: Don't ever do anything like this again. It makes your mama and daddy get old. We aged six months in the last two hours."

He walked to where Blaze stood and took the reins. "Come on, Blaze. Don't give me any problems. Your buddy needs to go inside and go to bed. I will put you and Dick to bed. Come along, Dick, you braying barnyard canary."

As Milton and Blaze headed toward the barn, Dick aimed his throat at the starry sky and brayed while his feet made quick steps in pursuit.

CHAPTER EIGHT
ON TO MEMPHIS

"Mr. Barney, when you marry my mother, I won't call you 'Barney' any more. I will call you 'Dad.' I had a daddy—a good daddy—and a good grandma, but that stuff they were drinking changed them. It was like they died, except worse." When Margaret made plans, she pursued them with a rare tenacity. If it meant that she had to bend others to her way of thinking, then so be it.

Immediately following the ambush by Nighthawk and his lackeys, she had decided that she wanted Barney to be her father. Of course, that meant that he must marry her mother. That they would like one another enough to marry, was just a foregone conclusion in her mind.

She had first inquired of Galen and the FBI agents as to whether her mother had remarried or had a man she intended to marry. She seem satisfied when they all told her that all the information they had indicated that she had not remarried. Nor did they know of any plans she might have to marry.

"Now Margaret," Barney demurred for the tenth time, "I would love to be your dad, and if your mama is anything like you, I am sure I would like her, but whether to marry is something that must be left to the adults. You can't decide that for us."

"But if I leave it to you and her, you are both too polite to say to one another what needs to be said. You will go separate ways when you would rather get married. I can't just leave it to the adults." She spoke the last several words in a voice rich with sarcasm.

"This Ford V8 has power," interjected Walter. "It takes the hills like a wild mustang." Walter and Cliff were taking turns behind the steering wheel while Janet, Margaret and Barney rode in the rear seat. Walter had just taken the wheel from Cliff about five minutes earlier.

"Well you know," answered Cliff, "that this is the same kind of vehicle in which Bonnie and Clyde were killed back in May? They didn't drive anything but the fastest."

"Well I don't intend to see how fast it will go," Walter responded, "but it's nice to have it climb the hills so easily. Galen will get there well ahead of us in that Ford Coupe, but we won't be far behind."

"Galen won't lose as much time with stops along the way as we do," Barney volunteered. "I'm glad he is going on ahead to check things out. From his experience in working under cover, he will see things that we would miss."

"He was very concerned about Chug Worley's younger brother, Tag Worley," said Janet. "He said Tag worshiped his older brother and would definitely be looking for revenge. He knows his hangouts and his mode of operation."

Janet looked at Margaret and weighed whether she should voice her next thought. Thinking of Margaret's statement that her Daddy's and grandmother's personality change was so drastic that it was as if they had died, she decided Margaret could handle what she wanted to say. "He believes that Margaret's father and his cousin will make an appearance. He wants to be a step ahead of them."

For the first time since Janet had met Margaret, she saw fear flash across her face. The mention of her father had prompted it. The girl had shown no fear during the ambush, but now the suggestion that her father might show up in Memphis, brought obvious dread and apprehension. Nevertheless, forewarned is forearmed, and she was glad that she had warned Margaret.

"Will you describe your father and his cousin to us, Margaret, so that we can be on the lookout for them?" Cliff asked.

"My father doesn't look much like he did two or three years ago," she answered. "Before he started drinking that stuff from the stills, he was a good-looking man, tall and handsome. He's still tall and dark-headed with a dark beard, but he doesn't keep his hair and beard trimmed like he used to. Wrinkles are coming in his face, and he is always frowning. He doesn't ever smile any more. Sometimes his eyes have a wild look. He is brown-eyed."

She sat up straighter as if she had just thought of something significant. "Last year he came back from a trip with a scab on his right cheek where he had been cut somehow. I never learned how it happened, but it left a scar on his cheek running at an angle like this." She placed her right index finger on her right cheek.

"It's about this long," she added. Again she used her right index finger and thumb to show the length.

"What about his cousin Delbert? What does he look like?" Walter asked.

"He is shorter than my daddy," she answered. "He is shorter and heavier, but he can run really fast. He likes to challenge people to a foot-race. None of the other men could run as fast as he could."

"What about his hair and eyes?" asked Cliff.

"Just like my Daddy. They favor a lot. His daddy is my grandmother's brother. If you see them together, you will know they are kin to one another. Sometimes people think they are brothers."

"Is there anything special we need to know about them?" Janet asked.

She thought only for a moment. "They both carried long skinny knives on this trip. My daddy usually carried the bigger knife that I have with me, but when he thought the trip might be dangerous, he would carry a long skinny knife."

"Arkansas toothpicks," said Walter. "That's not a big surprise."

Turning sharply toward Janet, she spoke with a sense of urgency in her voice. "Mr. Galen needs to know what I have told you about them!"

"I am sure he knows their descriptions, and he probably assumes that they carry knives," Janet said reassuringly. "He was briefed pretty thoroughly before he began the trip to the Ozarks."

"They throw those skinny knives," Margaret said. "They had knife-throwing contests in the front yard. Cousin Delbert almost always won."

"Well that is something we all need to know," said Cliff. "But I don't know of any way we can get the word to Galen. I am sure that he dealt with that more than once on the river. It won't be something new to him."

Janet became very thoughtful. She didn't trust her voice to make any comment. Somehow, the mental picture of a skinny knife flying through the air toward Galen was more than she could handle emotionally. She had failed to consider the possibility that Margaret's father and cousin would seek revenge against Galen. How could he survive so many people seeking his demise?

She had already acknowledged to herself that she had special feelings for Galen. She had never before experienced such pervasive emotions, emotions that persisted and grew stronger. Always having prided herself in maintaining careful control of her feelings, she thought of herself as a very logical person who thought matters through. She was trying to do that now.

Margaret interrupted her thoughts. "Mr. Galen likes you. He likes you a lot. I have seen it in the way he looks at you and talks to you. And you like him, too."

"Margaret!" Her strong feelings were causing her to over-react. She knew it, but she couldn't seem to help herself. "Margaret, you can't be playing Cupid all the time. Stop it!"

Janet had never before spoken to her in that tone, and hurt showed in Margaret's face. Janet hurried to apologize. "I'm sorry, Margaret. I didn't mean to snap at you. I'm just worried about Galen."

There it was. She had expressed a special concern for Galen and confirmed what Margaret had said. She didn't intend to do that. She was unable to maintain the usual careful control of her demeanor and her words when Galen was the subject.

Margaret recovered quickly. "What do you mean, 'playing Cupid'? I have never heard that before."

Her question helped Janet. It enabled her to regain her composure by getting into her schoolmarm mode. "Cupid is a character from Greek and Roman mythology who is supposed to be able to make people fall in love by shooting them with an arrow. People are said to be 'playing Cupid' when they try to get two people to fall in love with one another."

Margaret responded quickly and strongly. "That's not what I'm doing! I just pointed out what was plain to see by anyone with two good eyes."

Barney, Walter and Cliff began to laugh as Margaret looked at them with a puzzled expression. "What's funny?" she asked.

"Well, it just reminded me of something I told Galen when he first arrived in the Ozarks several weeks ago." Barney responded. "It's too long to explain." Then he began to laugh again.

"This road trip is going to be interesting." commented Cliff.

- -

"This was one of Al Capone's favorite hangouts," Walter commented as the group of five stood looking about in the ornate lobby of the hotel. Margaret's eyes were bigger than usual as she examined the details of her surroundings. It was as if she had walked into a different world, and she did not feel comfortable with it. She loved nice things, but she liked them to be simple and practical.

Every fiber of her being had emphatically rejected the squalor in which she had been forced to live with her seriously compromised father and grandmother, but this hotel lobby was the other extreme. She liked neither of those extremes.

Even so, she was very grateful that she had the opportunity to see the extravagant hotel, both outside and inside. Cliff and Walter had prepared her for what she was seeing. They possessed enough insight to know it would not be good to surprise her, nor for her to be unduly impressed by the grandeur of the Arlington Hotel in Hot Springs, Arkansas.

All four adults had acquired a very healthy respect for the amazing comprehension and good sense possessed by this nine-year-old girl. They did not want to do anything, anything at all, to soil that clean and pure mental outlook. That she had been able to come out of her two-year ordeal in such a stable emotional and mental state, seemed an absolute miracle.

Janet, herself, was a mature, composed and well-grounded young woman. Yet, the grandeur she was seeing threatened to throw her off balance. She realized it, and she resisted it. She had to remember the actual physical danger they had survived and still faced. She had to supply the emotional support Margaret needed until she was reunited with her mother.

She thought of how Margaret had her heart set on Barney marrying her mother, even though the two of them had never met. It was just a child's naïve dream, of course, trying to build a world to her liking. Or was it? Did she, perhaps, possess more insight and a deeper understanding than the adults around her? After all, she had said and done some precocious things that prompted Janet to review her own attitudes and priorities. An adult learning from a child? Shouldn't we all?

There was time enough before bedtime to take a tour of Hot Springs National Park, and still get the necessary early start the next day. Janet easily shifted to the role of school teacher and explained to Margaret the history of the park with its therapeutic hot springs.

She told of the special fascination it held for European pioneers since the Spanish explorer, Hernando de Soto, visited the area in 1541. They first learned from the natives that the waters had healing properties. In subsequent centuries, the warm springs drew an increasing flow of visitors. Some of them spent lengthy periods of time there, bathing in the very warm waters for lengthy periods of time on a regular basis. They drank the water as well.

Margaret showed keen interest when she told of how the influx of visitors was not limited by social status, but both rich and poor availed themselves of the benefits of the waters. Many of them spent several weeks at those hot springs every year. For several years some major league baseball teams conducted spring training near the park.

She noticed that Cliff and Walter were paying close attention to what she was telling Margaret. They were learning also. She loved to impart knowledge, and she had that rare gift that especially good teachers have. She conveyed the knowledge in a way that made her listeners really want to listen.

Although Margaret was not unduly impressed by the luxury to which she had never before been exposed, there was one thing that she particularly appreciated. After more than two years of trying to maintain personal cleanliness under difficult circumstances, she permitted herself to fully enjoy the big bathtub with ten to twelve inches of warm water. The bar of fragrant soap and the thick absorbent bath cloth helped make the experience especially pleasant.

There was a separate bottle of liquid soap for her hair, and she gave her dark locks the best cleaning they had received since she had been abducted from her South Louisiana home. She found sweet rest and deep sleep in a bed that was softer than any she had ever imagined. When Janet awakened her the next morning, she was not ready to get up, although around the camp she had usually been the first one to greet the new day.

When Janet and Margaret answered the coded knock on the door by Cliff, they found him, Barney and Walter with two other men dressed in dark suits. He explained that the two men were FBI agents going in the opposite direction. They all went to the hotel restaurant where breakfast awaited them in a semi-private area by previous arrangement.

From discussions on the trail, Janet and Margaret surmised that the two agents were headed to the county that was home to the Beans to investigate her kidnapping, together with whatever other corruption it might reveal. Janet noticed that Margaret became especially attentive. More so than usual. There was an air of expectancy about her, but she had to wait. The agents were determined to enjoy the breakfast without discussing business.

The initial fascination of the newly met agents with the beautiful young mountain school teacher, quickly shifted to Margaret. They had known that Cliff and Walter were escorting a nine-year-old girl, but they were not prepared for this nine-year-old girl. Her poise, together with her ready entry into conversation on the same level as that of the adults, quickly caught their attention. This was a child that one did not talk down to in even the slightest way.

Margaret anticipated that the two new agents would want to question her, but only after they had first enjoyed their meal. She was ready to be questioned, but she likewise wished to enjoy her breakfast first. She had some questions of her own. This meal was several levels above simple camp fare, although she had done the best she could with what she had.

Finally, Cliff turned the conversation to business. He told Janet and Margaret, "We have talked on the telephone with a young man named Kit Treadway. He rode quite a few miles to get to a telephone, and then it took almost two days before headquarters could patch him through to us. He persisted, though, because he felt that he had some important information for us."

Seeing that he had their full attention, he continued. "He didn't know either of you, so you will probably not know anything about him. Kit's family hosted that scalawag sheriff in their home for several days and helped him recover from a snakebite. He gave them a cock and bull story of how his horse had spooked, thrown him off, and then ran away. He passed himself off under a false name, a name that we checked out. It was the name of a man from that county who disappeared without trace several years ago."

"During that time the Treadway family received word of the attack on us that occurred only a few miles from their home. The sixteen-year-old daughter identified their snake-bitten guest as the sheriff when she was ironing his shirt. His badge had left holes in the shirt."

Cliff became intensely aware of Margaret's focus on him and each word that he spoke. After all, Margaret knew well how much time and effort the sheriff had put into the attempt to kill her. It was something that boggled the minds of experienced and tough federal agents. How could it not have a strong effect on this child of tender years against whom his evil attention was directed?

"He realized that they had discovered who he was, so he grabbed their shotgun and robbed them of a mule, horse and outfit for the road. He probably would have killed all six of them if he had not feared they would get to him before he got them all. The son, only seventeen years old, managed to slip away after nightfall without his parents' consent. Armed only with a pick handle, he pursued the sheriff and recovered everything."

"Good for him!" Margaret declared forcefully. "Evil people have to be stopped."

She quickly added, "Did he get away?"

Cliff nodded to answer her question in the affirmative. "He ran away in the dark with only the clothes on his back, and then he robbed again to get a horse, a pistol and an outfit for camping. However, he now has a broken left forearm in a cast, the result of a blow from the pick handle. He robbed the doctor who set his arm and put on the cast."

"That cast will be hard to hide. Have you put out the word so that people can watch for him?" The two newly introduced agents could not hide their surprise at the alert inquisitiveness of this little dark-haired beauty. Cliff and Walter looked at them and grinned knowingly.

"Well, have you?" Margaret asked impatiently. "He needs to be caught."

"Yes, we have." Cliff answered. "But you will remember what Galen told us about him. He has operated a theft ring on the river for years. He was dubbed 'Nighthawk' because he operates at night and is very elusive. He won't be easily caught."

"Thieves and robbers always get their due in one way or another," Barney volunteered quietly. "Consider Bonnie and Clyde. They got away repeatedly, but fate finally caught up with them."

"Y'all talked yesterday about Bonnie and Clyde driving fast cars and getting killed," Margaret said. "I have been shut off from the news for two years. Who were Bonnie and Clyde? Were they robbers?"

Barney, Cliff and Walter looked at Janet. She was the one to answer that question. She could do a better job of explaining, and she had the sensitivity to answer a girl of tender age in the right way. They were keenly aware that behind the brave front and obvious courage, Margaret harbored traumatic memories that required special understanding from the adults around her.

"Bonnie and Clyde were a young couple who went on repeated crime sprees across many different states for about two years. They lived off money they got from robbing small stores and service stations. They even robbed a few banks. They killed anyone who got in their way, and wound up killing thirteen people, nine of whom were law enforcement officers."

Janet watched Margaret's eyes for any clue as to how she was mentally processing that information. "As always happens with such people, they paid with their lives. Law officers knew from past experience that they would not obey a call to surrender, so a posse of officers ambushed them a couple of months ago south of Gibsland, Louisiana, as they were driving along a country road."

"That sounds like the sheriff and my daddy. I don't believe they will surrender. They will both be killed." She spoke the words without any apparent show of emotion, although the adults knew that underneath that calm exterior there were surely powerful emotions at work. Her comment showed that she was a realist, despite her seemingly unrealistic desire to pair Barney and her mother. Maybe that goal was not so unrealistic after all. Perhaps it just showed her ability to plan for the future.

The two agents who were headed to investigate the situation in the county from which Margaret had escaped, began to carefully and considerately ask Margaret questions about her captivity. They questioned her about information she had gleaned simply by listening and observing. Although she was very forthcoming and helpful, they found themselves being interrogated by this precocious child. She offered suggestions, good and practical suggestions, as to how they should conduct their investigation.

"I don't know whether my grandmother will still be alive when you get there. If someone doesn't move in and stay with her, and take care of her the way I did, she will drink herself to death in a short time. She won't cook for herself or even go to the spring to get water. If she is still able to talk with you, I doubt that she will make good sense."

She looked at the adults to weigh whether they were accepting the word of a mere child. She felt satisfaction in seeing that the two agents who were headed northwest were obviously mulling over her words. They looked at one another and nodded.

One of them said, "Margaret, you have been a great help. I am amazed at your insight and sagacity."

She quickly responded. "I have been able to attend school for only one year. There are a lot of words I don't know. What is 'sagacity?'"

"It means that you see and understand things missed or misunderstood by the average person," he answered. "Somehow, you have managed to progress well beyond the first grade in understanding the English language."

"I really liked school, and I missed it a lot when I couldn't go. My dead grandpa left some books he kept from the time he taught a children's Bible Study class. I would slip one or two at a time into my little room, and study them when I had a chance. My grandma would pass out from drinking before it got dark, and that would give me a few minutes to study those books. I was able to figure out quite a bit that I didn't understand at first."

"Well, you know what?" the agent responded. "You are an inspiration to an old calloused federal agent who has seen too much of the down side of human nature. We can't right the wrong that you have suffered, but we are going to do our very best to see some justice done in your case. We especially don't like people who claim to be law enforcement officers, but who break the law themselves."

- -

Galen began to feel uneasy as he waited for the gas station attendant to check the oil level and the air pressure in the tires. The attendant, a thick muscular lad of about sixteen, had taken longer than necessary to pump the gasoline into the clear glass elevated tank.

He had moved the pumping handle slowly to and fro as if preoccupied with other thoughts. Now that he was going from tire to tire, he was casting sidelong glances in the direction of an old tin-sided building located about thirty feet from the service station.

There was something familiar about the muscular teenage boy, although Galen was sure he had never seen him before. Suddenly, the realization jolted him as if he had taken hold of a spark plug of a running engine. He strongly resembled Chug Worley and his brother, Tag. In fact, his face had the same vacant expression that characterized the two of them.

Having paid for the gasoline before it was pumped, Galen quickly closed the open side of the hood and opened the door to enter the car. "Just forget those other two tires," he told the boy. "I need to be moving along." As he stepped to enter the car, the boy rushed him with arms spread.

Galen quickly side-stepped, pushed aside the boy's right arm that was reaching for him, and gave the lad a sharp shove to aid the movement of his thick frame in the direction in which he was
going. He sprawled onto the graveled surface, yelling in pain as the gravel ground into his palms.

Galen's revolver was suddenly in his left hand, and he looked about as he entered the car. The V-8 engine roared to life and he rotated his head to look in every direction as he pulled away. Suddenly Tag Worley lurched from behind the tin-covered building with a shotgun in his hand. He stood in front and to the left of the moving Ford Coupe as he raised the shotgun. Galen twisted the steering wheel in his direction and pushed the gas pedal to the floor.

The car jumped ahead, the rear wheels spitting gravel. One rock came from under the left rear tire at just the right angle to strike the teenage assailant on his forehead. Tag dropped the shotgun in a desperate effort to get out of the path of the automobile. Just before contact Galen twisted the wheel enough to miss him.

The rear tires squealed when they made first contact with the concrete surface of the street. Then they gained a firm grip to propel the vehicle forward as only the strong V-8 engine could. Three shotgun blasts sounded above the rhythmic hum of the engine, but he knew he had gotten beyond shotgun range. He was glad Tag didn't have a rifle.

He knew he would have to deal with Tag sooner or later, but he had not anticipated having to contend with another generation of that family. Was he the son of Tag? Perhaps Chug's son? He was still miles from Memphis, perhaps as many as one hundred miles away. He would have been more alert if he had been nearer to Memphis, which Chug and Tag had used as a base for their stealing and robbing.

Although he had stumbled into their lair and had a close call as a consequence, he had gained valuable information. He now knew where they called home. It was just one more lesson that a man in his business must always—always—be alert. But what was his business? He was a singing school teacher. Why should a singing school teacher always maintain hyper vigilance?

Sometimes one did not have the luxury of being just what he wanted to be. Circumstances often demanded other roles be filled. He had been just a deck hand on the tugs and barges when he was tapped to do undercover investigations. It had seemed exciting at the time, and he liked the additional money he was paid. He gained the deep satisfaction of knowing that he was performing an important function. Theft always hurts innocent, hardworking people.

Now his function, much more than being a singing school teacher, was to protect the lives of two of the most innocent of innocent people. Margaret and her mother had been victimized in ways that simply cried out for correction and retribution. Some crimes and misdeeds are so terrible that there can never be true justice.

Margaret's father and his cousin would probably have learned that Margaret was on her way to Memphis to meet her mother there. Would they ignore that meeting? Not likely. Frustrated by their failure to snatch the younger sister, Yvonne, they would look for a way to strike back. They would be concerned about the knowledge Margaret carried in her head.

Janet's safety and wellbeing stayed on Galen's mind day and night. There was something about that poised and seemingly self-sufficient lady that made him want to protect her—to run interference for her. Yet, she seemed to have no need of such care. She stayed busy looking to the needs of others.

His eyes continually checked the rearview mirror. Would there be pursuit? Would Tag call on others to help? He must have received word as to who pulled the trigger on Chug because he was obviously set to take vengeance on G. W. Broussard. Someone must have recognized him when he pulled into the service station and sent word to Tag. It was not in Tag's nature to take the time to go get a shotgun. He would have immediately accosted him if he had already been at the station.

It must have been the woman who worked the cash register. She was a large-framed woman, but she did not favor Chug or Tag. Tag's wife perhaps? During his encounters with Tag on the river he did not recall a female companion. Yet, she could easily have been with him in the background.

He would get to a phone a few miles down the road and make contact with the FBI. They would, in turn, contact Cliff and Walter. They needed to know where Tag and his family lived so they could avoid the stop that he had made. He had fully expected to see Tag in Memphis, but not a hundred miles before he got there.

Even though he had gotten hungry well before he reached West Memphis, he waited because he wanted to eat at a small café where he knew the owner well. He walked through the door of the little eating joint—that's what the owner, himself, called it—in the middle of the afternoon. There were no patrons except for three men in business attire sitting in a corner booth at the rear of the café.

At the sound of the squeaking hinges of the screen door, Cled Weaver turned from wiping the table just vacated by an older couple. They came in every afternoon for coffee and cake. He saw Broussard's eyes scanning the interior before coming to rest on him. The young man had given special attention, although very brief, to the three men in the corner.

He would have loved to have greeted his unexpected visitor loudly and enthusiastically, but prudence dictated otherwise. Instead, he welcomed him as if he were a stranger. "Young man, have a seat. If you sit at this table, you will be out of the sun and you will catch a bit of the breeze blowing through." He winked at Galen to let him know that he recognized him, and then he very deliberately turned his back on him and walked away.

The three men turned to look at the new arrival. They each looked at him long enough to size him up and to place him in some slot in their minds. Finding him of no interest, they resumed their conversation. But Galen did not so quickly dismiss them, nor did he so readily judge them and put them in a fixed category.

He was familiar enough with West Memphis, and with this particular eatery, to find the presence of three white-collar men unusual. His quick glances told him that they had not ordered a meal. Each one had a glass of tea and an empty ice cream bowl. A business meeting of some sort? Perhaps.

Cled returned with a glass of water. "What would you have young feller?" Clearly, he was not inviting any exchange of the sort of pleasantries typical of friends who had not seen one another for months.

Galen looked at the menu posted on the wall behind the lunch counter. It had not changed since his last visit there five months earlier, or for the past three years for that matter. His appetite tapered off in hot weather, particularly in hot humid weather, but he ordered the same thing he had ordered when he last stopped by during cold weather.

He knew that his order would require a longer time for preparation than almost anything else available. He wanted to wait out the men at the booth in the corner without seeming to do so. "While I'm waiting for that, bring me a big glass of iced tea and a small piece of potato pie. I eat dessert first sometimes."

Cled soon appeared with a pitcher of tea and refilled the large tea glasses of the men. He returned and gathered their empty ice cream bowls. "Would you like anything else?" he asked. They all shook their heads and grunted, totally engrossed in their conversation with one another.

Galen shifted his chair so that he could watch the windows that lined two sides of the diner as well as the entrance. The corner booth was in his peripheral vision where he could watch the occupants without looking directly at them or cutting his eyes in their direction. He ate his pie and sipped his tea slowly, after drinking all of his small glass of water.

When the broad-hipped and full-bosomed cook brought his ribeye steak to the table, the men were showing signs of concluding their discussion. She waited for him to check the steak to determine if she had cooked it to suit him. He assured her that it was just right, and she returned to the kitchen.

As the three well-dressed men walked to the cash register to pay their tabs, they all paid special attention to the nice juicy steak. They said nothing, but Galen could sense that they were recalibrating their first quick dismissal of him as someone of no consequence. They would see the new Ford Coupe outside, and that would raise additional questions in their minds.

Blue-collar workers lived in this neighborhood and constituted almost all of the customers of the café. Wearing denim pants and a short-sleeved blue chambray shirt, Galen's appearance was a good fit for the locale. If people knew shoes, however, they would recognize that the shoes on his feet were considerably more expensive than average. He wore shoes in which he could move quickly and deftly on all kinds of surfaces. He pointedly avoided giving them a good shine so as not to draw attention to them.

Cattle prices were low for the farmer, but steaks prepared in a restaurant were expensive enough that few hourly employees could afford them. That steak would be enough to persuade the three white-collar men that he did not fit into the hourly wage category. Of course any working man might decide to give himself a special treat, but the new Ford Coupe parked in front would dispel that thought.

The vehicle was rented, but there was no sticker or sign to indicate such, and he planned to continue driving it for at least another week. Cled would surely give a good clue as to who the men were and whether he needed to concern himself with them.

Weaver wasted no time coming to his table when he was satisfied that all three of their vehicles had pulled away. "Great to see you, G. W.," he said, through a broad smile. "I have been concerned about you. Those three men have met here three times, counting today. On their first visit, they got my full attention when I overheard them say 'Broussard' with an expletive in front of the name."

"Well now you have my full attention, Mr. Weaver. For a man who loves peace and quiet, I seem to have made some serious enemies. None of the three have a face that is familiar to me."

"I heard one of them say something about 'the trial,' and another one said, 'that ***** Broussard just dropped out of sight without a trace.' They talked about somebody they called 'Nighthawk,' but I couldn't make much sense of that. It seemed that 'Nighthawk' was a sheriff somewhere."

Cled Weaver was a thin wiry man of average height nearing sixty years of age. His movements were quick and sure, although unhurried. Galen had seen him move heavy objects with little effort. Before he opened the eatery some twenty years earlier, he had worked on the barges and tugs. Somehow he and Galen's father had met and developed a friendship. Galen had first come to the café with his father to deliver fish.

"I am very familiar with Nighthawk. He is a crooked sheriff back in the most rugged part of the Ozarks, but that was a cover for operating a theft ring on the river. That cover is gone because he is running from the FBI. If you see a tall, well set-up man with a cast on his left forearm, contact the feds. Nighthawk is on his way out of the Ozarks now, apparently on his way to Memphis. He will kill anyone without hesitation when it serves his purpose."

"It sounds like you are still at work. I thought you had lost your job after your cover was blown at the trial."

"I went into the Ozarks to teach a series of singing schools, but I was asked to keep an eye out for a nine-year-old girl who was kidnapped a little over two years ago. It just happened that she escaped into a community where I was scheduled to teach a singing school. Nighthawk and his lackeys tried to kill her, me, and four other people, including two FBI agents."

"Well take me for a one-eyed mule, G. W.," Cled spat. "You don't get out of one king-sized fracas before you get into another one. If I understood those white-shirt fellers, there is a contract out on you, and they are funding it."

After a brief thoughtful silence and a humorless sardonic laugh, he continued. "They got a contract out on you and you walk in on 'em just as plain as day. They don't know you from Adam. Just gotta laugh a little about that."

"They may figure it out, Mr. Weaver, and when they do, it may endanger you. You were careful not to show that you knew me, but I should probably not come here again. They may connect you to me through my Dad. You gotta be careful."

"Well, it just happens that I have been thinking of selling this place. I got a decent offer just a couple of days ago, and I've been turning it over in my mind. It doesn't take much for me and the wife to live. We are both pretty frugal, and we have put back a little nest egg. This just may be the time. I still own a little piece of farm land I inherited from my parents in the Missouri boot-heel."

Galen supplied Cled with sufficient details for him to know what was afoot, and he, in turn, gave Galen some useful information. They agreed upon a future means of communication.

"If they check back or send some of their men to check, I had better be gone from here, both for your safety and for mine. As it stands it's not likely they will connect you with me, but you gotta be alert to that possibility."

As Galen approached the Harahan Bridge to cross the river into Memphis, he was thinking of where he might rent a different automobile. Those men may have already put out a description of the coupe, including the license number, to gang members. If they checked thoroughly enough, they would learn that the Ford Coupe was rented to the FBI. That could be both good and bad.

The last rail car of a long train was coming off the bridge toward him as he approached the bridge. He was glad when the vibration and noise of the train receded into the background. The bridge had been originally built for trains only, but the general public persuaded the rail company to alter it to accept motor vehicle traffic as well.

Both he and the merchants who hired him to work under cover, had known that someone—maybe more than one—among the merchants was working with the thieves. Cled Weaver had just confirmed that fact. He feared for his longtime friend. If the mob connected him with Galen, a quick death might be the most merciful thing they would do. Some very helpful information had come out of the short meeting with Cled.

He must learn who the three men were. Cled had clearly understood that they were the ones who had put out the contract on him. Why? It must be more than just vengeance or to make an example of him. They must have some continuing fear of him. But what? Why? Did he know more about their operations than he, himself, realized? Or maybe they just believed that he possessed more knowledge than he actually had.

At this point he felt compelled to gain more knowledge. He was glad that he had come into Memphis alone. The mob surely expected him to arrive with Margaret and the federal agents. They would know the whole story about Margaret, the ambush and the killing of Chug. They would know that Margaret's mother was meeting them in Memphis, even the boat that was bringing her.

What would be their attitude toward Nighthawk when he arrived? It seemed to Galen that Nighthawk had quickly gone from being a substantial asset to them to that of being a clear liability? Would he realize that? Would he try to overcome that in some way, or would he find a way to drop out of their sight?

Not wishing to endanger any of the people upon whom he relied for information in the past, Galen would find room and board where they did not know him. The contacts with previous informants would be made very discreetly. And he must get information about the arrival of Margaret's mother.

Chapter Nine

MYRIAD MOTIVES AND MALEFACTORS

Margaret once again found herself entering a lavishly constructed hotel lobby. Janet had explained to her before arrival that the Peabody Hotel in Memphis would be even more extravagant than the Arlington in Hot Springs. She looked immediately for the five mallard ducks that she had been told to expect, but she learned that they had arrived too late to see them in the lobby. That would have to wait until tomorrow.

To keep her heart from pounding, she tried not to think of tomorrow. Her mother was due to arrive shortly after noon tomorrow, and mallard ducks would be relegated to the least of her concerns. As the actual moment of their reunion drew near, the anticipation was almost too much to bear. How would she be able to sleep tonight? How could she wait the entire night through?

As confident as she had been, doubts about the meeting of her mother and Barney pushed their way into her mind. Would they each like the other? Would they like one another well enough to marry? She resolved to insist, without accepting "No" for an answer, that Barney accompany them back to south Louisiana. That would give them time to get to know one another.

She remembered that different persons had often remarked as to how much she was like her mother. Barney had said that if her mother was anything like her, he was sure he would like her. That thought encouraged her.

The thought had not occurred to her that Janet might prove to be an ally in her quest. Little by little, Janet had learned what a lonely life Barney had lived for twelve years. She saw the loneliness that still haunted his visage at times. She noticed that the loneliness vanished when Margaret talked with him, to be replaced by the kindest and most serene expression she had ever seen on a man's face.

With the insight of a dedicated schoolmarm, she realized that Barney had filled a crying need for Margaret, whose biological father had been lost to adulterated alcohol. As she, herself, had put it so aptly, it was as if her real father had died. Her need for the love of a father still burned strongly in her breast. Perhaps, the need for her to love a father burned even stronger.

Sometimes when she thought of Barney placing that wood-carved and carefully painted Bluebird on the rail fence for a frightened and woefully mistreated little girl, tears welled up in her eyes. She had learned how much that gesture meant to Margaret, much more than even Margaret, herself, realized.

She felt that she knew much about Margaret's mother, beginning with her courageous journey to the home of her parents in south Louisiana with three little girls. She had endured daily hardship on the trip while fearing each mile of the way that her deranged husband would catch up with her and the children.

Surely, it must have been on that fearsome trek that Margaret, seeing the courage and determination of her mother, developed many of the striking characteristics that set her apart from other children. Her mother's example must have given her daily courage to endure the abuse to which she had been subjected during the past two years.

Because she knew Margaret so well, and because she believed that Margaret must be much like her mother, she felt comfortable with the idea of approaching her mother privately to insist that Barney be permitted to accompany them to their home in Louisiana. She believed that she could convey to her how important Barney had become to Margaret in the absence of a caring father. An abrupt separation would bring sadness at the least, and perhaps lasting insecurity.

Even though they would have the benefit of an FBI escort, Barney's presence would further secure their safety on the trip. He not only saw and heard things that most people missed, but he also had an uncanny ability to discern the significance of those things.

If any of the five of them had known what was occurring less than two blocks from the hotel, they would not have been able to enjoy the trip on the elevator to their rooms on the fifth floor. Margaret's father and his cousin were attempting to rob a man in the entrance of a dark alley. That man was Galen.

Somehow, they had managed to get a bath and shave and obtain nice new clothes. One of Galen's informants had identified them, and another had told him that they had somehow learned that Margaret would soon meet her mother at the Peabody. The two of them had been trying to enlist help to snatch Margaret. They were considering two or three different scenarios to accomplish their evil deed.

They were having no success enlisting help because their funds were not sufficient to entice anyone to accept the risk involved. The word had gotten around that Margaret enjoyed the protection of two federal agents. Mindful of the strict penalties that were a part of the Lindbergh kidnapping laws, the risks were just too great.

Additionally, even thieves often had standards they would not violate. One of these pertained to the abuse and misuse of children. In the prisons, when it became known that an inmate had been sentenced for abusing a child, other inmates shunned him. In many cases, they physically abused him.

But the Beans persisted in seeking help. "You only have to create a good strong distraction," they pleaded. "We will take care of everything else." Some of them dismissed their pleas by saying, "You just don't have enough money."

Not comprehending that they were actually saying, "There is no amount of money sufficient to hire me to participate in this shenanigan," they set their minds on robbery to get more money. Working out of dark alleys, they had already left two unfortunate men lying unconscious against a dark wall out of sight of passers-by. In each case, they obtained only small sums, but they persisted.

Learning of this, Galen made an offer to Memphis Police Officers. He would become a decoy in order to secure their arrest. Without success he went by two different dark alleyways, shuffling along as if he were inebriated. The third try succeeded.

Kelson Bean, Margaret's father, stepped out of the alley in front of him to block his progress. "Hey, friend, how about helping out a fellow who has lost his wallet? I need to get a meal and a place to sleep tonight."

The cousin struck smoothly and quickly. The club barely missed Galen's head as he pretended to stumble and almost fall. Recovering quickly, he slipped behind Kelson Bean and wrapped his arms around him, pinning Bean's arms to his sides.

Making his voice thick, Galen slurred his words. "He tried to hit me! He's got a stick! Help me!"

Margaret's father jerked free and pulled a thin-bladed knife from his belt. He lurched toward Galen to stab him in the belly, but suddenly his hand was between his shoulder blades and Galen was behind him. The knife clattered on the concrete sidewalk as Bean grunted in pain.

Delbert Bean stared stupidly, trying to understand what was happening. He decided to try again with his club as Galen used the taller Bean as a shield. He swung hard and struck his partner in crime a resounding blow on the head. Feeling him go limp, Galen lowered him to the sidewalk as three policeman closed in.

When their hands were in the cuffs, Galen pointed to the knife. "A piece of evidence there. Since the three of you saw everything, I trust that my presence as a witness will not be required."

"We appreciate your help in keeping our streets safe from this kind of vermin," the senior officer responded. "We have everything we need in court without you. The judge often excuses witnesses who are visiting from out of town. Thank you."

Galen wanted to warn the officers that their prisoners might not be safe in jail, that they knew things the mob didn't want told. His good judgment told him not to open that door. The officers knew that he had some kind of connection with the FBI, although he was not an agent himself. If he mentioned organized crime, that would raise serious questions about who he was and his motives in helping with the apprehension of the miscreants.

He had often experienced the disappointment of seeing prisoners released almost as soon as they were booked. For that reason, he couldn't permit himself to relax where these two were concerned. In the dim light, the Beans did not get a good look at him. Would they know him if he needed to track them down again? Hopefully that possibility would not become a reality as it had with Nighthawk.

When and where would Nighthawk surface? That he would indeed surface, he had little doubt. Criminal operations on the river had been his life for too long, and by his measure of success, they had been very successful. He dared not return to his home in the Ozarks.

The one big shadow hanging over Nighthawk's return to his criminal operations on the river, was not the FBI. It would be the white-collar managers in the mob. They would not like the increased efforts of federal officials that his presence would bring. They liked to steal in a measured and controlled way, not too much at one time and no activity that would draw special public attention.

The FBI tended to respond to news stories. They had a reputation to protect, and they would devote extra resources to any matter that might result in an unfavorable news story. The story of Margaret's return to her mother would likely make the news in a big way. The sheriff's name and his connection to mob operations on the river would be a big part of that story. The FBI stood to gain some very favorable publicity.

The mob, on the other hand, would have unwelcome attention drawn to their activities. The general public would want to see the dastardly sheriff caught and appropriately punished. If he remained at large, that would constitute a black eye for federal officials. His freedom to continue to steal and plunder would attract investigative reporters.

White-collar managers of the mob would be extremely sensitive to these considerations. Although informed people knew that mob operations existed, the absence of news stories kept them out of their minds. Most people were willing to "live and let live" rather than to incur any risk or bother. Gang leaders counted heavily on that mindset, and they feared anything that might arouse public concern.

As Galen mentally weighed these thoughts, his legs were carrying him to the Peabody Hotel. He must promptly make contact with Cliff and Walter so that the FBI could put a hold on the Beans. Otherwise, they might be released on bail before dawn. He would feel better when they became federal prisoners charged with kidnapping.

- -

Yvette Favre Bean stood at the railing watching the waves made by the boat as it plowed its way upstream, carrying her closer to her oldest daughter. Her heart had almost leaped out of her chest when she heard Margaret's voice on the telephone. In spite of the mechanical quality produced by the long-distance connections, she recognized the distinctive quality of her child's voice and her own special way of enunciating her words.

The tortuous days and nights of wondering how she was doing and whether she was alive came to a glorious end when she received that call from the FBI agent. What was his name? Cliff something? Not only had that amazing girl escaped from her captivity, but she had sent word ahead to spare her younger sister, Yvonne, from a similar fate. The word had come just in time. She shivered to think of what might have happened without that warning.

Having retained a superbly keen memory of her daughter during that horrible two years, she immediately comprehended Margaret's astonishing increase in maturity as evidenced by her choice of words and sentence structure. Her daughter's first aim had been to assure her mother that she was doing well and was in good hands. Then she had wanted to know how her mother and her two younger sisters were doing.

To see Margaret face to face, to hug her and to hold her! It seemed almost more than her nervous system would stand. She began to pace the deck, unable to stand still. She had come out on deck because she could not sit still. How long had Mr. Weber said it would be before they docked? About two hours? How much time had passed since he told her that?

Her mind raced. She tried to imagine how Margaret must look now, but she could not. Her mind would not permit her to alter the clear image from more than two years earlier. Margaret had told her that she had been forced to work really hard, but she would tell her nothing more of how she had been treated.

"I am fine now, Maman," she had said. Then she had repeated, "Je suis tres bien, Maman. That's all that counts now."

When she had come onto deck, the two FBI agents had appeared on deck also, but not near her. They did not let it become obvious that they were protecting her. One of them sat in a chair looking at a newspaper, and the other one wandered about on the deck checking out the passing scenery. She knew that their eyes saw much more than what seemed to be their focus.

That slender young man who worked with Mr. Weber walked onto the deck. According to Mr. Weber, who some people called "Patrick," he, Michael Harding, had been assigned to run any errands for her in order to minimize her exposure to people with bad intentions. It seemed that her ex-husband had developed many criminal contacts, and one never knew who might be working on his behalf.

Additionally, there were many rogues traveling alone who worked the river looking for ways to gain an unfair advantage. A nice-looking woman attracted them like a magnet attracts rusty nails. Three such men had been firmly discouraged by the agents traveling with her.

The boat sounded its horn, and with its strong clear resonance, a thrill ran through her that made her jump and shout like a teenage girl at a school ballgame. They were about to dock. She would soon go on shore to see her daughter. She had been told that the hotel was only a short distance from the dock, and transportation would be awaiting their arrival.

Yvette was not the only one who had been awaiting the sound of that horn. Like her mother, Margaret sprang from her chair and squealed when the long-awaited signal penetrated the walls of the hotel. She ran three quick steps to Janet and squeezed Janet's neck as Janet leaned forward in her chair. Then she began to spin and dance, her arms moving in rhythm with her feet.

"For goodness sake, Margaret! You almost squeezed my head off. You may squeeze the breath right out of your mother."

When Yvette arrived at the hotel with two FBI agents and Slim Harding, Margaret waited in the lobby with Barney, Cliff and Walter. She had been instructed to wait until her mother was well inside the building before she greeted her. "I will tell you when," said Cliff. "Just hold still until then."

At a signal from one of the agents escorting Yvette, as the other agent and Slim remained on the alert outside, Cliff said, "Now."

Mother and daughter ran to one another and hugged as if each one was trying to bury herself in the other. Yvette lifted Margaret from her feet and turned around and around. They clung to one another intensely. Sobs of joy shook their bodies. Abruptly, she put Margaret's feet back on the floor and backed away.

"Let me look at you! I want to look at you!" After looking her over briefly, she threw her arms around her again, and the sobs came once more. But they were softer and more subdued.

Barney looked at Walter through tears that were flowing freely. With a half grin, he commented on the tears in Walter's eyes. "What's a matter? Get something in your eyes?"

Walter choked out a response. "This makes it all worthwhile. The saddle soreness. Getting shot. Sleeping on rocky ground. Putting up with Cliff's wild driving. This makes it all worthwhile."

"I heard that," Cliff growled. Then he added, "It's not every day that I get to drive a car with a personality."

Margaret was pulling her mother by the hand, leading her to the three men. "This is Mr. Cliff and this is Mr. Walter. They are FBI agents." She placed herself between them and Barney, turning her back to him as if to set him apart. She waited for the exchange of courtesies between them, and then she turned to Barney.

"This is Monsieur Barney," she said. "It will take some time to tell you about him. He's a very special friend. I need some time to explain it."

"Now, Margaret," Barney said awkwardly. "Now, Margaret," he repeated as he felt his face burning. Yvette noticed his suddenly red cheeks, and they aroused her interest. What would this adult-sounding daughter tell her about this man?

Her quick visual examination of Margaret had revealed more to her motherly insight than anyone else would have seen. She had the advantage of remembering clearly everything about her daughter before the abduction, so she could quickly grasp the changes. She saw the marks on her face that told of ill treatment. The marks were not so obvious as to mar her beauty, or to even be noticed by a casual observer, but they jumped out at Yvette. They hurt her as only a mother can feel hurt for her abused child.

The most striking change was the poise and self-possession that usually characterizes a person only after years of adult experience. Without saying a word or making a movement, Margaret exuded confidence, determination and comprehension of the significant aspects of her surroundings.

Yvette's understanding of that change in her child also produced inward pain. She realized that circumstances had forced her daughter to forego her childhood qualities in order to cope with those adverse circumstances. And indeed she had coped. She had coped unbelievably, marvelously well.

Margaret took her mother's hand and led her toward Janet. Janet had waited well to one side, not wishing her presence to intrude in any way upon the joyous reunion. As Margaret guided her toward Janet, Yvette surmised that this dignified young woman with the warm smile must be the capable female companion the federal agents had told her about.

"Except for Miss Janet, I might not be here today," Margaret said. "She took me into her home where she lived with her mother and daddy when I was in the most danger. I was trying to make it to the Cockerel family's home where we stopped when we were all fleeing together. They had moved, and that house was vacant."

Janet said nothing, knowing that Margaret was not finished and she would tell it in her own way. "Miss Janet knew that a girl needs a woman to go along when she is making a trip. And she is just as much protection as any man. She yelled the warning when we were ambushed, and she returned fire. We all did."

That they had been ambushed did not surprise Yvette. The agents who accompanied her up the river had told her about it, although furnishing few details. She felt sure that Margaret would supply all the details soon enough.

That Margaret could speak about it so casually and matter-of-factly did surprise her. Her nine-year-old daughter had participated in a gunfight as if it was just one of those facts of life to be met and dealt with. And she had the means to return fire. She would have to ask her about that.

"Thank you, Janet." Yvette said simply. "Margaret and I owe you a debt we can never repay. I am so thankful she had a woman's company on the trip."

Cliff approached with the other agents, Barney and Slim. "I have reserved a separate dining area for all of us. We have a table large enough for ten people and a good meal coming. Let's go get it."

When they were all seated at the table, Margaret said, "I will move this chair away from the table so we can have space to spread out and Miss Janet can sit closer to me." Margaret got to her feet to move the empty chair on her immediate right that was between her and Janet. That Janet had chosen to leave an empty chair between them had worried her a bit. She wondered if the presence of her mother had prompted her to make that choice.

"No. Leave it there," Cliff said. "We have another person coming. I want him to sit next to you."

"Him?" Margaret questioned. Then her eyes brightened. "Mr. Galen? Is it Mr. Galen?" Excitement filled her voice.

Steps sounded at a side door. They all turned to see Galen walk into the room with a big smile on his face. Margaret rushed to hug him around his waist. Galen patted her on the back, looked down at her and asked, "Aren't you going to introduce me to your mother?"

She responded by hugging him again. "Thank you Mr. Galen for doing so much to get us back together."

"You must be the singing school teacher," Yvette said. "You don't look old enough to be all those things I have heard about you."

"I started young," Galen grinned. "When you get in the flow of the river of life, it will take you all kinds of places you never thought to go."

"He's a philosopher, too," Barney interjected. "He's my cousin, and I'm proud to say so, although he can be a little dense about some things. Especially women."

"Don't start anything, Cuz. Have a little respect for polite company." Seeing that there was only one vacant seat, and considering its location, he wondered if his cousin had anything to do with that.

Actually, he and Cliff had conferred about the seating arrangement. Barney took advantage of Galen's absence to sound out Janet's feelings for Galen. She had revealed enough that Barney felt comfortable playing the cupid role. After all, Margaret had taught him something about that.

Barney had mentally prepared himself for a trip to south Louisiana. His knowledge of Margaret's persuasive abilities told him that it was bound to happen. And his initial assessment of her mother told him that the trip would be an enjoyable one, even if nothing more came of it. In any event, he wanted to see Margaret safely home. That girl had won his heart.

Galen pulled back the chair and took his seat. He smiled nervously at Janet, and then asked himself why the seating arrangement made him nervous? They had all worked a lot and endured much to reach this point, the happy reunion of Margaret with her mother. He just wanted to enjoy it with all of them.

Another man at the table was feeling nervous. Slim Harding remembered all too well the last time he had met G. W. Broussard. Broussard had given no indication that he had recognized him, but after some light-hearted banter that included the women and Margaret, Galen looked directly at him.

"Slim, have you attended any good singings lately? Your Uncle tells me that you have been learning to read music." Slim understood that the remark was intended to put him at ease and to let him know that he had communicated with Jim Harding. He surmised that there may have been a reason Galen did not mention his uncle by name. For one thing, waiters with keen ears were putting food on the table.

"As a matter of fact I have." With a big grin he added, "And they have been doing me good just like you said they would."

Barney's eyes widened a bit. "Galen, I know you get around a lot, but it seems like you know everyone and everybody knows you. Both the good guys and the bad ones."

"I fall into that second category," quipped Slim. "At least I did until I met G. W. He showed me that I wasn't as bad as I thought I was. You can count me among his converts."

At the mention of those initials, one of the waiters froze for a moment, and then he continued serving the food. Janet noticed the hesitation, just as she had noticed the reactions of the crooked sheriff and his henchmen back at the mountain country singing school.

Galen had big news for them, but it would have to wait until after they had completed their meal. He, himself, did not want to discuss business during the meal. While working the streets, he had eaten sparingly and irregularly. He had looked forward to this good meal with good friends.

Having Janet sit beside him, and being able to talk with her without having to include everyone else around the table, was a special privilege. He intended to enjoy it. Janet seemed to enjoy his company as well, but he could tell that something was bothering her.

The news he had to share would evoke strong emotions from Margaret and her mother. It would be totally inappropriate to tell them until they had finished eating and visiting. The good thing was that each one would have the other from whom to draw strength while making their emotional adjustment.

In a different way, Yvette had suffered more than Margaret. She had endured more than two years of not knowing. She didn't know what her daughter was having to suffer or if she was even alive. And if she was indeed alive, how long would she continue to live? What kind of death might she suffer?

Given those considerations, the terrible situation had been resolved in the most satisfactory way one could imagine. Mother and daughter had been reunited, and they were obviously thrilled. Both were strong and resilient and they would face the future without permitting those terrible two years to blight the ones ahead.

The sheriff was still running free, and he might well pose a threat to Yvette and Margaret. He would return to his depredations on the river like a wounded animal to its lair. His natural viciousness would be multiplied. He would never blame himself for what had befallen him; his ego couldn't stand it. He would blame others and try to make them pay.

Tag was in town with Chug's fifteen-year-old son, two more people set on vengeance. They had made it known that they were looking for G. W. Broussard and anyone associated with him, including FBI agents. In many ways, their limited mental abilities made them more dangerous. Intelligent people learned to exercise caution. The lack of caution and common sense had led to Chug's death, and it would likely spell the end of Tag and Chug's son as well.

Cled Weaver had made contact with him to give him two important messages. First, he had sold his café and would be going back to his childhood home in the Missouri boot-heel within less than a month. Second, the three white-collar men had returned to the café to ask him questions about "that young man who ordered the big steak." One of them had commented on the new Ford Coupe he was driving.

"I been wondering about him myself," he had told them. "Probably into something illegal. Not many young men with that kind of money to spend." They didn't seem satisfied with his answer, and he didn't intend to leave any clues as to where he was going when he departed Memphis.

Galen had passed that information along to Jim Harding and Patrick. Their primary aim was to root out the top-most mob bosses who were passing themselves off as legitimate business men. Harding warned him—without telling him why or how—that his name had come up in a meeting of the merchants, and that three of their number had voiced an unfavorable opinion of him. They had offered no reason for their unfavorable opinion.

As hungry as Galen was, and as good as the food was, Galen ate slowly. Everyone else around the table also seemed to enjoy the conversation more than the food. It was, indeed, a happy occasion, and Galen felt deep satisfaction at having played a part in bringing it about.

Time passed all too quickly, and the time came to break the momentous news that would bring mixed emotions. The news was good, but it would remind Yvette and Margaret of what could have been and was gradually lost. Galen trusted that they would feel a deep sense of freedom to go forward to a fruitful and satisfying life.

He used a louder and different tone of voice that immediately caught everyone's attention. "I have big news for everyone," he said. "I saved it until we had all enjoyed our visit with one another because the news is both good and bad." Never one to beat around the bush, he cut immediately to the central point.

"Kelson Bean and his cousin, Delbert, are now dead. They died shortly before noon today in an attempted jail break here in Memphis. Their bodies are at the morgue. Yvette and Margaret need have no more fear of them. They are gone. Gone forever."

Galen scanned the faces around the table for reactions. He heard Margaret, who was sitting beside him on his left, spasmodically draw in a deep breath. In his peripheral vision, he saw her hands go to her face.

It was Margaret for whom he was most concerned, and it was with her uppermost in mind that he had decided to break the news in few words without trying to soften it. He had watched Margaret repeatedly confront reality in a straightforward way, and he had every confidence that she would do so this time.

He knew that Yvette and Margaret must have already gone through the grieving process. Margaret had stated that the changes in her father and grandmother were so drastic that it was as if they had died. Both mother and daughter had lost the love and support that they had every right to expect. Yes, they had already grieved.

Yvette turned to Margaret, and the two of them hugged one another tightly. "We are free now Maman. We are free." Margaret's voice was strong and clear.

"Why were they in jail?" Yvette asked.

"They were caught robbing people just down the street from this hotel. They were raising money to hire help to recapture Margaret. They had learned somehow that she was here." This time it was Yvette who sharply inhaled and put her hands over her face.

After Margaret, Yvette and Janet had gone to the room they shared, the FBI agents and Barney asked Galen for more details. He told of communicating with Slim's uncle, Jim Harding just a few minutes before joining them for the early afternoon meal.

"Harding and several other merchants are very suspicious of whether they were actually trying to escape. Both of them had been a part of gang operations on the river, and now they had become the subject of a kidnapping investigation. We brought that to a head when you asked that they become federal prisoners."

He noted the special attention Slim was giving to what he said. It appeared that he wanted to say something. "You know anything about them Slim?"

"I gave descriptions to Mr. Weber—Patrick—of two men who tried to rob me at Helena. Yvette said the descriptions fit for Margaret's father and cousin. Patrick has men on the lookout for them. At least he did have."

"Tried to rob you?" said Walter. "You got away from them?"

"They had a club and a knife. I had a pistol," he said simply.

Galen had received information that there was more to it than that. The cousin was nursing a swollen and injured jaw when he arrived in Memphis. Slim had acquitted himself well, and now he had passed up the opportunity to boast. He moved up a notch in Galen's estimation.

Galen continued. "There are three merchants here who meet with one another on the sly from time to time. There is reason to believe that they are a major part of the mob upper crust, and further reason to believe that they may have ordered the killings. One of them had just left the prison before it happened. The Beans had been escorted to a private area for questioning."

In Galen's peripheral vision, he saw Janet approaching. "Yvette and Margaret are finding it difficult to believe they are actually together again. They are having a great time talking about the two younger sisters. Margaret wants to learn as much as she can about them before she sees them."

Without pausing she turned to Cliff and Walter. "I would feel much better if you two were in your room next door. I will explain when I go back up. I want to say a word to Galen."

The two agents knew Janet well enough not to question her, and they headed to their room. Looking at the other two agents together with Slim and Barney, she said, "Y'all need to listen in on what I came to tell Galen."

She faced Galen. "When Slim addressed you by your initials, I saw one of the waiters stop in mid-motion. After a long moment of hesitation, he resumed serving the table. It reminded of the double-takes by the sheriff and his so-called deputies when Cliff identified you by your initials at the singing school."

Slim's eyes narrowed a bit as he realized he had made a mistake, one that might be serious. "As we women were leaving to go upstairs, I saw that waiter using his eyes and head to point you out to someone who had apparently just come in off the street. That man from the street immediately turned and walked quickly back outside."

"Which waiter was it, and what did the man from the street look like?" Galen asked.

"It was the older waiter, the heavier one with the scar on his left cheek. The man from the street was dressed in black trousers with a charcoal colored long-sleeved shirt. He held a nice-looking dark fedora in his hand. He was clean-shaven with dark hair, about the same height and build as Walter."

"A wool hat and a long-sleeved shirt in this hot humid weather?" Barney commented. "That could mean that he literally has something up his sleeve. He is dressed to move around in the dark without being seen."

Anxiety was written on Janet's face, an emotion that she almost never displayed. Galen permitted himself to entertain the thought that she cared enough about him to worry about his wellbeing. A woman like Janet would keep a man on his toes because she, herself, was always alert. "A woman like Janet?" he thought. "There is no woman like Janet."

"Forewarned is forearmed," he told Janet. "Thanks for warning me. I'm thinking that I know the man from the street. He doesn't know me, although I have seen him more than once. If I'm right, I know how he operates. But I will be prepared if it is someone else."

One of the agents spoke up. "Do you think you might need FBI assistance? Also, Patrick is going to hang around Memphis for a while, although he doesn't want it widely known. His men might be more readily available than ours if you need help quickly."

"I'm going to get back to Margaret and Yvette," Janet said. Galen watched her go with mixed feelings of admiration, gratitude and other emotions which he couldn't name.

Barney noticed how his full attention was riveted on Janet as she walked away. With twinkling eyes he said, "It's like I told you on your Uncle's and Aunt's back porch, Cuz. She has made her choice. All she has to do is slip the bridle on, and you will stand perfectly still while she does it."

Chapter Ten

MARGARET WEIGHS IN

"Maman, I have something to show you, something that helped me make it through some really hard days and months." Margaret opened her hands to display her precious wood-carved bluebird.

Yvette took the bird from her hand as if it was alive and needed to be handled tenderly. Her daughter had said that it helped her get through difficult days, and that made it precious. "The carving is so intricately done, and the coloring is absolutely perfect. I love bluebirds."

"Yes, Maman, I remembered that you love bluebirds. That is one reason it meant so much to me."

"It is great craftsmanship, Margaret! How did you get it?"

"Barney made it. He gave it to me."

"Barney made it? He has that kind of talent?"

"But how? When?" Yvette was mystified. "How did he get it to you when they wouldn't let you see anyone outside their circle of cronies? Was he one of their bunch?"

"Oh, no, Maman! When I went to the back of the pasture to get the cows, I would sometimes see him on the creek bank fishing. I became curious because he would have two poles propped over the water and held in place by rocks while he whittled on something with his pocket knife."

She saw a flicker of interest in her mother's eyes. Yvette commented, "Janet told me that he has been widowed for twelve years, and that he began to wander the mountains after his wife died. She learned that from Galen."

"When he noticed me watching him, he tried to talk with me, but I ran away. I had been warned that if I talked with anybody that person would be killed, and maybe me as well."

She saw her mother's muscles tense, and her eyes burned with anger. "He began to watch for me and wave at me. I would answer with a little wave close to my chest and then hurry away."

Tears were welling in her mother's eyes. She hurried on with her story. "One day I saw him waiting just outside the rail fence at a point where I passed close to the fence. I thought, 'Oh no! What do I do?' When he knew that I was looking, he held up this little bluebird for me to see. Then he set it on a flat place on the top rail and disappeared into the woods."

The tears rolled freely down Yvette's cheeks. "He was lonely, and he was reaching out to a lonely little girl. I can understand how that must have encouraged you."

"He's a good man, Maman. A real good man. I want him to go with us to south Louisiana."

"Oh, but Margaret. He may not want to go to Louisiana. He may not even like Louisiana. It's so different from the Ozarks."

Margaret laughed a deep and hearty laugh. To see her laugh did her mother a world of good. She remembered the pre-kidnapped Margaret as a laughing and happy child who found something to laugh about at every turn. The post-kidnapped Margaret exhibited a very serious personality. To see her laugh again was like a special balm to Yvette's spirit.

"That's the same response Barney gave when I asked him to come. 'But Margaret, your mother may not want me to come along,' she mimicked. You two would make a pair."

She saw suspicion in her mother's eyes. It delighted her that the suspicion was mixed with a twinkle and a grin. "Oh, but now I see. If you are not a cagey one! That kind of decision must be left to adults."

Again Margaret laughed heartily. Again she said, "That was Barney's response. Exactly." Yvette could not help but laugh with her.

"As to Barney not liking south Louisiana, try saying something to him in French. He lived four winters near Breaux Bridge. He said that he is torn between the mossy oaks and bayous of south Louisiana, and the clear streams and valleys of the Ozarks."

An opening door interrupted their conversation. Janet was returning from a visit with a man called "Patrick" who had come up the river on the same boat with Yvette. She had learned from Walter that Patrick was keeping track of Galen's work on the streets. It seemed that Patrick was trying to get to the source of mob activity on the river—to learn who was calling the shots at the top.

Now that they were in Memphis, one of the control centers for gang operations, the price on Galen's head never left Janet's thoughts. How many were there in Memphis who would go to extreme lengths to collect the mob contract money?

She talked frankly with Patrick about her concern for Galen, and he in turn spoke frankly about his efforts to pull the plug on that contract. He was getting closer to learning the source of the proffered money. If would-be killers received word that the contract money would not be paid, that would put the brakes on most of them— but not all. Some had their own motives for wanting to destroy Galen.

Patrick had been fighting gangland activity since the illegal whiskey mob in Kansas City had tried to take control of the county in which he lived ten years earlier. Now that whiskey could again be made and sold legally, the mob had lost much of its power and influence. They remained, however, a potent force, and they were trying to develop other areas for collecting big money dishonestly.

Learning that Stephen Weber, known as "Patrick" from his service in the big war, had organized broad opposition to gangland depredations, the merchants' organization for whom Galen had worked retained his services. Having lost the very effective services of "G. W. Broussard" due to his losing his cover, they turned to Patrick.

Three of their number, however, had opposed hiring him. They offered various reasons, all of which seemed flimsy. That aroused the suspicions of most of the other merchants. Then when several of the merchants, including Jim Harding, had proposed paying Galen a one-time bonus for services that had saved the merchants huge sums, those three merchants became openly angry.

Patrick, after sizing up Janet and finding her tough, honest and prudent, trusted Janet with the information. His men were methodically gathering information and closing the pincers on these three business men. They had determined that they had ordered the killing of the Bean cousins to prevent the FBI from questioning them.

He assured her that Galen was working closely with his men, and that Galen had the benefit of all the considerable protection that his men furnished. Janet learned that her warning to Galen two days earlier about the waiter and the man to whom he had identified Galen, had probably saved Galen's life.

Shortly after dark on that same day, an attempt had been made on his life, but knowing the modus operandi of the assassin had saved him. He had told Janet, "Forewarned is forearmed." The man in the dark clothes and dark fedora, seemingly preoccupied with something across the street, spun quickly as Galen was walking by him.

Expecting the move, Galen sprang back while pulling his abdomen away from the plunging knife. Knowing from his previous killings that he would follow quickly with additional thrusts, Galen had his pistol in his hand before his would-be killer turned. Two quick shots dropped him to the sidewalk.

Two of Patrick's men emerged from dark doorways to give policemen an eye-witness account of what had occurred. The knife with an eight-inch blade and his fingerprints, lay on the concrete near the body. The investigating officers immediately recognized the killer and one of them breathed a special sigh of relief. "He told me last week that he would get me. Just a matter of time, he said. He has a long rap sheet."

In his wallet they found a payroll check cut on that same date from one of the three merchants. Legitimate employees of that business man claimed to have no knowledge of him. They all declared that they had never worked with him.

Immediately upon Janet closing the door, Margaret turned her attention to Janet. "Did you find out about Mr. Galen? Is he okay?"

"He's okay, but that suspicious character I warned him about tried to kill him." She would have liked to tell them more, but Patrick had trusted her not to be loose-lipped. Many men did not trust women to keep confidential information nor to use it prudently.

"Have the two of you been having a good visit?" Janet asked.

"Oh yes," Yvette answered. "Margaret has been trying to play Cupid. She wants Barney to go to south Louisiana with us."

"Why am I not surprised?" Janet asked with a smile. She was making a mental effort to adjust to a light-hearted mood. She was not a worrier, but people were after Galen to kill him. That worried her.

Margaret had been good at changing her focus, and she did so now. "You accused me of playing Cupid and now Maman is accusing me of the same thing. The trouble with you grownups is that you don't face things head-on. You hope things will just work out on their own."

She saw the looks of amusement on the faces of her mother and Janet, and that irritated her. They saw Margaret's face suddenly acquire a look of fierce determination and heard added strength in her voice. "I should have been gone from grandma's place a year sooner. I just dallied around, hoping things would work out. Instead, they got worse. When they told me they were going to get Yvonne, I knew I had to do something."

She looked at Janet in a no nonsense way, and her voice retained its forceful tone. "You know you are in love with Galen, and he is in love with you. He may dally around catching crooks forever, just to avoid facing up to it. It's easier for him to catch thieves and murderers than to take a chance on you telling him, 'No.' And you are so polite that you will let him keep on doing it."

Margaret was not through. She turned to face her mother directly. "You and Barney haven't had time to get to know one another. He said if you were anything like me that he was sure he would like you."

She turned to address Janet again. "Are we anything alike? You have been around us long enough to know."

"Margaret, I can't argue with a thing you just said. To answer your question, I have been amazed as to how much the two of you are alike. I'm sure Barney would like your mother. He has the advantage of knowing and liking you first."

Janet looked at Yvette. "I'm a teacher, but this daughter of yours has taught me so much about living life, things you can't get from a book. It has been one of the greatest privileges of my life to spend days and nights with her in challenging circumstances."

Yvette was still feeling a bit dizzy from actually having her daughter back. "Thank you, Janet, for all you have done for Margaret. I will never forget and she will never forget. God sent you to pick berries that day so that you would be there when she came along. He sent you to meet her, and He hid you behind that big White Oak tree so that Margaret would not see you until you spoke to her."

Margaret was not going to let them change the subject until she was through. "Miss Janet, there is no way of knowing what Mr. Galen may get caught up in if you don't stop him. He told us it would be dangerous for him to come back to the river, but he just jumped back into catching thieves and killers as if he had never left. You are the only one who can stop him."

"But what can I do to stop him, Margaret? He has a head of his own, a very stubborn head."

"If the two of you were married, his first thought would be to protect you. He would get you away from the river to protect both of you. I heard him talking to Mr. Barney about wanting to find a farm in the Ozarks that was close enough to good roads that he could get his stuff to city markets. He just needs a nudge."

Yvette decided to weigh in. "That makes sense, Janet. He seems to be the kind of man who needs to look out for someone other than himself. You are worried about him, aren't you? I can tell."

Janet laughed. She needed that laugh. "Yes, mother and daughter are indeed alike. You are double-teaming me."

To Margaret she said with a smile, "Just a nudge, huh? Just a nudge? Do you have a suggestion as to how I might nudge him?"

The look she got from Margaret told her something of how she, herself, must look when a student would ask her a really off-the-wall question. "Don't be silly! You have a brain. Use it!"

Yes, those were precisely the words she had sometimes used—with the same inflections yet. To have those same words thrown back at her by a nine-year-old child, albeit a precocious one, did, in fact, make her feel silly. "Okay! Okay!" She threw up her hands in a gesture of surrender. "I will find a way to nudge him. I just may tell him you said so."

"If he was here, I would tell him now. He needs to think of the people who love him. He needs to consider them. Especially you."

She paused. She was thinking something serious. Janet and Yvette waited. With a faraway look she said somberly, "I thought I was a goner there at the singing school when that crooked sheriff showed up. He was going to kill me because Grandma wanted him to. I don't know what would have happened if Mr. Galen had not stopped him."

"Miss Janet, he will be the kind of husband that you can always count on to do the right thing. Nobody will push him around. Don't let him get away. You need him, and he needs you."

All three fell silent, each lost in her own thoughts. Then Margaret spoke up in a perky voice. "I want to come and see you and Mr. Galen when I am older. You will probably have children by then."

Yvette responded to her daughter's comment. "We three girls have Mr. Galen married with children, and he doesn't know a thing about it."

"He will find out soon enough," said Margaret.

"Barney and Galen are cousins," said Janet. "You get your mother married to Barney, and then you can tell him that you all need to go see his cousin."

Inexplicably, Margaret began to laugh, and she continued to laugh as if she didn't want to stop. Yvette and Janet loved to hear her laugh, and soon they were laughing with her.

Chapter Eleven
NIGHTHAWK AGAIN

The fugitive sheriff awoke refreshed and ready to get back into the game. He continued to take great personal pride in excelling at the game of stealing. Like baseball players take great personal satisfaction in being able to hit, throw or field at an exceptional level, he reveled at his ability to steal without getting caught. It was a game at which he had few peers, and it paid well.

When he saw sweat-drenched carpenters sawing and nailing, or dock workers straining to move heavy bales of cotton, his feeling toward them was contempt. Honest labor was too hard, and it paid too little. Only cowardly fools would punish themselves by engaging in it.

He liked the night hours when honest working men were sleeping. While they slept, he could take what he wanted of what they had worked so hard and foolishly to produce. They had to work almost every day. He could take what he wanted by working only one or two nights a week, and then take months-long vacations.

He didn't like having to kill a watchman or investigator from time to time, but he never hesitated to do so when it became necessary. For one thing, killing attracted attention, and it was something family members would never forget. Some of them would never quit trying to find the one who killed their father, brother or cousin.

It had been easy to enter a mercantile store and get the clothing he needed. He had gotten various sizes so that the owners would not be able to tell the investigators his general physical description. There was a stack of cotton sacks the owners had stocked in preparation for the upcoming cotton-picking season. Those clothes that did not fit he put into the sack. He would dispose of them soon, probably under a bridge.

Because he knew that people would have been alerted to watch for a tall man with a cast on his left forearm, he had to wear sleeves. Thus far he had stayed out of public view, slept mostly in empty cotton houses that no one would visit until the cotton-picking season began and stolen food from small country stores at night.

The locks were always easy to pick, and he took only what he would need for the next two days. If the storekeeper missed the items he would probably suspect one of his customers of shoplifting. He slept during the day and walked the roads at night. At one of the stores, he had acquired a .32 caliber pistol that could be easily concealed on his person and was easy to carry. A couple of nights later he lifted a box of cartridges for it.

One of the storekeepers kept a substantial sum of money in an old safe. He worked for only a short time before he succeeded in opening it. Elated at finding a bag containing almost five hundred dollars, he looked forward to traveling faster and more comfortably. The money was in a bag at the back of the safe, and a lesser amount was in a cigar box at the front.

He surmised that the cigar box contained the money used in daily operations and that the owner seldom opened the bank bag at the rear of the safe. He left the money in the cigar box as he found it and put a folded paper bag in the bank bag so that it would appear undisturbed. It might be days or even weeks before the owner discovered the theft.

It was then that he decided to present himself as a prosperous business man, and he needed the clothes to fit the role. He dared not present himself at a store to purchase the attire because of the cast on his arm. Because a shirt would not conceal the cast, he needed a summer suit. A suit coat would have sleeves large enough to conceal the cast.

After stealing the clothes, he walked steadily for the remainder of the night and located an empty cotton house located about three hundred yards from the road as the eastern sky began to show some light. By noontime, he was wide awake and unable to sleep because of the heat.

He walked outside and discovered a clean, running spring branch nearby. This would be a good time to make himself presentable. After washing the accumulated sweaty odor from his body, he used a pair of barber scissors, straight razor and hand mirror he had stolen from a barber shop.

At the time he had acquired them—and "acquired" was the word he used in his own mind—he had not yet "acquired" the .32 caliber pistol. The scissors, and especially the straight razor, would serve as weapons if the need arose.

When dusk came, he was ready for the road again. He had parted the weeds and shoved the cotton sack with the clothes of different sizes well underneath the cotton house. It would not be discovered until cotton-picking time, if then. One of the two summer suits he folded very neatly and put in the duffle bag. The other he carried over his shoulder on a hanger together with his shirt.

There was a town large enough to have an automobile dealership a few miles ahead. He could easily make it before daylight and have time to change into the clothes of a prosperous business man. He looked forward to eating a fresh-cooked breakfast at a cafe. No more canned sausages, bologna sandwiches, peanut butter and crackers.

"Yeah, my brother had to rush back home to see about his sick horse," the sheriff said. "I told him I could buy a car here good enough to get me to Memphis. His son thinks he can repair the one that broke down on me, but I'm thinking it needs a new motor. I told him it was his to do whatever he could do with it. That lad is a fine boy, and I hope he can make it run like new."

The salesman had been a little too inquisitive about where his brother lived. "I know most of the people up in that part of the country, but I don't know anybody by that name."

"Well, he hasn't been there long. My brother likes to move around. I don't guess he will ever settle down. He is always looking to move. He is always thinking the grass is greener on the other side of the fence."

"Yeah, some people are like that. I have known a few like that. Me? I like familiar surroundings and to chew the fat with people I have known for years."

Nighthawk soon decided on a 1933 Ford Coupe that matched his pose as a prosperous business man. It left him with sufficient money to eat at nice restaurants and sleep at decent hotels for a week or two. When he felt it safe to do so, he would access the stash he kept in Memphis for just such a time as this.

People shouldn't do him the way Broussard had done him, the way Kit Treadway had done him nor even the way Janet Williams had done him, and think they could get by with it. He had always evened the score and a whole lot more when anyone got in his way. While the arm healed, he would have time to gather information and consider his next moves.

Only one thing bothered him. He had to meet with the three musketeers—that's what they called themselves—and get his business back in order. These three merchants controlled everything in the Memphis area and a lot more things up and down the river. He had to clear his jobs with them before he pulled them off, and then they told him where to take the goods.

When they had an opportunity to inspect and inventory what he had "acquired," he would receive his pay, usually by a cash deposit to one of several bank accounts he maintained under fictitious names. They would know by now that he was wanted by the FBI, and they would not be happy about that. That was the only thing that worried him.

Nevertheless, he had major confidence in his ability to persuade people—to bend them to his will. The ability to lie convincingly had served him so well that he seldom gave thought to what the truth really was. He thought instead in terms of what he might get people to believe, things that would serve his purposes.

No one had come close to making as much money for the three musketeers as he, and he was sure that they would be greedy for more. They were big spenders, and they liked to gamble. Like many who liked to gamble they were not good at it. Nighthawk knew two gamblers who depended on losses of the three musketeers for a steady income.

He didn't have to go to them or even to Memphis. He had other people with whom he had done business both up and down the river. Memphis was the place he liked best and the place where he could more quickly be up and running with a good flow of income. Memphis had the women he liked best.

Coming off the east end of the Harahan Bridge he felt good. He was going to miss Chug Worley. He had learned about him from the doctor who set his broken arm. Perhaps Tag would be around and he could use him for the same sort of jobs he had used Chug. He would line up all his men before he contacted the three musketeers so that he could convince them that nothing had changed.

Yes, he would have to be careful about the feds, but that would soon settle down as they moved on to other things. He had used numerous aliases as it became convenient to do so, and he could come up with more as necessary. In fact, he didn't really know his real name. His father had adopted a new name when he moved to the Ozarks. On the river, there were many men who fit his physical description.

Arriving at a boarding house he had often used, he carried inside his newly-bought luggage. If the woman behind the desk recognized him, she did not make it known. She had seen him many times, but she had long ago learned that the less she knew, the better. She politely checked him in as she would any well-dressed business man. Not an eyebrow was raised when he gave her his newly adopted alias.

He was soon eating his evening meal at a restaurant frequented by people in summer coats and ties. As he looked about, he considered how recently he had been sleeping in cotton houses during the day and traveling at night. He congratulated himself upon making the transition so quickly and smoothly.

The sawbones had told him that he must wear the cast for four weeks. The inside bone, the one connected to his thumb, was okay. It was the outside bone—he called it the ulna—that had been fractured. He said that it was a severe fracture, but fortunately not completely broken.

"You will get tired of wearing it in this hot weather; it will be uncomfortable," he had said. "If you want it to heal, you've got to do it. Be careful not to fall on another rock."

Seated at a small table in a corner, he had a good view of the restaurant, but he saw no one he knew. Mildly disappointed, he returned to the boarding house to sleep. The next morning he hit pay dirt. One of his best men was staying there as well.

Within a few days, he had gathered information about the little girl and the adults with her who had come and gone at the Peabody. The information was contradictory and he had difficulty getting a clear picture. It was clear that the girl and her mother had caught the southbound boat, still in the company of two feds.

There was a third man who went with them. One source said he was G. W. Broussard, but the only other source said he was not. In any event, it seemed that Broussard was gone and that schoolmarm was gone. He concluded that they had probably headed back together to the Ozarks. He would take his vengeance in due time when they least expected it. For now, he had to get his operation up and going.

He received one welcome bit of information. "Striker," a local hit man had been killed while attempting to strike another man dead with his knife. Striker dressed in dark clothes, operated at night, and was likely to kill just because someone had looked at him wrongly. Everyone feared him.

His method of operation was almost always the same. He would casually wait until his victim walked by, preferably in dim light. Turning quickly, he would stab repeatedly with a long-bladed knife until his victim fell. One of his informants believed that G. W. Broussard had been his intended victim when he was killed. He was trying for the contract money.

Having gotten his men lined up and ready, he considered how best to make contact with the three musketeers. They were very sensitive about how contact was made, and he wanted to be especially careful because of his status as a fugitive from the FBI. While he was pondering, they made contact with him.

As he left a nice restaurant in coat and tie, two men suddenly appeared, one on each side of him. In a low voice one of them said, "The bosses have an assignment for you. Come and go with us." A sedan pulled up by the curb, and the men opened the doors. The three of them sat on the back seat with him in the middle, even though the passenger seat in front was unoccupied.

An effort to make conversation received no response, so he remained silent. With every block he grew more apprehensive. He tried to make conversation again, but was met with dead silence. The vehicle stopped at a stop sign to wait for cross traffic to pass. He jerked his right elbow up against the chin of the man on his right, used the weight of his body to pin him against the back of the seat and threw open the door.

As he exited, he pulled his small pistol from his coat and fired into the car, just something to discourage them from following him. He raced down the sidewalk of the mixed residential and small business neighborhood. He knew the area, and he knew where he could conceal himself.

Finally feeling safe in the storage room outside a private home owned by people he had boarded with, he thought of his automobile and of his belongings at the boarding house. He could return to neither of them. They would be waiting. He was in the streets again with no place to sleep.

He had the advantage of being able to withdraw money from a bank safe at a bank they would not connect him with. He had to change his appearance. He had to get out of this light-colored summer suit. For the next several hours, he picked at the cast on his arm with his pocket knife.

He was removing it sooner than the sawbones had said, but it had to happen. The cast was a dead giveaway. Dead? Yeah, that was the right word. He would just have to be careful with the arm.

The next afternoon found him on the docks dressed in stevedore clothing, an old hat worn in such a way as to cast a shadow on his face. The next morning found him stowed away on a tug headed downriver.

CHAPTER TWELVE
SOUTH LOUISIANA

Grand-Pere and Grand-Mere Favre stood behind Yvonne and Lynette with their hands on their shoulders. A cavalcade of vehicles produced a cloud of dust as they rolled slowly in their direction along the tree-lined dirt road. Limbs from the big oak trees overhung the road, and moss hung from those limbs. For at least the twentieth time Yvonne said, "I can't wait. I can't wait."

She turned again to Lynette and repeated what she had told her several times before. "Margaret and I helped Maman take care of you when we came back from the mountains. We did a lot of walking, and we slept outside at night a lot of times."

The two slender, dark-haired girls, ages eight and six, bore striking resemblance to one another and to their mother. Lynette struggled to remember all the things she was supposed to know about Margaret. She had seen pictures of the family when Margaret was still in the picture, but she wanted to remember more clearly.

In order to spare the girls the agony of their sister being gone, Yvette and the grandparents had focused their full attention on them with little mention of Margaret. They feared she was dead, and they would discuss their sister with them when they were older. Although they never gave up hope for Margaret's return, it was just that. Hope.

And if they did get her back, how would she be affected by her ordeal? What kind of bad ideas might have been pumped into her head? But the grandparents had learned that their granddaughter was amazingly fine. Margaret had declined to talk with them on the phone. "Your voice didn't sound right on the telephone," she told her mother. "I want to talk to them face to face and hug them. I want to see them when I talk to them."

The FBI agents had instructions to see Margaret and Yvette all the way home and then to maintain surveillance of the home and surrounding area for forty-eight hours. The sheriff and one of his deputies led the way in the first car. Neither of them wore a uniform or any insignia indicating their law enforcement capacity.

Everyone in the Ascension Parish area knew the story of how a sheriff had tried to kill Margaret while she was in the protection of FBI agents. It might be a while before Margaret could again place confidence in any sheriff. At her homecoming, she probably should not be looking at a man wearing a badge. The sheriff would first let her get to know him and win her confidence before displaying a badge.

Yvette and Margaret rode on the back seat of the second car with Cliff driving. Walter and Barney followed them with all the luggage on the back seat and floor. "I'm going to miss you and Cliff," said Barney. "We have walked through the fire together, and it's coming to a really happy conclusion. Mission completed successfully."

"I'm sort of sorry it's coming to a conclusion, Barney. I'm going to miss that girl. I have never seen anyone like her. Think of what she went through, and it just made her stronger. She will be an inspiration to me for the rest of my life."

The other two federal agents brought up the rear, hanging back to check the countryside and to avoid some of the dust. They were taking extra precautions because they knew Nighthawk had come into Memphis and made contacts. Now he was headed downriver. His fixation on a nine-year-old girl puzzled everyone, and they were taking no chances on what he might have in mind.

The vehicles pulled to the left to enter the front yard and stopped with the left sides of the vehicles toward the house. Margaret sat on the driver's side behind Cliff and looked out the window at once familiar surroundings. She spied Grand Pere and Grand Mere Favre standing behind Yvonne and Lynette. How they had grown, especially Lynette.

She opened the door as soon as the vehicle stopped, and both she and her mother exited through that same door. They all moved slowly toward one another, their faces exhibiting deep emotions. Soon they were all in one another's arms. Tears flowed freely.

Margaret began to go from one to another with personal words for each one. She reached Grand-Pere Favre last. "Grand-Pere, I didn't do what you told me. I left my pistol at home when I went berry-picking that day. They would not have gotten me if I had carried the pistol with me."

That remark prompted Yvette to volunteer more information. "The firearm lessons you gave them enabled Margaret to stop a despicable pervert from abusing her. She found a .32 caliber pistol by the spring and hid it. On the second day after she escaped one of the men sent to find her, came upon her where she was sleeping. The pistol and your training made the difference."

"I aimed between his eyes like you told me,' Margaret said, "but he lunged at me just as I pulled the trigger. The bullet hit him at the top of his forehead and knocked him out. I was able to get away." Her grandfather held her close for a long time.

Her grandmother said, "You are back with us now. That's what counts. We have a lot of living to do to try to make up for those lost years. We can't make up for them, but we can try."

Yvette turned and beckoned to Barney. As he stepped forward, she took the wood-carved Bluebird from her purse. "That's where it was!" Margaret exclaimed. "I was afraid I had lost it!"

"This is Barney. He became very special to Margaret before they ever talked with one another. Now he has become special to me."

She smiled self-consciously. "Margaret insisted that he become very special to me. Margaret told me that he helped her make it through some difficult months."

At this juncture, Margaret could not resist. She interrupted her mother. "Every afternoon I had to go to the back side of the pasture to drive the cows to the barn for milking. Quite often I would see Mr. Barney sitting on the creek bank fishing about fifty paces down the hill from the rail fence. He would prop two fishing poles with rocks and watch them while he whittled. One day he saw me watching him whittle, and he waved at me."

Her facial expression became more serious, and her voice reflected it. "Papa and Grandma had told me many times that if I ever talked to anyone when they were not around, they would kill that person. And probably me as well. When he waved to me, I held my hand close to my chest like this"—she demonstrated the covert wave—"and waved back. Then I ran away after the cows."

"He started walking toward me one day while motioning for me to wait, but I ran away. Two or three days later I saw him waiting by a section of the fence close to the trail where I always walked. I was afraid for him and was ready to circle away from him."

Margaret grasped her mother's left wrist with both her hands. She raised that hand, which held the bluebird, for all to see. "He held this Bluebird high so that I could see it, and then he set it on a flat place on the top rail of the fence. He disappeared into the woods."

She looked at her mother as if to say, "Now, you take it from there."

"I have learned from Barney that he understood her situation, but he was afraid she would not go with him if he made an effort to rescue her. His cousin, a singing school teacher who you had hired to look for her, inquired about her to Barney. They were developing a rescue plan that would not endanger her when Margaret escaped on her own."

She had to pause and control her emotions before she uttered the next sentence. "Margaret escaped so that she could get to a telephone and warn us that they were coming to get Yvonne."

She paused again to compose herself. "Barney has been with her since the crooked sheriff of that county tried to take her from a singing school. She was attending the school while waiting for FBI agents to escort her to Memphis. The sheriff intended to kill her to please her grandmother. Barney helped those agents protect her all the way to Memphis."

Barney had stood looking about, scanning the countryside, as if he was not aware that he was the subject of their conversation. With his right hand extended, Grand-Pere Favre stepped toward Barney. As he firmly grasped Barney's hand he said, "Thank you for protecting Margaret. Merci tres beaucoup!"

"Il n'y a pas de quoi, Monsieur. Your granddaughter is a pure delight. Adults learn from her."

When he heard the French words, Grand-Pere's head came up just a bit and his eyes grew a little wider, but he gave no other indication that he noticed. Yvonne did not hold back. "You speak French!" she chirped excitedly.

"Un peu," Barney responded. "Je parle un peu de francais. You three sisters look very much alike. I believe you are all on your way to looking just like your mother looks now. Grand-Mere Favre, you must be really proud."

The sisters wandered off to one side and began to pepper one another with questions. The adults took great satisfaction in seeing the bubbling excitement of the girls. Grand-Pere Favre asked some rather penetrating questions of Barney. His reactions to the answers seemed to indicate that Barney was giving the right answers.

On the way down the river, Yvette and Barney had stood on deck near the rail while Margaret had fascinating conversations with the federal agents nearby. They sat in deck chairs in a semi-circle with Margaret doing most of the talking. Occasionally Walter or Cliff would glance at the other two agents as if to say, "Didn't I tell you how she is?"

Yvette and Barney had taken to one another as quickly as Margaret had thought they would, and soon they were talking about the practical aspects of making a home together. As always, there was the problem of money. Three growing girls had definite and continuing needs.

The FBI agents had brought the reward money for Margaret's recovery to Galen, and he had shared it equally with Barney and Janet. The amount was substantial, but much more would be needed to establish and maintain a home. With the depression hanging on, he could not expect to get much at all for the sale of his Ozark farm. He had not worked the fields for the past twelve years, and they would need to be cleared of brush and briers by any new owner.

One happy circumstance was the ready access to good markets for agricultural produce in and near Ascension Parish. The entire family would work together to produce and sell eggs, butter and vegetables. Barney had several colonies of bees that he could sell for a few dollars. He would use that money plus some more to establish new colonies in Louisiana.

Although he had given up farming after his wife's death, Barney had devoted considerable time to his hives. He enjoyed working with the bees almost as much as his fishing. He didn't sell the honey, but gave most of it to appreciative neighbors. Most would find some way to return the favor.

He had improved his beekeeping abilities during his stays near Breaux Bridge. The beekeeper he had worked with there, produced queen bees to sell to beekeepers throughout the country. He had learned new techniques for starter hives and new methods for swarm control.

He knew it would take as much as three to four years before he could make the hives pay, but he also knew he could produce significant income from them. Moreover, it would be a labor of love. He enjoyed every aspect of honey production. The girls would enjoy uncapping the combs and spinning the honey out of them. He could imagine their delight at seeing rows of full honey jars produced by their own efforts.

At noon on the second day, he carried hot meals and some good strong Cajun coffee with chicory to the four agents, who had stationed themselves at various vantage points near the house. They had begun to look forward to the good Cajun cooking each day, and they were not anxious to see the end of this assignment.

Barney made his way toward Cliff, the last of the four agents to be served. Cliff had stationed himself in a wooded area where he would likely see anyone coming from the direction of the river. A voice from behind him stopped him in mid-stride. "Turn around slowly, Barney, and look at me." Barney knew the voice, and he knew he was in trouble. He turned slowly to face Nighthawk and looked into the barrel of a .38 caliber pistol.

"This is going to give me special satisfaction for the trouble you caused me. I want to see the look on your face, and I want you to see who is pulling the trigger. I didn't come looking for you. Had no idea you were within a hundred miles, and you just came walking up with a picnic lunch. I can use that lunch."

He was bringing the pistol level, aiming for the head. Barney tensed to leap toward him when a shot rang out behind him. It was Nighthawk's head that suddenly had a hole in it, just above his left eye. The right back of his head seemed to explode and he crumpled to the ground.

"To paraphrase you, Mr. Nighthawk, that is for the trouble you caused us." Cliff said grimly. He stepped forward and visually examined the body.

"I was waiting for him behind that tree. He was working his way deeper into the woods. He must have been looking for a place to rest until he could pull off a robbery. I didn't really think this watch was necessary. It just goes to show that you never know."

"I should have been more careful," said Barney. "You saved my bacon. I thought my time had come. Merci tres beaucoup!"

"Well, the only reason we set this watch was the information that he had stowed away on a tug headed downriver. That came
from Patrick. He and his men are good. Real good. You need to thank him."

"Look. There is a packet of bills," said Barney. "He must have dropped them when he pulled his pistol."

Barney lifted the packet from the leaves and thumbed through the bills. They appeared to all be hundreds, and the packet was more than a half- inch thick. Barney tried to hand them to Cliff, but he shook his head.

"You found them. They are yours. I can't connect the money to Nighthawk. I didn't see them fall. It looks like the Good Lord gave you a wedding gift."

"Then split them with me. You take half."

"I would just have to turn them in, and it would mean a lot of paper work for me. Like I said, I have no way to connect that money to Nighthawk. Put it in your pocket and be grateful for your good fortune. Take good care of Yvette and the girls."

CHAPTER THIRTEEN
MEANWHILE BACK IN MEMPHIS

Janet was restless. She tried not to let her restlessness morph into anxiety. That was not her way to deal with life. Her approach to life required action. She enjoyed lengthy periods to read, think and reflect, but then action must soon follow. She had read, she had thought, she had reviewed her thoughts, and now she needed action.

Galen and Patrick had chosen the boarding house for her. The owner, a middle-aged widow, catered to working women, and she admitted only those who convinced her that they were self-disciplined and reputable. There were four other women, three of whom had made the house their home for more than a year. They were all congenial and easy to talk with.

Everyone lingered at evening meals to visit with one another around the table. Janet had no reason to go anywhere to meet her physical needs; all her needs were met within the four walls of the house and the enclosed patio garden behind it. This was her twelfth day there, and she had grown very restless.

Not knowing. That was the worst thing. She had always thirsted for knowledge, to be informed, to know. Not knowing was hard.

Patrick had told her that he needed Galen. The two of them were packed and ready to go back to the mountains—she to her parents' home and he to see his Uncle Louis and Aunt Mary. When their party of six was riding horseback to take Margaret to Memphis, she knew then that Galen was her man. He didn't know it, but she did.

Why was Galen so indispensable that Patrick had to have him? He had several good men. Galen had said so. He had excellent contacts with others. Why did he have to have Galen? That business man, Jim Harding, had been there, and he insisted on having Galen.

She had the keys to a new sedan and a blank bill of sale with his signature at the bottom. "The car is yours if anything happens to me," he had told her.

"But I want you," she had responded emphatically. "I don't want the car without you!"

He had looked at her long and warmly. If she never saw him again, she would remember that look. If a man could show love in his eyes and on his face, his love had shown forth so strongly that it enveloped her and held her in a warm embrace. He left then to go with Patrick. She didn't realize until later the full import of what she had said to him under the stress of the moment.

In a vague way Galen had hinted that they had "things to talk about" on the way back to the mountains. "We will have hours to talk," he had said.

Finding it almost impossible to sit, she was strolling about—or more accurately, pacing restlessly—in the patio garden. She heard footsteps, a man's footsteps, in the hallway of the boarding house. She knew those steps, firm steps as if on a mission, and she ran to the screen door that opened into the hallway.

They each saw the other at the same moment. "Galen! Galen!" That was all she could say as they held one another tightly. "Galen! Galen! Galen!"

"For a schoolmarm, you have a very limited vocabulary," he teased.

"That is all the vocabulary I need right now," she retorted.

"Oh, you will need a rich and extensive vocabulary. We have miles to go and a lot to talk about. We have plans to make—decisions big and small. As my wise

Cousin Barney once told me, I must find out what you want. But first I have big news, good news."

Janet stepped back and waited for him to tell her the news. "It will take some time to tell it," he said. "That is time that we can use to get across the river and on the road. How long will it take you to pack?"

"I have been packed and ready to go on a moment's notice since the first day. Help me get my luggage."

Mrs. "Dottie" met them as they came out of the room with the luggage. "Here is the unused portion of your deposit," she said. "You have been an exemplary guest. When you visit Memphis again, check with me. I will likely have a vacant room. If not, I will be happy to see you and just say, 'Hello.'"

As the smooth-running new sedan carried them westerly from West Memphis, Galen looked at Janet while keeping one eye on the road. "I don't want to take too much for granted. I have a very important question to ask you." Janet waited expectantly while Galen seemed to be framing the words in his mind.

Galen finally decided to make it simple. "Will you marry me? Will you make a home with me for as long as we both shall live?"

"I have already given you my answer, and you know it. Thank you for asking, anyway. When you handed me that blank bill of sale for this new automobile so that I could write in my name if something happened to you, I gave you my answer. It just came out of my mouth. I told you that it was you I wanted, not the automobile."

"How well do I remember! Those words kept ringing in my ears throughout all the hectic activity of the past several days. They made me stronger and more alert. You affect me that way. From the very first, you have affected me that way."

"Without you, this new car wouldn't mean much," she said. "As you well know, no one owns a motor vehicle where I was raised, and we have all gotten along quite well without them. Whatever we share together has meaning, whether it is a mule and jack, or a car."

Galen responded in a more serious tone, almost solemn. "Janet, our Lord has been especially good to us. So good that I am just astounded. He has brought us through dangers where people wanted to kill us, and would not have given it a second thought if they had succeeded. During the past few days, those people who decided to become our enemies have, themselves, bit the dust."

"Well it does seem that you have some big news to tell me."

"Oh, that is just part of it. Bear with me. It's going to take a while to cover it all."

"It's like you said. We have hours and hours together in this car. I was so restless this morning that I could not sit down. I was just pacing to and fro in the patio garden. Then I heard your steps in the hallway. Now I can patiently listen to your voice. We are together. That is what matters."

"I was with one of Patrick's men at the docks just after nightfall when I saw Nighthawk steal aboard a tug. That was the night after we checked you into Ms. Dottie's boarding house. I had been watching him lurk in the shadows near the boat, and I knew that it was Nighthawk. As you know, he has a distinctive way of moving."

"Oh no! Him again? He is a blood-thirsty wolf!"

"Worse. A wolf is more honest and straightforward. Excuse my correcting you. He was a blood-thirsty wolf. No one has to worry about him any longer."

"He's dead?"

"Cliff reported to the Memphis office by telephone yesterday afternoon. He shot and killed him near the residence of Margaret's grandparents. He was taking dead aim on Barney and was about to pull the trigger, but Cliff pulled the trigger first. It was a head shot. Instant death."

Janet brought her right hand to her chest just below her neck, and her left hand followed it to the wrist. She closed her eyes and held her breath. After a few moments, she breathed a prayer of thanks. "Thank you, Lord. Thank you. Thank you."

She jerked stiffly erect and looked at Galen. "That devil! How did he know where Yvette's parents lived?"

"He may not have known. We will never know. He told Barney, 'I had no idea that you were within a hundred miles, and you just came walking up with a picnic lunch.' Barney was taking lunch to Cliff. It's hard to believe that his presence there was just coincidence."

"Why else would he leave Memphis?"

"Oh, that? That's another story. He was running from mob kingpins. He thought he could just move back in and pick up his operations where he had left off in the spring. The mob bosses thought otherwise."

"They wanted to kill him?"

"Right. They did not like the fact that he was implicated in a kidnapping and had tried to kill FBI agents. That made him too hot to handle. He was drawing unwanted attention. Since he had gotten back to Memphis, his regular attire was a summer business suit and tie. When I saw him on the dock, he was dressed like a dock worker with a weather-beaten hat pulled low over his face."

Galen veered to avoid a bad place in the road. The new four-door Plymouth PE Deluxe took to the road better than any vehicle he had driven. The salesman had explained that it had a new improved suspension system, but he had discounted the statement as salesmanship. He had not exaggerated.

He also liked the steady strong straight-six engine. It did not have the pep of the V-8 engine in the rented Ford Coupe. It was just strong and steady. Of course, the additional weight of the sedan worked against quick acceleration.

"Barney and Yvette are getting married. Right away. That was also part of Cliff's report. I can just see all those Cajuns celebrating Margaret's return along with Yvette's marriage to the man largely responsible for getting her there. It's bound to be a great event with

Cajun music and dancing. And there is no food in the world like Cajun food. There will be plenty of that."

Janet gave him a mischievous smile. "We Ozark Mountains folk know how to throw a good party too. Fiddles, guitars and banjoes. We also cook good food. Do you think you are up to that?"

"You can bet I am! I can hardly wait. That brings me to the really important thing. Where will we make our home? What do you think? Before you say, let me tell you what I have in mind. Then I will listen to your thoughts and desires."

"Hey, you are jumping ahead, but I suppose I'm the one who got into that subject. When we are married, we will need a home. Okay, I'm listening with eager ears. I have not really thought ahead to where we will make our home, but I will tell you this. I am a country girl. I feel strongly about that."

"Our financial situation is considerably improved. The merchants for whom I worked until the trial blew my cover, decided that I deserved a nice bonus. I believe Jim Harding was primarily responsible for the idea. He sympathized with the fact that I suddenly lost my job at a time when jobs are scarce. He reminded the merchants that I lived each day with a price on my head."

"Oh, Galen! We will always have to be on the lookout."

"We need to always be on the lookout anyway. One never knows what malice is in someone's heart. More often it comes from the fact that you have something someone else wants."

"I have been fortunate to have lived among decent accommodating people. It's difficult for me to imagine what you must have dealt with in your undercover work."

"One big part of the good news is that the contract for my scalp disappeared with the death of those who were offering it."

"It sounds as if a lot happened during the twelve days you left me with Mrs. Dottie."

"There were three merchants who opposed my bonus, even got real angry about it. After events of the past few days, the remaining merchants unanimously agreed to make the bonus even larger."

"Should I ask, 'What events of the past few days?' Do I really want to know?"

"Patrick's men had begun to suspect that those three merchants were the ones who had let the contract on my head. At some point, Patrick discussed it with Jim Harding. He brought another merchant into the discussion, and they put their heads together. By reviewing past occurrences and by bringing together what each one of them knew, they became firmly convinced that those merchants were mob bosses."

"And they were privy to all the information you developed while you were working undercover."

"No, not all. Not by a long shot. I learned that information I gave to the merchants soon leaked to the wrong people. I had a couple of close calls that could be explained no other way. I gave them information after property had been recovered and arrests had been made."

"Whew! They are going to wreck that truck and kill themselves." Janet exclaimed. Two young men had passed them in a stripped-down pickup truck that obviously had been modified by the installation of a souped-up big engine.

As they disappeared from sight around a curve, Galen continued. "Even though they kept hounding me for preliminary progress reports, I gave them only summary reports after the fact. I knew that some of them were unhappy with that, and now I feel sure that the unhappiness originated with those three."

"Mr. Harding insisted that you work with Patrick's men. Why was your presence so important?"

"Questions would come up that I could answer because of my experience on the waterfront and among the warehouses. Finally, though, I became the bait that baited the trap and drew all the rats to one location."

Galen heard Janet gasp. "Are you sure you want to hear all these details?"

"Don't expect me to sit here like a school teacher listening to a book report!" she retorted. "You are talking about the man of my dreams, the man I am going to marry. Nevertheless, I do want to hear the details."

"The word went out that I would be at a certain location near the waterfront at a certain time, and the price on my head had gone up. That drew almost a dozen people that Patrick had been looking to apprehend. Among them was Tag Worley and Chug's teenage son. I feel really bad about a teenage boy getting killed, but he was spraying bullets with a Browning automatic rifle, shades of Bonnie and Clyde."

"We had a conversation with Margaret about Bonnie and Clyde. She heard the names and wanted to know who they were. She pointed out that she had been cut off from the outside world for more than two years."

"I don't know how they managed to get them there, but those three mob bosses, the three merchants, also showed up. I didn't ask any questions, and they didn't tell me."

Galen fell silent. He, himself, did not want to share the gory details. There was no way to find what might be called, "the right words."

"Are you trying to find the right words to tell me the gory details?"

His next thought was, "I'm going to be living with a woman who can literally read my mind."

"There are no right words, Janet. Let me just say that it was not pretty. There is nothing romantic about crime, whether it's Bonnie and Clyde or Nighthawk. And there is nothing romantic about fighting crime, even though there is nothing that is more necessary."

"I am happy to hear you say that—for more than one reason. I don't want you to miss it and want to go back to it."

"I have had enough crime-fighting to last a lifetime, but sometimes we don't have a choice. The man who can't find something worth fighting and dying for is a poor excuse for a man."

Janet became thoughtful for several long moments. "I have never heard it said quite that way, Galen. We both jumped right in to help an abused and endangered little girl. Who knows what other challenges we may face and when we will face them? Jesus said, 'Sufficient unto the day is the evil thereof.' We will take each day as it comes."

"Well, so long as we are quoting scripture, Solomon said, 'Let us hear the conclusion of the whole matter.' At the conclusion of the shootout with fully automatic weapons, the three mob bosses, Tag, Tag's nephew and two other criminals had been killed. Our side sustained three non-fatal casualties. The other criminals were arrested."

"Are you feeling hungry yet? It was almost lunch time when you came to get me."

"I saw that sign, too. It should be a decent place to stop."

To keep fresh air coming through the sedan on the hot summer day Galen had lowered two windows halfway before leaving the boarding house. He had learned that letting the air flow into the front window on one side and out the back window on the other side, served to minimize the sound of the wind. Out of consideration for Janet's hair he lowered the front window on the driver's side.

As soon as they got out of the car, the late summer heat made them miss the moving air that had dried their perspiration and made them feel cooler. Upon entering the building, they were pleased to notice that the restaurant had a very high ceiling with open windows near the ceiling. Hot air near the ceiling flowed out the windows to keep the air stirring among the patrons.

The restrooms were clean, and the food was excellent. Soon they were back on the road. They talked about the scenery, the cotton fields they were passing, and politics. Soon the conversation returned to their own hopes and dreams.

"You declared yourself on the matter of city living. You are a country girl and feel strongly about it. I have long wanted to be a farmer, even though I have no experience at all. I have spent countless hours gathering information, reading and talking to farmers. I have heard many discouraging words. Farmers have been having a tough time, but so has almost everyone else."

Janet responded with a broad smile. "No matter what you set out to do, someone will discourage you. You don't know how good it makes me feel to hear you say that you have that dream. I will help you with it. I won't discourage you."

"It sounds like we have resolved something that is important to us both." Galen grinned back and spoke in a teasing tone. "Did you think I might want to take you to a houseboat?"

"I have heard you speak fondly of your childhood on a houseboat. That crossed my mind. If that was the only way I could have you, I would do it."

A sudden thought ran through her mind. "We have to make plans for me to meet your mother and daddy and the rest of your family."

"Janet, when I combine my savings with my third of the reward money for getting Margaret back home, and with the nice bonus I got this morning, we have enough money to buy a decent farm, build a home and have money to live on until we can make the farm pay. At some point, we may have to borrow some money to get the farm started, but I don't want to go whole-hog into anything. We will work into it slowly."

"You can count my third of the reward money. I know how to live thriftily. I wouldn't be wasteful even if I had plenty of money to waste. I can find a job teaching until the first baby comes; then I want to stay home with my children."

Galen's head swiveled toward her quickly. "Thinking ahead! I like that! How many?"

"Who knows?" she laughed. "Time will tell."

"My cousin got off to a running start. He starts with

three girls. If they are anything like Margaret, he has an interesting life ahead."

"It will be a drastic change for Barney," Janet observed. "He goes from living alone and roaming the countryside to having the responsibility of a wife and three daughters."

"He and I had a serious talk when I first arrived in the Ozarks. He confided to me that he was very lonesome and ready to find a good wife. He had prayed about it, and the Lord has answered that prayer in a big way."

Galen thought of something he had not told Janet. "Oh, by the way, Margaret demonstrated remarkable foresight on another matter. Her grandma Bean is dead. She died just the way Margaret said she would. Without Margaret there to see after her, she drank herself to death. The FBI agents discovered her in bed just the way Margaret said it would happen."

"So sad. Margaret said that both her grandmother and her father were decent people until they started drinking that home-made brew."

"Margaret and her two sisters are now the owners of an Ozark farm. Carlton Bean wishes to help his son, Robert, purchase the farm. There are also four cows, two horses and three mules. Carlton and Robert are caring for them. You or I may be called upon by Yvette to help with the transaction."

"How would we help?"

"Yvette doesn't want to make a trip back to the Ozarks. She would sign a power of attorney giving one of us the authority to act for her as guardian of the three children. Barney wants to sell his place as well, and he wants to stay busy in Louisiana making a home for Yvette and the girls. He will handle the transaction by mail, but he wants me to retrieve some personal belongings from the house."

Soon they found themselves approaching the little river town of Dardanelle, located northwest of Little Rock on the Arkansas River. Galen's mother and father liked to spend time on the Arkansas River, and he had visited Dardanelle several times as a child.

When he had visited Uncle Louis and Aunt Mary as a twelve-year-old, he had met Uncle Louis at Dardanelle. He remembered so well how amazed he had been as they made their way north. The landscape had become increasingly rugged, and recent rains had made some of the stream crossings hazardous. It was just the kind of adventure a twelve-year old boy needed.

The late afternoon heat had taken its toll on Galen and Janet in spite of the constant flow of fresh air through the vehicle. They were ready to find rooms for the night, and they had become hungry again. "Let's get something to eat first," Galen said. "I want a big glass of iced tea."

"That's a good idea. If we wait too long, the eating places may close for the day."

"There is a place just ahead where I ate with my family when I was a boy." They happily found it open with several vehicles parked in front. From force of habit, Galen scrutinized the vehicles and looked up and down the street. As he escorted Janet through the door, his eyes were searching the interior just as they had examined the area outside.

Suddenly his whole body jerked as his eyes stopped on a man and woman sitting at a table near the back of the café. He smiled broadly as a thrill ran through his entire body. "Janet, I see two people who I know really well. You absolutely must meet them." He took her arm and guided her to their table.

Engrossed in conversation with one another, neither of them looked up until Galen and Janet stopped at their table. "Did I hear you say, 'G. W.?'" Galen was looking at the woman, a pretty woman who sat tall in her chair.

Before she turned her head to look at the one who spoke to her, she sprang from her chair. "G. W., G. W.! Oh, G. W.!" She threw her arms around Galen and reminded him once again of how strong she was.

Galen looked over her shoulder and said, "Hello Papa!" His father added his arms to those of his wife. They squeezed so tightly that he had to make a special effort to draw air into his lungs.

"Don't squeeze all the air out of me. I'm glad to see you two, also. And just as surprised."

Suddenly Janet found two pairs of curious eyes fixed upon her. Galen's mother wasted no time. With a smile she asked, "Would you like to introduce this pretty young lady to us, G. W.?"

Galen responded with special flair. "Maman! Papa! Please meet the woman of my dreams. She has graciously agreed to become my wife. And your daughter-in-law."

With a teasing look at Janet he added, "She's a schoolmarm, so she can help correct the deficiencies in my education."

"A man never knows how many such deficiencies he has, Son, until he gets married."

Grace Broussard playfully slapped her husband on the arm. "Hush, Galen! I have been very considerate in helping you understand those things that all men find difficult to comprehend."

Janet took a step forward. "My name is 'Janet Williams' and I learned to love your son while we were sharing some challenging experiences together."

Grace looked at her husband. "You see, Galen? Janet had to tell us her name. I tried to teach my son how to properly introduce people, but you men just need women to help you grasp basic things."

"Well I can understand this:" the elder Broussard retorted. "We need to sit down and let this waitress take their order." A lady stood waiting a respectable distance from them holding a tray with two glasses of water on it.

Soon they had ordered the special of the day shown on the chalk board in large print, together with large glasses of tea. Father and mother Broussard eagerly listened to Galen and Janet fill them in on the events of the past months.

"When I heard your voice," his mother said, "we were speculating on where you were and what you were doing. We have been worried sick about you because we heard that after the trial, the mob put out a contract on you."

"We have been spending a lot of time well upstream on the Arkansas River and away from the big water, because we were afraid they might try to get to you through us," his father added.

"Put your minds at ease. The three mobsters responsible for the contract died in a firefight with FBI agents last night. FBI agents and people working with them are busy putting out the word to everyone that there is no more contract. We can all get on with our lives."

When Galen and Janet had slaked their thirst and satisfied their appetites, Galen said, "I would like for Janet to see your houseboat."

"Spend the night with us," Mrs. Broussard invited. "I will prepare breakfast for us in the morning. Would bacon, eggs, biscuits, gravy and honey be okay? We have some ham too."

The parents enjoyed the ride in the new Plymouth sedan. Happiness characterized their every gesture and every word they spoke. They were happy for the prosperity their son had achieved, but most of all for the relief they felt upon learning that the price on his head was gone.

Upon seeing the boat, Janet expressed her surprise at its size. "My goodness, you have a roomy home on the water. I had not expected it to be so large."

"The one on which G. W. was raised was not this large," Grace answered. "He helped us buy this one after he went to work on the tugs and barges."

Janet slept lightly but well, enjoying the slight movement of the boat throughout the night. Mosquito netting over the breakfast area enabled them to enjoy a delicious open-air breakfast without the worry of those little pests. Janet looked forward to getting back into the Ozarks where mosquitos were few.

"Galen," Janet said, "I would like to have your mother and daddy come along with us to meet my parents and be present at our marriage ceremony."

Galen noticed that his father and mother thought that she was speaking to his father when she used his first name. He owed them an explanation. He told them of how Janet had known him only by his first name, and of his decision to use his name instead of his initials when he arrived in the Ozarks.

Janet told them of the reactions of the sheriff and his lackeys when the FBI agent addressed him as "G. W. Broussard." "I had suspected that he was much more than a singing school teacher, and when I saw their reactions to the name he used on the river, I knew my intuition had served me well."

Grace Robinson Broussard had longed to see her brother, Louis, and his family. It was a trip she had discussed with her husband. To combine such a visit with attending her son's marriage would be special. Soon they were on the road headed north into the Ozarks.

Before they left town, Galen and Janet visited the little shop of a jeweler and watch maker. "I want just a simple gold band, Janet said. I want something I can wear while I do all kinds of work. It's the kind of wedding ring your mother is wearing and the kind that my mother wears."

The hills grew steeper and the curves became sharper, but the happy foursome enjoyed every mile of the way. The strong six-cylinder engine was just the right powerhouse for steep slopes, and the hydraulic brakes worked perfectly. Trying not to overuse the brakes and get them hot, Galen used the gears. Between climbing and going downhill, he used the clutch and gear shift almost constantly.

Finally they arrived at the farm where they had left Emma, Jack and Janet's horse. Beyond that point, the use of a motorized vehicle posed too many problems to be feasible. The automobile age would arrive in this part of the Ozarks one day, but first many rocks must be dynamited and bridges must be built.

No sooner had they stepped out of the car than Jack greeted them with braying that rang across the countryside. The farmer came from the barnyard where he had been repairing a gate, and his wife stepped onto the front porch. Then a tall, broad-shouldered young man followed the farmer.

"You arrived just in time to eat," the farmer said. "Come on inside."

"We didn't want to surprise you with more than you could feed," Galen said. "We brought along some food, and we will add it to what you have."

"Janet and I will help fix the food," Grace told the farmer as Galen took a card-board box from the rear seat.

"Please meet my mother and father," Galen said as the farmer's wife came to the car. "My mother's name is Grace, and my father and I share the same first name."

"This young man is Kit Treadway," the farmer said. "He is my sister's grandson, my great nephew. He is working to earn money to go to college. Wants to be a civil engineer."

"I want to see roads and bridges constructed into these mountains," Kit said as he admired the new Plymouth PE Deluxe. "It would be nice to drive a car like this all the way to where I live with my parents. I want to be a part of designing bridges and laying out roads."

"You are good with math?" Galen asked.

"My teacher said I am. I know I love it. I love to design and build things."

"I have heard your name mentioned in a favorable way," Galen told him. "Armed with only a pick handle you recovered your family's mule, a pistol and a shotgun from one of the worst criminals to ever operate on the Mississippi River."

"I still worry about him,' Kit answered. "He may come back and take revenge on my family. That makes me hesitate about going to college. I'm thinking that maybe I should stick around to be there if that happens."

Galen placed his hand on Kit's shoulder. "You don't have to worry. He's dead. An FBI agent shot him in

Ascension Parish, Louisiana, just a few days ago." Kit's relief showed on his face.

Turning to the old farmer Galen said, "Mr. Alston, we are going to need two good horses for my mother and daddy to ride. We will need them for about three or four weeks."

"I have a good mare, and my neighbor has three geldings that you can pick from. They are all gentle, but still young enough to take the steep places. We can ride over there in your car after we eat. It's a bit over two miles."

As they ate in the large dining room with a triple window facing northwest and overlooking a clear mountain valley, the Alstons eagerly sought any news their guests could share with them. Galen kept looking at the pasture land and the cattle grazing there. There was a free-flowing creek that flowed into the pasture at the northwest corner, made a wide loop through the pasture and flowed out about midway on the west side.

Galen was thinking of how he would like to locate a farm in that general area when Mrs. Alston said that she and her husband were thinking of selling the farm. "I know we can't get as much for the farm as we would like in these tough times, but every year gets harder on both of us. My rheumatism hurts me really bad in cold wet weather, and George has two bad knees."

She had Galen's full attention. This farm lay close to passable roads, and it was near enough to the Arkansas River to give access to big-city markets. The barns, pastures and fields were well maintained, and the well-built house was no more than ten years old.

"We have looked at small tracts near Russellville," she continued. "We have found one we especially like, but I doubt that it will be on the market for long. The house is really nice. If we can get a decent price for this place, we can buy it without dipping into our savings and have enough to buy a car or a pickup."

"We could borrow and buy it, and then pay the money back when we sell this place," George Alston said, "but we don't feel comfortable doing that. We don't want to put ourselves in the position of having to accept whatever price someone offers us."

Galen glanced to the side at Janet and found her looking at him. He raised his eyebrows to communicate an unspoken question, and she responded with a barely perceptible nod. The attention of the Alstons was focused on Galen's parents.

He had to wait a while for a break in the flow of conversation between the farm couple and his parents, but finally he asked in a casual tone, "What kind of money would you feel is a fair price for a farm like this?"

George Alston didn't hesitate. He gave a figure. "That's lock, stock and barrel. Everything. All the equipment and the livestock. Not the chickens. We will take them with us. We just want chickens and a garden. That's all."

"George can't plow a mule anymore. His knees won't take it. We will hire someone to plow the garden, and then we will work it with a hoe. Between the garden and the chickens, we can make out pretty good."

"I can find some good fishing spots, and we can eat fish once or twice a week," George added. "I don't know how we are going to make out here when Kit goes off to college. I ride my old horse as much as I can to stay off my legs, but there's not much work that can be done from a saddle."

Soon Galen and Janet had made a deal with the Alstons. Janet asked for paper and pen. She put their agreement into writing, which agreement included a cash deposit against the purchase price. The Alstons would ride with Galen and Janet the next day to Russellville, the county seat, to see an attorney.

"How long have the two of you owned this farm?" Janet asked. Mrs. Alston went to another room and returned with a conformed copy of the deed bearing a date of 1899.

"Have you lived here and used the entire 240 acres since you bought it?" Galen inquired.

"We have had about seventy acres fenced for pasture since about three years after we bought it," Mr. Alston answered. "In one way or another we have used it all since we owned it."

"It should not take long to check the title," Janet commented. "We might even be able to close the deal tomorrow. We can take you to start the transaction on the property you want to buy, if it is still available."

Two days later Galen sat astride Emma, following Janet and his parents. He had thought to have Jack follow at the rear while he led the way on Emma, but Jack had a different mind about that. He insisted on following immediately behind Emma. Both Emma and Jack showed enthusiasm for the trip. In fact, Emma was a bit frisky at first, but she soon settled down.

With each passing day Galen's mother and father grew more animated. They actually seemed years younger. His mother, especially, looked forward to seeing her brother and his wife. "Won't Louis and Mary be surprised?" she said to Galen. "They will be almost as surprised as I was to hear your voice in the café."

Kit Treadway would remain at the farm to help care for everything until he left for college. Galen and Janet looked forward to moving into their home about three weeks later. "I really love our house, Galen," Janet had told him. "I wouldn't change a thing about it if we were building it new."

When Galen thought of the events of the past two months, he marveled at how life had changed for better for so many people in such a short time. He promised himself that he would never forget and that he would always remember to thank God for it.

www.ingramcontent.com/pod-product-compliance
Lightning Source LLC
Chambersburg PA
CBHW051958150726
47999CB00004B/1433